Love and Crime

stories

V.S. Kemanis

Cover design by Eeva Lancaster

"Collector's Find" and "Journal Entry, Franklin DeWitt," were first published in *Ellery Queen's Mystery Magazine*, and "Collector's Find" is included in *Ellery Queen's Mystery Magazine's* anthology, *The Crooked Road, Volume 3*.
"The Zephyr" was first published in *The William and Mary Review* and is included in *Dust of the Universe, tales of family*.
"Cactus Flower" was first published in *Iconoclast* and is included in *Everyone But Us, tales of women*.
"Cat" was first published in *Lynx Eye* and is included in *Malocclusion, tales of misdemeanor*.

ISBN-10: 0-9965909-8-6
ISBN-13: 978-0-9965909-8-3

℞ Opus Nine Books
•New York•

All works published by Opus Nine Books are dedicated to the nine members of the family headed by John and Kate Swackhamer at 3 South Trail, Orinda, California—a large world under one small roof.

Praise for story collections by V.S. Kemanis

"Rich in metaphors and intensely provocative descriptive passages, these stories are to be tasted, savored, enjoyed and read over and over again. *Your Pick: Selected Stories* is a powerful tribute to this author's mastery of the art of creating not just a good story, but a story that needs to be read many times to appreciate the full power of its presentation." — *Readers' Favorite*

"Eleven compulsively readable short stories… Anyone who appreciates supple writing and fine storytelling will enjoy every minute spent reading these stories… A good deal of the pleasure in the collection comes from the writing itself. Kemanis knows how to build a story and keep it going." — *Foreword Reviews* on *Love and Crime: Stories*

"[Kemanis is] unarguably gifted…a great talent… There are stories here that I think I will remember forever. They've stayed with me in the weeks since I read them and make me smile even now as I call to mind their wonderfully flawed characters, their gentle humor, their twists and surprises and, without exception, the compassionate insight at their core." — *SP Reviews* on *Dust of the Universe*

"V. S. Kemanis is certainly one of the most intelligent writers I have read. Her insight into human behavior is truly unusual… These are believable stories and believable characters… Unwaveringly fascinating." — *The Kindle Book Review* on *Everyone But Us*

"Quietly effective… Perfectly paced and brimming with mood and insight into our darker moments… Kemanis pulls off the difficult trick of imbuing the humdrum with a subliminal disquiet." — David Antrobus, author of *Dissolute Kinship*, on *Malocclusion*

"[A]ny reader with a love of fine writing in short story format should find pieces to savor among these well-written offerings." — *BlueInk Review (Starred Review)* on *Love and Crime: Stories*

"Little miracle stories…profoundly touching and at other times hilarious… Writing of this quality is rare." — Grady Harp, author of *War Songs*, on *Dust of the Universe*

CONTENTS

love stories

crime stories

love and crime reprise

epiblog

These stories are about love and crime,
but...
reader beware.
You may find love in the crime stories
and crime in the love stories.

love stories

℞ *Rosemary and Reuben*

ANDERSON IS SINGLE by choice and always has been. True to his one love, he treats himself to an epicurean delight every Saturday night. At this stage of his life, he's indifferent to money and mortality and gladly indulges to excess. Only the finest restaurants in Manhattan will do.

Before stepping out, Anderson trims the goatee and puts on his evening best. Invariably he dines alone, although he isn't without a list of possible companions, female and male. Still, there's no wish for a lover to dine with. On his evenings out, he indulges a craving of a different sort, the sensual experience of taste, texture, and aroma, the heft of silver and gleam of crystal, the lengthening and savoring of time. For a few hours he forgets his life—everything it is and is not. A full belly and a buzz from the grape will do that.

On this particular Saturday, Anderson is fortunate to have a reservation at the celebrated Ole Factory in the Village. Competition is high. It's rumored that, after thirty-five years in business, Rosemary and Reuben Blandrigard will soon be retiring.

At seven o'clock, Anderson alights from a taxicab,

braves an icy blast, and darts over the frozen pavement into the restaurant. The small foyer is square, dim, and hushed like a confessional, with a single, warm light directed from the ceiling toward the opposite wall. Anderson is drawn to the sepia-toned photograph of the owners, framed in a simple mahogany rectangle, displayed on the eggshell wall. Rosemary lovingly gazes at Reuben, and Reuben gazes at Anderson with a look of glazed contentment.

Past the foyer and over the threshold, a young hostess looks up. Anderson squares his shoulders and announces his name. She seems to know him. "How are you this evening, Mr. Anderson?"

"Fine. Just fine, thank you." He strokes the goatee and drops his eyes to her neck.

"Is this your first time at the Ole Factory?"

"Yes, indeed it is," he informs her neck. "I've run the gauntlet successfully it seems."

"And you've earned your reward."

"I look forward to it."

He senses her amusement, feigned or real, from the tension in her neck.

"Right this way, please." She turns, sending her long skirt into a gentle swirl, and guides him at a leisurely pace through the well-spaced dining room of about twenty tables. The décor is spare but pleasing. In the far corner, a small, round table awaits him. The single chair is backed into the corner, allowing him a view outward into the room—a thoughtful arrangement. At some establishments he's made to face the wall, and at others, an empty, second chair stands in silent rebuke of his social failings.

Anderson sits and orders an aperitif. Glancing at the menu, he senses, in the periphery, the sexual murmurings of a young, starry-eyed couple at the next table. Against his will, he's aroused by a fleeting emotional stirring. The moment passes, giving way to the pleasing texture in his hand—the single sheet of cardstock. This is the message printed on the front:

"Welcome to the Ole Factory. We've created a unique menu for tonight's meal. Let your server know if your pleasure is One or The Other. Your hosts, Rosemary and Reuben."

Always a surprise, always superb. (The critics agree.) Each meal at the Ole Factory is specially created for the clientele, a process that begins with a telephone interview to vet personal aversions and food allergies. Simpatico tastes of prospective patrons are carefully matched, and a guest list is compiled for each sitting before any reservation is confirmed. It can take a year to get on a list.

As a successful applicant, Anderson has won the right to ponder his two options for the evening. Without much thought, he selects "The Other" before flipping the card over. Printed on the back is a short paragraph entitled "The Story of Rosemary and Reuben." *Legend* might be the more descriptive term. Everything about them is legend, including their habit of circulating through the dining room during coffee and dessert. They appear at the kitchen door, wrench apart like cloven chopsticks, and weave different routes through the tables, separately greeting their guests.

As he sips his aperitif and reads The Story a second time, Anderson silently hopes that Rosemary will be the one to visit him at the end of his meal.

Two and a half hours later, he gets his wish. At nine thirty, she emerges from the kitchen with Reuben. Nearly touching, they suspend all movement for barely an eye blink. Reluctantly they part. With a quick, light step, Rosemary toes a straight line along the wall to Anderson's table. She's a roundish, dwarflike woman of about Anderson's age, with silvery-gray hair pulled tightly back into a doughnut at the nape of her neck, exposing delicately lobed, naked ears. Coming to a halt in dramatic proximity, she's not much taller than Anderson as he sits. With a familiar air, she regards him from beneath jet-black eyebrows. *Hold still please*, says the creator of that sepia-toned photograph.

"Mr. Anderson. We're very glad you could come this evening."

His heart races in confusion. Her visit to his table fulfills his dearest wish, but everything else has been less than expected, troublingly so. He doesn't understand the meaning of the past two and a half hours. He wants to tell her, but the words are bottled under a well-aged cork.

Before Anderson can speak, Rosemary lifts a bent index finger and rests the knuckle on the tip of her sharply pointed nose. The finger covers her nostrils, the fisted hand covers her mouth.

Anderson searches for polite words but finds only the single, obvious truth. "The service was excellent, thank you."

With a nod, she removes her hand. "It's been our pleasure. Is there anything else we can get for you? Anything at all?" Pausing after the last word, the silence that follows announces her omission. She hasn't inquired whether he enjoyed his dinner.

In the middle of the night, Anderson lies awake, puzzled and unsettled. He remembers eating but feels hollow and unsatisfied. More than anything, he's deeply ashamed. The words of The Story march relentlessly across his brain like sturdy, soldier ants. Between the permanent black bits, the holes wait to be filled.

Staring into the lightless room, he mourns the passage of time. In 1975, the three of them shared this city, unaware of each other. For Rosemary, it was the year The Story began. For Anderson, it was the middle of the sameness of his life. In the inky stillness, he conjures her in the predawn streets of Midtown, January of 1975. Where was he, and what was he doing at that hour?

It's six forty, still dark. Rosemary scurries along the pavement on her way to work. She's a girl of twenty-five but looks older in her nappy wool overcoat and sensible, rubber-soled shoes. Winter is her friend, a time when outdoor offenders are put on ice. She avoids any close, overheated indoor space. She avoids the subway with its coffee spills, underarms, garlic, perfume, earwax, intestinal gasses, hair, breath, mothballs, greasy take-out, and aftershave.

Rosemary walks a mile to the forty-six-story office building of her employer, a monstrous insurance underwriter. Her cubicle on the thirty-third floor is stacked with claim forms. Check, check, check. She's the first employee ever to be granted flextime—a special medical dispensation for a disability of an indeterminate nature. In by seven, hungry by eleven, Rosemary takes her lunch every day at that early hour, avoiding the crowd. Food is not permitted in her cubicle, but the company offers more than one option for dining in the building.

On the second floor, a cafeteria exudes tumultuous, clashing odors. Spaghetti and meatballs. Fried chicken. French fries. Pizza. Turkey, gravy, and mashed potatoes. Hot and sour pork. Tacos and enchiladas. Rosemary avoids the second floor. On the third floor, the options are less fragrant. There's a lunchroom for brown baggers, offering a perfume of burnt crusts from the toaster oven, and an automat, where the food is pre-packaged in cellophane bags, neatly slotted into machines. Sterile, odorless, chrome, glass, plastic. Refrigerated. Rosemary always eats lunch in the automat, where her usual choice is American cheese on white and a bottle of sparkling water.

On the first day of The Story, another early lunch taker sits alone at a small table on the other side of the room. Rosemary has seen him before and feels embarrassed by her interest in him. She lowers her head and nibbles one corner of the white sponge in her hand, barely able to swallow the marble. Surrendering to an irresistible urge, her eyelids flutter upward, but he's gone. Disappointed, fighting tears, she drops her eyes to the table, unable to eat. Her nostrils prickle. There's a shift in the atmosphere, a softening of the air, and her nose relaxes. When she looks up, he's suddenly there.

"Hello," he says in a pleasing voice, clearly nervous. He's gaunt and pale, a sign of ill health, but his eyes burn with the desire to overcome his frailty. She smiles at him as she clutches a napkin in her lap. If he were someone else, that napkin would instantly be pressed to her nose in her usual pretense of needing to stop a drip. But something about him elicits the opposite need. She wants him to come closer.

"Hello," she replies.

He glances at the half-eaten sandwich while the fingertips of his right hand stroke the tabletop in round movements. "I had the same one today. American. I'm also okay with cream cheese."

In this, she hears a confession more exciting than any pickup line, but she holds back, not wanting to assume. "You're fond of milder cheeses then?"

"Fond?" He laughs heartily, revealing his true nature. "Those are the things I can barely eat!"

She laughs along with him, suddenly sure of his meaning. When silence falls again, their eyes meet in a sustained, intuitive gaze. It makes her feel daring, and she invites him to sit.

"My name is Rosemary," she says.

"I'm Reuben."

They shake hands across the table. "Forgive me," she says, "but, just now, I couldn't help wondering. Do you suffer from hyperosmia?"

He shakes his head, but his eyes sparkle. "No. Hypergeusia."

Sudden joy! Their teeth have never been so whitely exposed to the world.

Late at night, Rosemary lies awake at Reuben's side, thinking of Anderson sitting alone at the corner table with shame written on his face. Framed by his two forearms, the cranberry sorbet melts into the tuile cup on his plate, barely tasted. He's a curious character with a precisely crafted goatee, cherry-apple cheeks, and alarming intensity.

The Ole Factory has seen many solo diners over the years. Every sitting includes at least one, despite the lost revenue from an empty seat that easily could be filled. It's a tradition rooted in kindness. Recalling their many lonely sojourns in the automat before they met, Rosemary and Reuben feel an especial fondness for those who, by choice or necessity, must dine alone. These people, more than any others, are deserving of a sumptuous meal, or at least, the effort to deliver such a meal to them.

Anderson's ill-concealed torment haunts her. She feels no fondness or affinity for this man. She blinks him away and recalls other faces of single diners from times long past. A gallery of aging lonely hearts. Kindness? Is that truly her motivation? For the first time, she suspects something else. Arrogance. Maybe even cruelty.

A teardrop descends, carving a path along her cheekbone, making a final plunge into her ear.

In his coal black room, suffering from reflux, Anderson pulls the covers up to his chin and welcomes the chilly air on his cheeks. The Story is momentarily interrupted by a recurring image. He sees that dark-haired young man at the next table, depositing lascivious whisperings into the ear of his tawny-skinned lover. His lips touch the outer curve of cartilage, moving warmly and moistly against the opening of the auditory canal.

In his youth, Anderson had a handful of failed affairs. He was naturally timid with the opposite sex and moved slowly, afraid of rejection. Women usually left him even before he contemplated a move. Analyzing his failures, he resolved, in one instance, to move faster. That, too, resulted in a stinging rejection. *How dare you!* Her face is still vivid in his mind. She's the marching majorette with the thrusting baton at the head of his life-long parade of humiliations.

His gratitude for the carefully placed corner table is fading. To be sure, that sexy couple was deliberately placed in close proximity. Why should Rosemary be entitled to make such arrangements? Shame might have been her fate too, if not for the fortuitous arrival of Reuben in 1975. Everything about her today might have been the same—the roundness, the tight bun at the nape of her neck, the skin translucent like filo dough—except for her brow, which might have been crimped and hard as a rim of crust instead of smooth like the uncooked pie shell that it is. It could have been.

But no, Rosemary meets Reuben a second time in the automat, and a third, and then it's on to greater things. A sexual conquest isn't on their minds, or even possible in light of their disabilities. Not immediately. They set foot on a cautious path toward healing.

Rosemary refrigerates all her food to mask the smell, but the ingredients are not always flavorless. The first night that Reuben visits her apartment, she serves a chilled pasta salad. What could be blander? White shells barely greased in the lightest virgin olive oil with green peas and a tiny shaving of red vegetable for flavor. It's cold and odorless, but Reuben nearly gags on the pimento.

"Dear Reuben! I'm so sorry."

Tears fill his eyes, and his fingertips race hectically along the tabletop. "Please don't be sorry. Let me try it again."

He clutches the fork in his right hand while touching her forearm with his left, girding for the excruciating hypersensitivity of his taste buds. But something magical happens. With the next bite he relaxes, and the magnificence of tang hits him in all its glory. "Pimento! So *that's* what it is!" He takes another bite. "Excellent. Give me more."

For dessert, they have vanilla ice cream. He encourages her to let it melt a bit, releasing the sweet fragrance. She leans toward the bowl and sniffs at the vanilla, cream, and sugar, but immediately she turns away. His heart goes out to her. Reaching across the table, he takes her delicate earlobe between thumb and index finger. She turns her head toward him, bringing her nose closer to the hand on her ear.

"Your skin is very soft," he says, like whispering in a closet.

She's intoxicated by the smell of his skin and the sound of his voice. How can it be? "Say that again," she says.

"Your skin…"

"Wait until I get a spoonful."

"No, *you* wait!" He drops his hand. "We'll do it together. Just… You'll have to, I mean, will you let me touch you?"

"Yes, please." She blushes.

They each scoop up a spoonful of ice cream. He waits while she holds her spoon under her nose, and he takes her earlobe again with his free hand. "Your skin is very soft." Her head clears and the nausea vanishes. With their eyes locked, they open their mouths to receive the cool sweet at the same time, each knowing the pleasure of every sense in perfect balance and proportion.

Standing at the edge of Anderson's table, Rosemary is suddenly in the grip of a revulsion she hasn't felt in years. The pong he emits is foul indeed, despite the cardamom in his coffee, a bad-breath neutralizer. His cup still holds most of the liquid, growing cold. She's compelled to cover her nose and mouth. He sees and understands. If this is kindness, it's the cruelest sort. She exerts the will-power she once needed so desperately, and her hand falls away.

"It's been our pleasure. Is there anything else we can get for you? Anything at all?"

She pauses, hoping he'll say no. She'd rather move on to that young couple at the next table. Their juicy bodies telegraph their enjoyment of each other and their complete satisfaction with the culinary masterpiece they've just consumed.

At Reuben's apartment, the food is bland and spiceless but warm, releasing its aroma. On her first visit, when he opens the front door, the smell hits her. Something is cooking in the kitchen. Later, she'll confront it on her plate: the boned and skinned chicken breast, no grease, no salt, no pepper, no herbs. But first, all she knows is an overpowering smell of gamey flesh. Her head tightens in pain and her stomach does backflips. She covers her nose with one hand while the other hand clutches the string of a boxed apple pie she's brought for dessert. It's still cold, and she's anxious to get it into the refrigerator.

"Rosemary," he says, moving toward her, touching the hand that covers her nose. It's enough. The smell of his skin replaces everything. In this way, she's leaping ahead of him. She has the scent and sound of him, but he doesn't have the taste of her. Only touch.

That evening, they take new baby steps. For Reuben, the chemistry of touch starts to regulate the pain and pleasure of taste. During the meal, he holds Rosemary's forearm with his left hand while eating. "It's as if I've never touched the skin of another human being before," he muses.

Batting her eyelashes mockingly she says, "You expect me to believe that?" She's acting the coquette, wanting to provoke a response so that his words will diffuse the molecules of cooked bird invading her nose. The mellifluence of his voice regulates the pain and pleasure of scent.

"If I've touched anyone before, it's never been like this. My fingers are melting into your skin. I have a feeling I could eat *anything*!" He sprinkles a bite-sized piece of chicken with salt and pepper, forks it into his mouth, chews and swallows, all the while holding onto Rosemary's forearm. His taste buds are calmed by the touch. "Almost too easy. Maybe even a little bland."

After dinner, in their anxiety about the pie, he insists on heating it because he loves the bouquet, a mixture of warm apple, cinnamon, and butter. She's able to tolerate it only because he's near. She no longer needs his hand next to her nose because his pheromone is released into the air, traces of his skin and everything it oozes—the oil, perspiration, and foods he's eaten. His thoughts and desires.

They sit down to their dessert. "What a delicious aroma," he says. But she notices his hesitance in taking a bite. He distracts her with a question. "Have you ever made a pie before?"

"I'm afraid not. I purchased this one because I've heard it's the best." She glances at the box, which bears the logo of a famous pie shop. Fearing a seizure if she set foot in the shop, she ordered it by phone for delivery to her apartment. "I'd like to be able to bake a dessert, but I'm sure it's impossible. Maybe I could handle the dough if it's cold enough. But it would get warm in my hands, wouldn't it?"

"Warm or cold, I think you could do it. You're surviving this heavenly scent right now, aren't you?"

"But you're here with me."

"Then, maybe we should cook together."

Briefly, her eyes reflect disbelief, and in the next instant, her face lights up. "Yes. I'd love it!" No one is more surprised than Rosemary to be excited at the thought of baking with all of its sensory consequences. Reuben makes anything possible. She notices then her mouth has started to salivate heavily. Her enjoyment of the apple-cinnamon smell is translating into an urgent desire for a mouth-stuffing bite. Eagerly, she chops off a hefty forkful and shoves it in, clumsily leaving a morsel of crust and apple goo on her lower lip. She lifts her napkin to wipe it away, but he stops her.

"Let me do it." With an index finger, Reuben gently wipes at the crumb, taking it up with a bit of saliva from her glistening lip. He sticks his finger in his mouth, and his eyes go wide.

He's discovered the taste of her.

At the end of their evening together, they stand awkwardly in the tight space near his front door. She hopes to have stored enough of his essence—inhaled and deposited on her skin and clothing—to last until the next time they meet. Tentatively, he takes her in his arms and gently touches his lips to hers. The kiss deepens and calms his throbbing taste buds as he sucks and drinks her taste. They each take enough of the other to last until morning when, at eleven o'clock, they will meet again in the automat.

Someday, the cafeteria? With Reuben, anything is possible.

Rosemary sees the artery throbbing in Anderson's throat, telling her that their conversation isn't over yet. He's working himself up to ask The Question. It's a predictable inquiry that many solo diners have posed, but tonight, she's not in the mood for it. Not from him.

The color rises in his cheeks. "I *am* curious," he begins. "I'm wondering, is it true?"

She knows exactly what he means. A thousand people have asked it, and she has never been annoyed—

until now. The odor emanates from his mouth as he speaks, hovering in the space between them. She does her best to ignore it while she smiles and waits for him to explain, as if she didn't understand.

"The Story. On the back of that card, the menu. I'd like to know. Is it true?"

The Question is an insult. Why has it taken her so long to know this? From the point of view of the inquisitor, two answers are possible: yes or no. Even odds. Anderson is suggesting a fifty-fifty chance that, for thirty-five years, she and Reuben have promulgated a lie on the back of their menu.

Perhaps no one else has ever seemed as earnest as this Mr. Anderson. Her answer to everyone else is always the same, cheerfully given, maybe with a little laugh. *Yes, every word is true. Life is stranger than fiction, wouldn't you agree?*

This man requires something else. She echoes, "Is it true?" in a musing tone. "Let me put it like this. We've distilled our Story into about fifty words on the back of that card. The words decorate the page like the garnish on your plate—they're indispensable to the presentation, but only a small part of the meal."

As soon as the answer leaves her mouth, she's unsure if she actually said it. At any rate, it's what she wanted to say.

Only a small part of the meal. By three in the morning, The Story is well underway, and Anderson doesn't have much difficulty completing it.

After the exciting apple pie night, Rosemary and

Reuben are inseparable. The symbiotic lovers are on their way to achieving the complete synthesis and perfect harmony of taste, touch, smell, and sound.

Every afternoon, at the end of their workday, they walk out of the building together, headed for his apartment or hers. "What shall we cook tonight?" They discuss the contents of their refrigerators, the ingredients they desire, and whether a trip to the market is necessary.

At first they keep it easy, nothing pungent or biting, piquant, sharp, or spicy to burn the tongue or sting the nostrils. Mashed potatoes are safe. Gradually, they start to add things: garlic or fresh grated parmesan, mushrooms or onions, sour cream and butter, lots of it. Chicken is safe. Later they add sage and start to experiment with paprika, green chili, shallots and white wine, stewed tomatoes and oregano. Fish is not safe, but eventually it makes the list. Filet of sole, unseasoned. On to salmon, broiled with Dijon and dill. Whiting with capers and lemon. Lobster with jalapeño and lime.

One evening, in the sixth month of their union, Reuben takes a cold shrimp by the tail, scoops up the tangy cocktail sauce they've crafted, and inserts the curled body into Rosemary's mouth. The offering is cold, but the horseradish penetrates the nasal membranes. Her nose, with its sharply pointed tip, has changed in the past months. The nostrils, which once appeared painfully sucked in, white rimmed, and narrow, have relaxed to their full, round circumference.

She chews, luxuriating in the zesty taste, and scolds him, "Didn't I tell you, Rube?" She scrunches her nose for emphasis. "Only a dash. You're trying to kill me with this stench." Her eyes shine, more from loving him and kidding around than from the odor of the horseradish.

"I didn't add any more than a soupçon, my love."

"Let's see about that."

"Testing me, are you?"

She takes up a firm piece of succulent white flesh with its painted coral stripes and applies a liberal layer of sauce. "Open your mouth." It hovers near his opening. Reuben has also changed. His lips are still slender, but the inside of his mouth has emerged from its shriveled constriction, pushing his lips out to their maximum fullness. A sexy mouth, Rosemary would say.

He pulls back, like the old days. They like to tease each other this way. All a prelude.

"Come on, now," she says.

Like a dutiful little boy, he opens his mouth to receive the acerbic treat. "Ouch! It does have a kick, doesn't it? I need a kiss." His favorite excuse. Their kiss turns into unbridled passion, and they make love for an hour before serving the entrée.

Indispensable to the presentation, but only a small part of the meal.

Rosemary doesn't follow the usual script with this man. She doesn't ask him, "Did you enjoy your dinner?" because she knows he wouldn't follow the usual script either.

Most of her solo guests are circumspect in their compliments. They tell her that the food is "just fine" or "very nice." Everyone else uses adjectives that range from "superb" to "heavenly" to "delectable." Because of this difference, Rosemary has every right to impart a bit of advice to the singles: "If you return, bring a companion next time. I guarantee, the experience will be improved."

But, no, she doesn't ask this man whether he enjoyed his dinner. In the aftermath of her statement about The Story, Anderson perks up and shows his indignation. "I've read some things about this restaurant that I don't find to be true."

"Oh? And what are the untrue things?"

"'Always a surprise, always superb.'"

"Well, you can't say it wasn't a surprise."

"Yes, certainly a surprise, but very far from superb."

"I'm sorry to hear that. Perhaps, Mr. Anderson...," and she's about to impart the usual advice to dine with a companion, when she realizes it would be wasted on him. "I can see that you expected more."

"I expected something with flavor, that's for sure. Taste. Aroma. Texture."

"And you got none?"

He screws up his nose and shakes his head in disgust. "Your server told me that the thing on my plate was a duck confit of sorts with *pommes de terre sarladaises*. Is that true?"

Again, with the "true." She says nothing.

"Indigestible grease. And the vegetables. Carrots, of all things. I know. You're going to say that the oyster mushrooms and onions make it special." He's working himself up into a lather. "I *did* taste the peppercorns, but in theory only. Actually, those little pebbles were like the grit on unwashed asparagus. And the thyme. Stuck in my teeth like shards of crabgrass."

Is this man saying these things? He looks as if he's unable to speak, yet Rosemary hears it all, feeling the heat of that sexy couple on her back.

He continues. "You call this a treat, a delight, a savory meal? You call yourselves chefs, master cooks?"

These are his last words. He gets up, steps away from her, and stumbles over his chair. The single chair at his table.

"Rube." It's three in the morning. She gives him a little squeeze on a fleshy love handle. "Reuben."

He rolls over to face her. "Wha...?"

"I can't sleep."

His eyes pop open in the dark. They're lying on their sides, his right, her left. The gauzy curtain filters the light from the street. Searching for his eyes, she discerns only a spectral gleam. He takes in a deep breath, puts a hand on her shoulder, and asks, "Why not?"

"We're getting old."

"Hmm. Old people sleep very well, thank you."

"No, I mean it's bothering me. That we're getting old."

"We're sixty-five. That isn't old."

"We're getting there."

"Like everyone else."

"And something else is bothering me. I don't want to retire."

"We don't have to. No one says we must."

"Okay. But we haven't talked about what happens to the person left behind when the other one dies. I can't bear the thought of it."

"Aren't you jumping the gun a little bit?"

"We have to think about it."

"Then we won't."

"I can't stop thinking about it."

"I mean we won't die one at a time. We'll go together."

"That's impossible."

"Suicide pact maybe?" He's been stroking the top of her head, and now he's running his hand along the side of her face and down to her neck.

"Not that. Not now."

"You need to forget."

"I can't."

"It's that man again, isn't it? The one you told me about earlier."

"Maybe it is."

"Why does he upset you so much?"

Rosemary visualizes the face with its need and dismay and accusation. "Why do we keep inviting the singles?"

"We always have."

"It seems terribly wrong to me."

"You've never thought like this before."

"Are we gloating over ourselves?"

"Not in the least."

"Maybe I just didn't like him. He isn't like the other single patrons. They're all a little sad maybe, but appreciative and accepting."

"You're wrong, my dear. I remember another one like him. At least one, maybe more."

"I don't remember."

"Maybe five years ago. A woman."

"The woman who wrote to us afterward?"

"Exactly her. She was just as confused and jealous."

"I don't think this man is jealous."

"If not jealous, he's in pain, so he took it out on you. It's the kind of pain that comes when…" Reuben stops to think a moment, "…when you've just been given a hard pill to swallow."

"You're saying he's starting to understand."

"That's my guess."

"Well." She stops to think. "I suppose that's the good of it, but we're still responsible for what happened to him."

"You analyze too much, my dear."

"But we're responsible, and I'm worried."

"About him?"

"No. About my lack of love or caring for him."

"Pity isn't a good foundation for love, or for any kind of good feeling."

She ponders this, and the room becomes darker in its silence.

Finally, Reuben says, "Even though you're *not* worried about him"—he's mocking her—"there's no need for worry anyway. That woman turned out all right."

"How so?"

"Her letter of apology. She explained what happened to her, and how her life became better. This man is like her in some ways. You'll see."

"He'll never write us a letter."

"It doesn't matter. I could see it in his eyes and that little self-righteous swagger. Maybe he'll keep his little protections, but he'll get over us. It's only a matter of time. He'll taste and smell again. And maybe more."

"You're sure of that?"

"Very sure."

"But it won't be at *our* restaurant that his taste returns."

"And why not?"

"He won't be asking for a return visit."

"That's true," says Reuben. "It will be somewhere else then. At a senior social, when a blue-haired lady offers him a stale cookie. The taste will be like heaven."

She laughs softly, cheered by the image.

"Come here now." Reuben pulls her close and blocks out everything in the world but him.

₪ *Weeping Willow*

AN AUTUMN MORNING in my fortieth year marked the delayed start to my life. At about four o'clock, someone was breathing in my ear—having difficulty breathing. I was jolted awake, my body clenched and rigid in the cold bed. Across the room, red numbers blinked into a new minute, 4:03.

I closed my eyes again and let the breathing drift off to its resting place. Still, our voices whispered in the dark.

Trisha.

Jesse.

Tell me this is over.

The feelings were pleasant. His arm circled my shoulder, and his forehead rested on my temple, making a tender spot of living warmth. A thick, sandy curl of male hair tumbled onto my cheek and trembled into view. More than trembled, it vibrated and shook and the air became thick with the pungent odor of red wine and fear.

By then I was really up, stumbling around the apartment, turning on the lights. I waited until a decent hour to call Phoebe.

"Still having those dreams," she said. "Double-oh-seven." Her tone was sensible but not uncaring. *Time to wake up.*

"I haven't had one for a while but, I know, it's been a long time…"

"Twenty years."

"Almost twenty-one." I could tick off the days, months, and years that had passed since December 18, 1971.

"We were only kids. What did we know?"

"We knew better than that."

She exhaled an audible sigh. "This is old news, Trisha. I don't know what to say to you anymore. Did you ever go to that therapist I recommended?"

I didn't want to answer that question, so I just gave a little laugh and changed the subject. I inquired about Phoebe's job and listened quietly, harboring my envy of her smarts and steadiness. She led a very organized life as a nurse practitioner at a respected hospital in Chicago. Even her short-lived, failed marriage had been a success. She and her ex-husband were best buddies and cooperated amicably in raising their daughter Sarah. They'd just celebrated her Sweet Sixteen.

"Sarah's only three years younger than we were," I observed. A slip into forbidden territory. Quickly, I resurfaced and offered a few positive things about my flip-flop of a life in New York City. My boyfriend, perhaps the tenth since college, wasn't half bad. My income was up a few dollars after starting a new job—also the "nth" since college—as a social worker in a battered women's shelter. Life in the Big Apple was exciting, dangerous, and distracting. These were my needs when I arrived here in 1974, and I still needed the distractions. I couldn't survive without them.

The five of us met in 1970 as freshmen at U.C. Berkeley, where we lived in coed housing known as the Ridge Project. L.B., Jesse, Alex, Phoebe, and I. Soon, we became fast friends, inseparable, sharing everything that anyone was talking about during that era of change and unrest.

At the close of freshman year, ready to break out on our own, we pooled our resources and rented a house: a ramshackle, two-story Victorian in a downtrodden area of town. The lease started in August 1971, so we moved in early for sophomore year. We were The Full House, three boys, two girls. We assured our parents that the arrangement was purely platonic, as indeed it was. A few of us didn't report home at all, having pretended to disown our parents on principle, while a few others simply kept quiet about being homesick.

Alex's parents, the establishment figures he disdained, gifted him their used nineteen-inch black-and-white TV, a former fixture of the family room in their upscale home in the Berkeley Hills. Alex propped it on a wooden crate in our shag-carpeted living room, a few large pillows the only other furnishings. On August 5, 1971, we piled onto the floor, a writhing mass of human flesh in cutoffs and tie-dye shirts, buried in bags of potato chips. L.B. had procured the six-packs of beer and the weed. This seemed to be his job. Leonard Bartholomew, also known as "Laid Back" or "Lucky Baby" (because he was the youngest), was a happy, carefree kid, brilliant without the ego, and in love with everyone. I loved him back, but loved Jesse more.

The TV program that night was interminable. There was a restless energy, and as the minutes ticked, our human amoeba wriggled around the room, changing shapes. My favorite spot was next to Jesse. He was gentle, melancholy, and introspective. His pale blue eyes beamed a tender light, and the skin at the crease of his neck had a musky scent. He majored in philosophy and I majored in sociology—proof that we belonged together.

A fat joint was passed and everyone partook except Jesse, who said it made him paranoid. On the TV was a man in a suit with a somber face, heavy black-framed glasses, and sideburns to mid-ear, in a sorry attempt at style. He inserted his arm into a huge glass fishbowl, made a show of roiling the sea of blue plastic capsules, and extracted the first one. Go fish. A game show. "December 4. The fourth of December is 001." A lady with a beehive put the number on the board. There were 365 more slots to fill because 1952 was a leap year.

After the first number I let out a sigh, suddenly aware of just how fast my heart was beating. The heckling, hooting and wisecracking began.

"Hey, I've had one of those blue capsules!"

"Looks like a huge upper."

"Eat it, baby!" someone shouted at the beehive. "You know you want it!"

After a few numbers, a premature relief set in and the comments got nastier. "Next one's your son, asshole." Alex came up with that one.

I remember that comment because double-oh-seven

was next. At that moment, I was sitting alongside Jesse with our legs stretched out in front, our bodies touching lengthwise. "June 27. The twenty-seventh of June is 007."

Two things happened at once. A quick, coughing laugh spurted from Alex's mouth, and a zing of electricity shot into my arm where it connected with Jesse's. We all immediately shut up and stared at the TV like zombies. Jesse separated himself from me. It wasn't until number 010 that I noticed the chant in my head: *May 17. Let it be May 17.*

We kept drinking and smoking. Soon enough we were raucous again, tumbling over each other, screaming "Shhh!" whenever the man was about to read a number. It took a very, very long time to get to number 270, May 17, and number 366, November first.

Afterward, we were all good and drunk and, some of us, stoned. Alex leaned over, grabbed the nape of my neck, and kissed me full on the lips. He pulled back with a challenge in his eyes. I turned away to wipe my mouth. Jesse was off in a corner, but we'd hugged a few times in silent commiseration between 150 and 175.

Alex sprang to his feet, pumped his fist, and cheered. "Right on! 270! Ten strike! Whatcha say Lucky Baby? Leap Boy? Number 366! What a load off!"

"Shut up," said L.B., his eyes darting over to Jesse.

"Yeah, shut up!" Phoebe chimed in.

"It's okay," said Jesse, sotto voce. I went over and took his hand, but he tensed up.

"You win some and lose some," said Alex smugly.

"Come on, Alex. Go make us some spaghetti," said Pheebs.

"Hey, I can't be happy? It's forbidden to be happy?" But he wasn't talking to Pheebs. He was looking at me. I avoided the eyes of this boy, trying to forget that time, almost a year ago. My first time. In those days, we were supposed to pretend that intimacy had no emotional significance, except in a universal sense. Love the one you're with. I felt sick just remembering it.

"Go ahead and be happy," said Jesse quietly. "I'm fucked."

"You don't know anything, man," taunted Alex. "You'll get a deferment."

This made no sense. Even then, Congress was considering a repeal of the college deferment, and Alex knew it. He was the political science major, fascinated by the inner workings of government, yet inconsistently spewing rhetoric about revolutionary change. He was the one who persuaded us to miss a week of school so we could make a cross-country trek to D.C., where we participated in May Day 1971. Our polite anti-war banner and good manners kept us out of the sweep: thirteen thousand arrestees, the largest number in U.S. history.

No one responded to Alex's bluster. We were feeling bad about ourselves. It was our fifth day as housemates, and we suspected a mistake.

Alex started laughing wildly and broke into song. "*O Canada! Where pines and maples grow...*"

Under the noise, Jesse growled low, "'Whoever fights monsters should see to it that he does not become a monster.'"

I didn't know it then, but Jesse was, more or less, quoting Nietzsche.

* * *

The next day, after we'd slept it off, Alex didn't apologize. Maybe he didn't remember. He was, again, the boy we adored. Black hair, green eyes, so good looking he might have stepped out of a magazine. Quick, funny, persuasive, charismatic. These were the qualities that made him a leader and served him well in later years, early in his law career. Sometimes there was no winning against him, so you simply gave up. Then he would laugh, and it was all a joke.

He got up early, before any of us, and made a huge cheese omelet. He was always cooking, and we loved him for it. Five bleary-eyed youths sat on the grease-encrusted linoleum floor and ate from sagging paper plates, discussing the dinette set on display in the window of the local Salvation Army outlet.

Life went on, and no one mentioned the draft. Our initial shock had worn off, and January 1972 was almost five months away. The boys would be inducted in order, by lottery number, during the year they turned twenty. We tacitly hung on the sliver of hope that the law wouldn't change, that Jesse could defer until he was twenty-six and too old to be drafted, as long as he stayed in college. Then, on a day near the end of September, the draft bill was signed, and college deferment was reduced to a single semester.

That night, I came home to a quiet, dark house. No one was in the living room or kitchen or the two downstairs bedrooms, Alex's and L.B.'s. I walked upstairs and passed Phoebe's room. Empty. I stopped at Jesse's open doorway. The overhead light was off, and a single flame flickered on a fat candle on the floor. Jesse was staring into it, sitting cross-legged on his bed. All our beds were just futons or mattresses on the floor.

I stood in the doorway, my eyes wandering. His few possessions were stuffed into two crates, philosophy textbooks in one, clothes in the other, dirty laundry scattered around. He looked up, and our eyes met. I hesitated, but then he said, "I'm glad it's you."

I came in and sat on the futon next to him. We both gazed into the flame. Finally, I said, "I heard the news. I was hoping—"

"'Hope is the worst of all evils because it prolongs the torments of man.'"

"I don't agree with that," I said, daring to look him in the eye. "Hope is good, especially when the thing you're hoping for comes true."

"When does *that* ever happen?"

"Lots of times!" But I couldn't think of an example, and we fell silent again, staring at the flame.

After a while, I looked up and was surprised to see his face wearing an expression of deep contentment. He said, "There's nothing at all except you and me and this flame. Nothing." Beyond the circle of yellow light, the world was dark. Jesse's window faced the backyard with its giant weeping willow tree. On the other side of that pane of glass, the dangling, wispy limbs blew in gentle waves, a mysterious river against the inky sky.

"Do you believe in eternal life?" I asked.

"No. Not if you mean the life we're living now."

"I mean in the spiritual sense."

"I don't believe in the spiritual. I believe in matter,

physics, and chemistry. Everything we think and do and feel comes from these."

I thought for a minute and said, "All those things are eternal. Maybe you *do* believe in eternal life."

"But the word 'life' isn't right." His mouth stretched into a broad smile with his eyes fixed on the flame. "Or maybe it is. Life is just a series of reactions anyway. Your heart is pounding. Your brain is thinking. Everything you say and do touches another life and changes it, and that life affects another one and so on and so on. All the chemical reactions you created, all your thoughts and emotions, are left behind in this world, spread around to a million people and carried forward to the next generation and the next. *That's* your eternal life."

My heart swelled with the terrible beauty of his words.

A door slammed, blowing the moment to bits. "Hello!" It was Alex, downstairs. "Why doesn't anybody turn on the lights?" Alex never worried about things like his twenty percent of the electric bill. His trust fund money covered it. "Where *is* everybody?"

We heard footsteps on the stairs, and seconds later, Alex stood in the doorway, a silhouette in the dark. He said nothing for a minute, and I felt him looking at us, our faces, arms and hands and crossed legs. His body slumped childishly, like the kid who was picked last for the team. "What're you doing?"

"Talking about chemical reactions," I said.

"I thought you'd be talking about the news from Washington." He shifted forward and his eyes grabbed the light of the candle. They glittered, on fire. "I just wanted to tell you I'm sorry about it," he said in a rehearsed way.

"'Pity makes suffering contagious.'"

"There's nothing to pity. We all knew this would happen. But maybe I'm more of a pragmatist than you."

"Pragmatist, fatalist, what does it matter? Shit happens. Good night, Alex."

It stunned me, the way Jesse said that. His words were strong, but I heard only resignation and sadness in his voice.

With a wave of his hand, Alex left us and went downstairs. We heard him rummaging around in the kitchen before he slammed his bedroom door, a distinct, final sound.

A while later, L.B. came home. We heard his heavy footsteps and bearlike rumble. "Honey, I'm home!" He stumbled around downstairs, and finding no available signs of life, he came up and filled Jesse's doorway. He was the biggest teddy bear alive. "Jesse, my man!" he bellowed and dove onto the futon, delivering a manly hug. Then, with Jesse squished between us, L.B. hugged me too, and the three of us tumbled around on the bed, laughing. A while later, Phoebe came home, and the tumble was repeated, a foursome. No one suggested that we include Alex.

When the fat candle was down to an inch and permanently puddled on the floor, L.B. and I announced that we had to go study. Pheebs stayed behind with Jesse. I didn't mind, because I knew it would be a healing session. Even then, she had a way about her that carried people through their times of crisis, a foreshadowing of her later work with cancer patients. I imagined that she and Jesse could talk about chemical reactions. She was, after all, a chemistry major, psychology minor.

When I ran out of my fake, cheery-voiced news, Phoebe was the one who returned to the forbidden territory. "You've just proved it."

"Proved what?"

"That you're stuck. Won't settle down with any man. Still having the same dreams. You turned forty this year."

"Thanks for the reminder."

"Life begins at forty. We're all there, except Lucky Baby. His birthday is coming up." *November one. The first of November is 366.* L.B. was a high school teacher in Salinas, California, married, with two grade-school kids. The cool "Mr. B." was one of those fun, eternally young teachers revered by his students. Alex, at forty, was a moderately successful lawyer in the Bay Area and still lived in Berkeley. His early professional potential had sparked, flamed, and fizzled. He never married.

I corresponded sporadically with L.B. but hadn't spoken to Alex since 1974. Every May, for a few years after we graduated, I sent Alex a birthday card, each one with a new message artfully concealing the three digits of his lottery number. "Just zeroed in on the date—two days past the seventeenth! Happy belated!" Around 1978 or so, I confessed my habit to Pheebs, who convinced me to stop for my own good.

She kept in touch with the boys and would update me periodically on their news. After making the remark about our birthdays, she reminded me: "L.B. suffered from guilt for a long time. Lost a lot of weight, but he's back to bear size again. He's over it, and you're still stuck."

"I need a memory wipe."

"I don't think that's possible. But we can find a way to reverse your chronic pain."

"It's incurable."

"Not the kind you have. Pain management is tough, but not impossible when the source is external."

"We're going to hold a lottery," Alex said during one of his charmingly persuasive days. "Low number...no, *high* number is the control."

It was early December 1971, and we'd been tossing around ideas for celebrating the end of the term. We must have been drunk. Otherwise, no one would have tolerated the mention of the word "lottery."

We were lolling around, watching *All in the Family*, half listening to the show, half in a daze. "Outta sight. A lottery," I intoned, trying to show Jesse some support.

Jesse was quietly drinking his red wine. He liked wine, but not much else.

"There has to be a control person," Alex directed. "We can't all drop at once."

"Why not?" I asked naïvely.

L.B. looked at me with a screwy eyebrow, pushed way up into his high forehead. "Alex is right." L.B. had dropped before, so he knew.

"You're right, Alex is right," mimicked Phoebe, the scientist. "We need a control to make sure no one looks in a mirror. You'll freak out."

"I'll get four hits," offered L.B. "I know where to get them."

"For such a square, you sure have the connections," said Pheebs.

"Trust me," said L.B. "It'll be the best. The cleanest."

Alex slithered next to Jesse and got up into his face. We were feeling good that night and thought we saw the love in him. He rumpled Jesse's thick sandy hair and persisted in making eye contact until Jesse looked up. "This'll be good for you," Alex insisted. "A magical mystery ride."

"No lotteries," said Jesse. "I volunteer to be the control."

"But I'm doing this for *you*, man. This is the lottery that *isn't* a lottery. This is the anti-lottery. Everyone wins."

"I don't mind being the control."

"You don't get it, do you? This is a win-win. One through four, you drop and have the trip of your life. Later, you write a philosophy book about it. Five, you're the control and get off watching four people doing crazy shit. You're the protector, the big brother. You still get to write a philosophy book."

Jesse broke into a broad smile, but his eyes were filmy, unfocused. "What the hell…"

Alex took this as a "yes." He jumped up, found five sheets of college-ruled paper, and wrote a number on each.

L.B. said, "We need a fishbowl!"

"We don't have one. Wait!" Phoebe ran into the

kitchen and returned with Alex's spaghetti pot. Alex crumpled the sheets into compact balls and threw them into the pot. "Number five is the control! Take one, but don't open it yet." He passed it to Jesse first, and then the pot made the rounds.

"Drum roll please!" ordered Alex. We all pounded the floor, the soiled shag carpet muffling our thunder. Then, we opened our papers.

Jesse was number one. Alex was number five.

On Saturday, December 18, in our cozy little home, four of us dropped acid.

A few days after my cry for help, Phoebe called back and said, "I've spoken with the others. We're going to meet in Berkeley to observe the anniversary of our drop."

"December 18."

"Not exactly. It's too close to Christmas for L.B., the family man. So we're doing New Year's Eve. Alex is okay with the date."

"We'll have a grand old time watching the fireworks over the Bay."

"It'll be good for us," Phoebe said. "You'll see. I'll take care of everything." My private nurse knew what I needed, and I decided to trust her.

With plans in place, on December 31, 1992, Phoebe and I took flights from our separate cities to the Bay Area. Although Berkeley was still Alex's town, he didn't invite us to his home. Instead, he made a dinner reservation for eight o'clock, and we agreed to meet at the restaurant.

Phoebe and I arrived early. She was standing outside

the restaurant when I walked up. I hadn't seen her in five years, but she hadn't changed much. We hugged, and I clung a bit too long, awash with relief. She was my backbone that night, the person who would make all of it come right again. We went inside, and a hostess showed us to our reserved booth in the back.

We sat down across from each other, my stomach fluttering up in my throat. I could imagine what I looked like. "This isn't the time for cold feet," she scolded. "We're here to confront our demons. We'll get through this." She reached across the table and touched my hand.

"It'll be a test. We'll keep quiet and watch him." I was mimicking her words, the things she'd said to me on the phone when she suggested the plan.

"Exactly. And then, we'll put it behind us." She looked at her watch. "Ten minutes to eight. Since this is the night of confessions, there's something I ought to tell you before the boys get here."

My butterflies were forgotten as I perked up to receive her secret.

"You never spoke of it," she said, "but we all knew about you and Alex, freshman year. Your crush on him was so obvious, and he just gloated afterwards. I understand completely what it must have been like for you."

I searched her eyes for a clue.

"I understand from experience," she explained.

"You? You and Alex?"

"Freshman year. Only once. I'm guessing my night with him was similar to yours. It was horrible. There was no affection or even respect. Only failure and frustration and…" *Anger. Punishment.*

I shook my head in disbelief. Phoebe, strong as a rock, practical, scientific, the controlled caregiver—how could she have been so vulnerable? The way she looked now, it was doubly impossible. Rancor simmered where the compassion of a nurse once reigned.

I had to ask. "I'm confused about this. It doesn't seem possible."

"Remember what it was like when we were that age? All that hype about 'free love'? We all bought into it. I know I did."

"I suppose so," I agreed. "But why would we let this boy be our housemate? How stupid was that?"

"We weren't supposed to care about it. And we were taken by Alex on so many other levels. He was magnetic and strong and we needed a leader. He found the house, negotiated the lease, arranged the utilities, everything." I considered this and concluded that she was right. Phoebe was always right, and it made me a little angry.

At eight o'clock straight up, L.B. lumbered in, bigger than ever with a higher forehead and half the hair. Phoebe and I stood up to greet him. His arms enveloped me, and I became lost in his chest. When I let go, he gave Phoebe a hug and sat down next to her, across from me. I enjoyed looking at him but felt anxious about the open seat next to me.

"Phew, thought I'd be late!" L.B. stared at the empty seat. "Haven't done that drive for a while." Salinas was about two hours from Berkeley.

We ordered drinks. L.B., our former recreational drug supplier, ordered a Coke and sipped through a straw as he caught us up with family news. He described his wonderful wife, his boy and girl aged six and eight, and the bright high school kids he mentored.

"Sorry to take you away from your family on New Year's," I said.

"Christie's fine with it. She goes to all of her own high school and college reunions. Tonight she went with the kids to a party at the home of family friends. They'll try to stay up, and everyone'll fall asleep by ten!" His exuberance renewed me. I fell into a fairytale longing that our evening might end right then, on a perfect, trans-formative note.

But the time passed and tension tightened our group. Was Alex going to show? At eight thirty-five he strolled in. We stood up to greet him without hugs or handshakes. He was very changed and appeared shrunken. The jet-black hair was streaked with gray, and the rumpled business suit hung from a skeletal frame. His eyes were jittery and dark-circled. When he slid into the booth next to me, I smelled the drink on him.

"Sorry I'm late," he apologized. "Rough day at the office!" Not very convincing this late on a New Year's Eve. "Been trying to work out a settlement for a matri-monial client. His wife wants everything—the house, the savings, the kids. Hah! They always do! Any wonder I never got married?"

We chuckled politely, and then the waitress came to save us. We ordered appetizers.

During our three-course dinner, we tiptoed around the elephant in the middle of the table. Phoebe and I each had a glass of wine, L.B. had another Coke, and Alex had three glasses of wine. For dessert, Alex ordered brandy, while the rest of us drank coffee.

Finally, our superficial chatter flagged and Alex leapt into the silence: "We're still doing the drop, aren't we? The fake one? The ceremonial one?"

"Sure. I thought Tilden Park might be a good place to do it," Phoebe said. "We'll ring in the New Year with our private séance in the dark."

Alex slapped the table with an open palm, making the silverware jump. "What did we ever do in Tilden? We never went there!"

An awkward silence fell on the dregs of Alex's belligerent tone. We didn't need to speak, but maybe Alex did. "You were waiting for me to bring it up, weren't you?" His eyes randomly searched our little group. "Well, let's raise our glasses! Here's to Jesse! May he rest in peace."

Coffee cups and brandy snifter met over the table. As drunk as Alex appeared, it wasn't a bad beginning for him, I thought.

"Here's to Jesse," we all said.

Alex turned to me. "The love of your life!"

"We all loved him," I replied.

He kept his glittering eyes on me. "So, why don't we pay him a visit?" Another stunned silence gelled around us. Jesse was buried in his home state, Oregon. "My God, you're thinking…?" Alex laughed, scanned our faces, and banged the table again, this time with two palms. "I meant, let's go take a look at the old house!"

A pause. Murmuring voices, clinking glasses, and scraping chairs were the only sounds. I couldn't judge how this would change things. Phoebe looked me dead on, her eyes saying, *Yes, let's give it a try*. It was easy to grant her this authority. "I think we should go," she agreed for me and L.B. "It will be good for all of us." Foreboding crept in on slippered feet, taking me in its grip.

My heart was beating fiercely as we launched into our impromptu plan. We fumbled with credit cards and cash, split the bill, put on jackets, and walked outside. Alex lurched along the row of parked cars and stopped at a late model sedan, fishing for the keys in his pocket. L.B. piped up, "Let me drive! My car's over on the next block." Phoebe and I didn't have cars; we'd taken taxis from the airport.

Alex was having trouble finding the lock. Phoebe walked over to him and motioned to L.B. over the hood. "We'll take your car, Alex, but let L.B. drive." Her voice was calming, indulgent. Gently, she took the keys away, and he surrendered without a fight.

Ten minutes later, L.B. pulled into a neighborhood I didn't recognize. We drove through a brand-new development and entered a dark block with all the original houses, uninhabited. Deserted. Our old house lurked in the middle of the block. Its lifeless hulk was slated for demolition, boarded up with a dumpster in the driveway. As we stood under a dim streetlamp near the weedy front lawn, Phoebe took my hand and squeezed it. On her other side, she clutched a bulky handbag, its strap slung over her shoulder. Gently, I pulled away.

Alex swayed like a reed in the wind. "She's still standing!"

L.B. walked up to the front door and called back, "It's locked up. No way in." He came back and said, "Let's get out of here."

"Not yet," Phoebe said. "Let's walk around back."

Internally, I suppressed a scream. *Stay quiet and see what he says.* My blood was pounding with my own guilt, everything that'd happened, everything I could have prevented.

Alex gave a drunken chortle and staggered forward, leading us. We walked around to the backyard and stood near the trunk of the weeping willow as our eyes adjusted to the faint ambient light.

The sight of it was too much for me. Helpless again, I dropped to my knees, tripping back in time to that night. L.B. and I sat cross-legged on the ground watching the mysterious wave and ripple of the thousand finger-thin branches, swaying, beckoning and receding. They pulled us in, expelled us, and flew away in the wind. A deafening sound split the air. Glass exploded outward from the hurled crate of Descartes, Sartre, and Nietzsche, diamond shards glistening, raining down from the sky. A beautiful boy took flight, gliding toward the willow like an eagle, into the drooping arms that were unwilling to hold him.

Alex looked up at the tree and dizzily jerked a few steps backward.

"God help us," L.B. muttered. "Poor Jesse!" He got down on his knees next to me and put his mighty arm around my shoulder.

Phoebe spoke, standing above us. "I was inside near the front door and Jesse ran upstairs behind me. I couldn't move. I couldn't stop looking at that doorknob. It was psychedelic, swimming in colors and patterns, and then your hand was on it." She turned to Alex. "You walked *right* out that front door, Alex!"

"Pheebs!" Alex spat the name like a curse. He swiveled around to look at us. "Okay. So you want to go through all this again? You were tripping for hours. I had to take a walk."

His excuses drifted away in the cool night air. We said nothing.

"He *wanted* to take the shit. No one forced him."

The winter-bare branches rustled.

"And you blame me. All of you." He spun right and left, looking for agreement.

L.B. spoke up from his heart of gold: "Jesse was vulnerable. We were all responsible—"

"But you always blamed *me*," Alex cut in. "And you like to forget. He was on death row anyway! He was *al - rea - dy* dead."

In my ear, Jesse quoted: "'There are no facts, only interpretations.'" Nothing had changed.

"All right." Phoebe took charge. "That's it. This is the place. We're doing it right here."

She pulled out a flashlight, illuminated the contents of her shoulder bag, found what she needed, and handed each of us a ceremonial tissue, a tiny blotter soaked with LSD. Only it wasn't.

Phoebe set the round base of the flashlight on the ground with its beam shooting up to the heavens. Tilting her face up to the light, she started to preach. "Jesse, you were an exceptional person. We love you, we miss you, and we beg your forgiveness. We're dropping one last time to feel your pain, to feel our own pain, and to move on. We're doing this for you, Jesse, and for us, the living." Phoebe slowly raised her hand to her mouth and placed the tiny sugar-soaked blotter on her tongue.

Stop. A feeble resolution to interrupt the ceremony bubbled up in my chest, powerless against the mesmerizing influence of the weeping willow tree. I lifted my hand. The blotter hovered over my tongue. L.B. licked and swallowed. Alex grumbled, "Ridiculous!" and stumbled over to the base of the tree. He sat down heavily and cried, "Jesse! This is so goddamn ridiculous!" He slumped over and began to shake uncontrollably, howling like a wild animal.

The sound of his grief alarmed me. A moment ago he'd failed the test, but now he was proving us wrong with his contrition and remorse. Sorrow. Hadn't he been showing it to us all along?

I felt the rumblings of a call to action just as Phoebe started to preach again. "You're wrong, Alex. You were always wrong. It wasn't certain that Jesse would go to Vietnam, or that he'd be killed if he did go. But he was in pain. And the end to his pain wasn't bad. A quick, clean break of the neck. Instant darkness. It wasn't a bad end for him."

Her cold truth made me shiver.

"But *your* end isn't going to be so clean," she went on. "Look at you! Slowly drinking yourself to death!"

I jumped to my feet, afraid I was too late. A special blotter for Alex, she'd said. A little jolt, a scare, some palpitations, shortness of breath. Nothing serious, is what she'd promised. A small punishment to make him a better person. But now, the way she was talking and the way he'd been drinking…?

I knelt in front of Alex and took him by the shoulders. He was pushed up against the base of the tree, his body another twisted root in the ground, arms limp and loose at his sides, palms open. "Are you okay? Alex, are you all right?"

He juddered and convulsed. "How could I? Oh God, how could I?"

Twisting around, I yelled at her. "Phoebe! Tell us what to do!"

In the second before she answered, I saw her as she truly was, as she always had been. Solid as a monument, she stared into the night, her spectral face in the beam of light. She stood on a higher plane, always above us. Nothing could ever touch her. Even at nineteen she was like steel, holding up through the investigation and the following years while L.B. and I were crushed by guilt, every form of therapy useless.

"There's nothing *to* do."

I scooted over to her feet and grabbed the flashlight. As I inspected Alex in the beam, L.B. came over to us.

"He'll be fine," Phoebe said. Another part of the plan: leave him to work it out on his own, just as he'd left *us* alone. "I think we should go."

L.B. ignored her and sat down next to Alex, putting his arm around his shoulders.

"Do you have the keys?" she demanded, holding out her hand. "It's time to go."

"We're not ready to leave," L.B. said.

Alex bore up under my inspection. He was still sobbing, still drunk, but I didn't see any troubling physical symptoms. In a lucky sweep, the beam of light caught and fixed on the tiny blotter, stuck fast to his index finger.

"All right. Do what you want. I've done everything I came to do, and I'm going to walk back to town."

As her final contribution, she abandoned the flashlight to us. We watched her go. Then we settled in, a tight group under the tree. We sat for a long time holding each other, keeping warm against the Berkeley fog.

At midnight, a loud explosion shook the air as the first rocket burst high over the Bay. The fireworks couldn't be seen from our backyard. I looked up into the underside of our broad umbrella and imagined the next bomb bursting high over our heads, spreading its tentacles of red, white, and blue.

₪ *Conference*

MY WINE GLASS, the second, has been empty for some time, and I'm not quite sure of their names, a man and a woman, acquaintances from conferences past. I'm talking and maybe they're listening. My words hover between us, eyes wander. When we drift over to the dining hall, I see my mistake. Territories are already staked, tables full, every empty chair spoken for. The head table is reserved for the "names," and the most skillful schmoozers are sprinkled in among the lesser panelists. At the threshold, my conversation buddies abandon me for saved spots, leaving me with a smile plastered on my face.

A successful latching-on is the objective for these conferences, a shameful purpose that often kicks me awake on the night of the last day. I've missed my targeted panelist by a long shot and look to cut my losses. Flight is an option, briefly entertained and dismissed as cowardly.

So late! The wine is to blame. The dining room is abuzz, a labyrinth of tables topped with half-eaten salads and crusts of buttered rolls, the conferees amiably leaning into one another. Far off in a dim corner, a small table offers three salads and a single diner munching the fourth. He's about my age, maybe a little younger. Most of us conferees are on the other side of middle age, nearing our respective professional peaks. I've reached a certain stature, a place of respect if not recognition, but it's a precarious perch. At times like this, the solid edge of my overlook is liable to crumble underfoot.

I've never seen this man before—perhaps he's new to the circuit—and I'm not blind to the opportunity. A magnanimous gesture of welcome could salvage the wreckage. I'm halfway there when he looks up, mouth full, chewing with gusto, the tail wagging. Complacent, observant. Maybe he doesn't need a welcome, but I'm on the path now and something about him keeps me on it.

At table's edge I say, "Hello. Are these seats taken?" Too late, I regret the sound of it, the unintended insult.

"Not at all! Be my guest!" Genuinely sweet. His nametag says "Courtney Stone" and nothing else, blank where an affiliation should be printed.

He extends a hand, something between an offer to shake and a gesture of invitation toward the empty chair across from him. I decide on the former and accept his hand assertively, in the spirit of a colleague. We share a friendly clasp, a brief pump that's swollen with more feeling than I expected. His blood-filled veins bulge under my fingertips, the coarse hairs bristle. It's a large hand, square, dry, and warm. "Abigail Priory," I say. My own nametag fell off an hour ago.

"Abigail. One doesn't hear that name very often." It's an inappropriately intimate remark, revealing that he hasn't heard of Dr. Priory. I take no offense.

"There are more of us than you think." My cheeks are suddenly warm as I take the seat opposite him. To avoid his eyes, I turn sideways to drape the strap of my handbag over the chairback while directing an oblique nod toward his nametag. "For that matter, I haven't met too many Courtneys."

He laughs. "Male Courtneys, you mean!"

I smile, merely.

"My friends call me Court."

An invitation to friendship? "All right, Court. You may call me Abby."

He grins at that, and our eyes meet undeniably for the first time. He's the first to lower his eyes as he gathers up a forkful of salad. I look down at my own plate. "Now that I think of it, I'm very hungry." I stab a bite. "It's been a long afternoon."

"Mm-hmm," he agrees. We chew for a while until he swallows and asks, "Have you been to many of these conferences?"

"Too many to remember. I come every year. It's the place to make new connections and share ideas." Or crib them, I could add.

"This is my first time. Maybe you can tell."

Does he expect a response? I slip a slice of cucumber into my mouth instead.

"I'm very excited to be here," he explains. "I'm writing a paper now. You might say I'm a neophyte in the field. You're published, I imagine?" He gives a little embarrassed laugh.

I name only the most recent article, and he seems impressed. His large eyes are heavily lashed, his cheeks smoothly shaved, his lips minutely tremulous. A sign of nerves, I think. His interest is showing with a hundred questions poised on the tip of his tongue. The first: "So, you're affiliated with—?"

"Yes, that's right." Maybe he *does* know something of Dr. Priory after all, or at least he recognizes the article I mentioned. "And you?"

But his attention is diverted. A server has arrived with a dish in either hand. "Chicken or salmon?"

We make our choices, one of each. I hardly notice which is mine because the server has interfered with my need to place this man. "You were saying…?"

"Oh, yes." He names an institution I've never heard of, causing the edge of my overlook to crumble. I nod agreeably—a tiny fraud—and take a bite of the entrée. Court explains his educational background and degree, which he earned at the age of forty-seven from a university of unremarkable standing. This time, I recognize the name.

Before I can think of something positive to say, he turns the tables. "Tell me about your research." It's a welcome diversion, a relief.

The highpoints of my professional life are swiftly assembled and laid out in organized fashion. Court is drawn to my story like a daisy to the sun, all eyes and ears, listening and inquiring with enthusiastic smiles, friendly words of agreement, and occasional sounds of muted awe. I rattle on despite the discomfort of a small doubt. This is far too easy, and many of his questions are prefaced with "Abby."

Abby, listen to me, Abby, Abby…

I silence the voice. *This* man doesn't want me to listen. He wants me to tell, and he doesn't seem to notice how I struggle to make it new and shiny. The hovercraft delivers many of the same words I spoke to that woman and that man in the cocktail lounge before dinner, the pat phrases so easily repeated to nameless people who have their own ideas and never ask for mine. In the white noise of my brain, that pair of conferees and a hundred others engage in self-promotion, the content now blurry.

Court, maybe, deserves more from me. He's a man who grants permission with apparent sincerity. It's a refreshing change, even as the red light flicks on.

"An amazing study," he says. "Tell me, Abby, how did you develop your theory?"

When a person repeats your name, is he interested in *you*, or does he hear only himself intentionally creating an impression of his interest in you? In this instance, I have no doubt. I'm finding it easier to meet his eyes. My answer, this time, goes deeper, and I find myself reliving the exhilaration I felt at the beginning of my career, the excitement and hope. My narrative creeps into the years of trial and success and setbacks and frustration. Recently, there've been hours at my computer attempting to build an online network, typing into a vacuum composed of a billion people screaming "me" into cyberspace. God knows I've expended every effort to light a fire in the popular psyche, to create a groundswell of support fueled by the promise of the early studies. If only...well then, the momentum would virtually guarantee the recognition needed to tap the bottomless well of government grant money to fund more assistants, technicians, graduate students, analysts, clinicians, therapists, programmers, ghost writers, and statisticians, to solicit more test subjects, to conduct more blind studies and run more correlations. I'm not asking for much. It doesn't have to be penicillin. A modest panacea will do, enough to spur an opening of the public coffers, allowing my project to feed and branch and grow. Then they would see. Everyone would see.

Court sees it. His eyes tell me so.

Of course, I haven't stated my thoughts quite so crassly. My work stands on its own. This is my project. This is where it could go.

"Fascinating!" he says.

But I begin to exhaust myself and come to a stopping point. I glance down at the table. How long have I been going on? My plate is still nearly full. The effects of the wine should have worn off by now, but I'm feeling slightly ridiculous and lightheaded. The end of my last sentence still resonates on a high pitch that could be mistaken for neediness or resentment instead of exhaustion.

Perhaps Court didn't notice, or else his change of subject is deliberately tactful. "This is pretty good," he says after a bite and a swallow. Gazing at him, I'm put off balance, made dizzy. The wall behind his head forms a shimmering halo. Luminous eyes caress my face as he blinks in slow motion, long lashes going down, going up. "How's your [salmon] [chicken]?" Going down, going up. Incomprehensible. With just a blink or two, the dining hall fills with strutting chickens and flying salmons.

I say something like this: "As good as can be

expected, whatever it is."

He laughs heartily. Apparently, my confusion is delightful. My palate awakens to the taste in my mouth—most definitely salmon. "At least they've managed not to overcook the fish."

"I wouldn't know."

And why would he? *Here*, I almost say, picking up my fork. A bite to prove it. How silly! But it doesn't matter; he's already on to the next thing. "What about tonight?" he asks. "The panel discussion should be good. Are you going?"

I've been keeping my options open. "Yes," I say, without hesitation.

"Great! I've been looking forward to it. There may be something for me to learn. Something to help me in writing my paper."

There. He's done with the flattery, a premeditated return to self. This would be my usual assumption, but Court is different. Court is guileless, transparent, and hint-free. There's no obligation to ask him anything, but I want to know, and I've reacquired my professional bearing. "Tell me about your idea, Court." Borrowing from him.

He begins an earnest, if disjointed, presentation. His voice is rich and male, his manner hopeful and inclusive, conveying the idea more completely than his words. I'm feeding myself the salmon while trying to yank my eyes away from him, to let them skate around the room as I did with those other conferees before dinner, the people whose faces I've forgotten, whose ideas I don't care to know. But here is someone different, unknown, fresh, new, untested. Undistinguished. Why, then, do I want to hear this? His manner is alarmingly open and irresistible, inviting another plunge into a bizarre unreality. "How did you arrive at your thesis?"

"I'm not completely sure, but I can trace it back to a starting point." His face shines in beatific centeredness as a fleeting smile of remembrance graces his lips. "Years ago, I had an experience that...well...sort of changed me...set me on a certain path." He pauses with his hands open, palms up, on either side of his plate. His face, shoulders, torso, arms and hands create an air-brushed image, vaguely beckoning.

"An experience...?"

"Yes, during one of my trips abroad. I've traveled quite a bit, you see..."

"Traveled? Where have you traveled?"

"Asia, Africa, Europe, South America. Afghanistan."

I take a mental inventory of the times I've been to Europe—three trips, one of those for a conference. "What was the nature of your travel?"

"When I was young it was mostly volunteer work in Third World countries. Later I was in the military, stationed around the globe, dragging my family with me. Except for Afghanistan. They didn't come along for that." He gets sidetracked and starts to talk about his family. Midway through, I remember that I didn't ask him for this, a topic with absolutely no relevance to our purpose in being here. At these conferences, I've sat through more than my share of volunteered information, the tedium of it. Endless recitations about projects, theorems, data, techniques, and the ironies of causation versus uncorrelated coincidence. Never has any conferee offered up such a personal account, but I want Court to go on.

He describes his wife, a psychologist—a marriage counselor, actually—and their three children, all boys, now young adults, aged nineteen, twenty-three and twenty-five. Perhaps Court is older than I thought, or else he and his wife were fairly young when they started having the children. How old were we at the beginning, trying so hard and failing? When the reality set in, Nathan and I captioned ourselves the divine, childless couple. My husband is my go-to, my sounding board, now even more so in his speechlessness, after losing his vocal cords to cancer two years ago. I still hear Nathan's voice…heard it again only moments ago, not in its most pleasing iteration. Something harkened it. Something Court said or did…

I've never spontaneously told any conferee about my home life, yet Court is blithely unspooling his. The wife has a name: Regina. He doesn't describe her physically, but I know the type of woman she must be. I see them together, a tight pair, so close they can read each other's thoughts.

While I fight the envy, Afghanistan floats into consciousness, a place the family wasn't dragged into. "Was your family involved in this, what was it, this life-changing experience, you say?"

He doesn't answer immediately but gazes past my left shoulder, into his transformative past. Would he back out now? "No. I was very young. It was 1979, a time before I met my wife. I was working for a humanitarian organization in South America—in the mountains of Peru to be exact. We were in a small Quechuan community in the Ayacucho region of the Andes. It was very remote. We had to hike in at eleven thousand feet—so breathtakingly beautiful."

Catching my own breath, I can't find any, all the air sucked away. I pick up my sweating water glass, ice melted, and gulp thirstily. The water leaves an aftertaste of rust on my tongue.

"There were four of us volunteers, myself, another boy, and two girls. Our leader was a man from the organization who managed the project. His name was Roberto. He was much older than us, and I regarded him almost like a parent. Looking back on it now, he might have been only in his mid-thirties or so, but the four of us were so very young. I was only nineteen. We were building a schoolhouse for the community and developing lesson plans. Members of the village shared the physical labor. At night, Roberto and the four of us had endless discussions about everything that these people didn't know. We were deciding, for them, what we thought they *should* know. Nineteen-year-olds and a man not much older!"

He smiles to himself and looks down at his plate, pushing a roasted potato around with his fork. It rolls, he pushes. At my back, a hundred bodies press into us in our little corner. The din swells and breaks with jagged punctuation: a person laughs, another coughs, a man makes a loud point, cutlery dangerously clicks against china, ice cubes tinkle inside glasses. I'm unaccountably repulsed by my participation in this conference, yet in need of it, my safe harbor. "They grew potatoes," Court says, still looking down. "Small, multi-colored potatoes." He inserts the bit into his mouth, chews, and swallows. He punctures another cube of potato with his fork and points it at me. "This one isn't as good, but then, that was a time when everything tasted so delicious. I was idealistic and in love with the world and so sure that I could change it. You know what I mean, don't you, Abby?" His eyes are full and searching. He puts the potato down, not giving it another thought.

"Yes...of course." I'm nodding but can't say that I've ever felt that way before. Never. Not at age nineteen, not at thirty, not now, although I believe that my work has had, and continues to have, an impact on the community of ideas in a theoretical sense. A trickle-down effect. Not the same as building a school for the impoverished and ignorant.

"We were too young, really, to understand anything at all. We came from middle class homes in the United States. These people were poor farmers and herders, but they had something far greater than I'd ever seen. They were descendants of the Inca, an ancient people. What were we doing there? What right had we? But I fell in love with them. They were small and brown and robust in their colorful clothing, walking miles of trails that snaked around the mountains. It took me a week just to be able to breathe."

I shift in my seat, trying to get enough of the rarified air. I'm openly staring at him now, ascending his mountain, annoyed by the pebbles in my shoes, feeling the heat and constraint of my nylon pantyhose and the tight skirt squeezing my thighs. These clothes were chosen with a purpose in mind: to display my legs, still my most attractive feature. At the moment, it seems a ridiculous costume.

"I was there only a few days when a man in the village took a liking to me. It seems he was impressed with my nascent Quechuan—"

"Please!" I interrupt. It's a sudden, almost desperate, sound. "Please," I repeat in a quieter tone. "I'd like to hear the language."

Court's eyes open wide. I've surprised him, and he seems pleased by it. "I didn't think you were... Well, here goes." He sends out a string of foreign sounds that could be anything at all. I have no way of knowing.

"What did you say?"

"Do not steal, do not lie, do not be lazy."

"I can assure you, I'm not like that." My lips twitch upward in a smile to go along with the facile cover-up for my violation of the middle precept.

He pretends not to see. "Then I predict that you will live an eternal life in the warmth of The Sun." He says it just like that: "The Sun."

"Thank you. I like that." Me and my undeserved place in The Sun. Court has that look again, the fullness of life, and he's certainly no stranger to the sun. It shows in the crinkles around his eyes.

The server is back, depositing white saucers with thin rectangles of cake and scooping up our dinner plates. Another server follows with two coffee pots, regular and decaf. Choices are made, sugar stirred. "Go on with your story. Please go on."

"Yes, I will. The man I was talking about…his name is Cuyuchi. Was. I suppose he's no longer in this world. The year after we left, the Shining Path launched a civil war, and most of the people in the region were slaughtered. But I can still see Cuyuchi's face. He was an elder, not so very old, perhaps sixty-five, old enough not to be engaged in the hard labor of building the school. I remember noticing him from my first day. He seemed to be everywhere, curious about us, listening, observing, always in the background. His expression was unreadable. They were a shy people, so I suppose I was the one to initiate our conversation. I can't remember how it started, but…" Court stops to take a sip of his coffee, thinking back. "I'll never forget him."

Another sip. "He was stocky, almost a foot shorter than me, and his face was like tough, brown leather. He slowed his Quechuan just for me, using the simplest words so I could understand, and somehow I always did. His eyes and gestures had a way of communicating every point he was making in an understated way. The very first thing he said to me was: 'My son. You are different from the rest.' I didn't know what to say. I suppose I said, 'Thank you.' I know I felt honored and chosen. I didn't know what this man could possibly want. He would simply come up to me when I was alone and stand quietly, very close, giving off his distinct smell, a mixture of damp alpaca wool, coca leaves, and mountain air. My eyes and ears and nose were always instantly attuned to him.

"One day he said, 'Your leader, Roberto. You always listen to him.' He was right. All of us kids, the volunteers, hung on his words, especially when we first arrived. We were a little scared. The people of the mountain were the opposite, secure and serene. When Roberto spoke to them, they listened, and when they replied, Roberto would stare at them intently and nod in agreement. It was a very intimate look, almost an intrusion. After a while, I started to think it was all for show.

"The day after Cuyuchi made that comment about Roberto, I was with the two of them when they had a conversation. I understood only half of it. Roberto was fluent in Quechuan, so Cuyuchi spoke faster than he ever did with me. As usual, Roberto wore his intent look and said 'Yes' several times. After Roberto walked off, I asked Cuyuchi, 'What did you say to him?' Cuyuchi didn't answer directly but said just enough to tease me. 'If you ask him, he will not be able to tell you.' Of course, it proved to be true. When I asked Roberto, he failed the test. 'Something about the school,' is all he said. Then he quickly changed the subject to talk about his own plans for the school.

"I was puzzled and annoyed at Roberto, but more curious than ever about Cuyuchi. He always seemed to gather up his thoughts in silence before speaking. A few days later, we were at the building site when he came up and stood quietly at my side. The next thing he said was, 'Roberto's children will not be going to this school.' He spoke in an offhand way, as though it wasn't important, but of course it was, and I was powerless to address it. What could I say? That I would intervene? I had no control over Roberto. Cuyuchi remained silent for perhaps a full minute, his face a complete blank. Then he said, 'Come,' and turned away, taking a few steps toward the dirt road in the center of the village. I didn't know what he intended. He kept walking and seemed to assume I would follow. 'Come where?' I called after him. He turned around to face me and said, 'Come,' a second time. Still I hesitated, until he gave this final command: 'You should come with me.' His voice was calm, nearly emotionless—it was simply so, nothing to debate. He turned and started walking again, and I followed."

At last, Court breaks for another sip of his coffee. I've eaten the cake, he has not. He's been talking non-stop. He looks at me over the edge of the coffee cup with eyes like spinning corkscrews. I hardly know where I am. I whisper, "Where are we…? Where did you go?"

His lips curve upward in the smallest of smiles. "Let me tell you. I followed him through the village and onto the nearest mountain path. I'd only been up this path once before and had stopped well before the end—if there *was* an end, because it seemed infinite. We walked and walked until my lungs burned, my feet grew sore, and my hands were swollen. I couldn't predict our destination. The summit was at least fourteen thousand feet, and we'd gone maybe a thousand up from eleven. He didn't speak, just kept going. Parts of the path were treacherous and steep and narrow on the face of the mountain, where any misstep could send you tumbling into oblivion, but he wasn't slowing down. The hard walking was an integral part of who he was, a mountain animal, life of the earth. Trust flared up inside me without even a thought. There was no way to make this journey without that implicit trust and complete abandonment of self. If I turned around to go back to the village, I wouldn't be able to make it on my own, ignorant of the safe places to step, the correct way to move. His arms didn't swing but held him in perpetual balance; his footsteps were so sure that they naturally picked the secure toeholds, avoiding rocks or outcroppings that could lead to catastrophe."

Court pauses, letting a shadow of embarrassment pass over the earnest expression in his gentle features. "I was fearful, I admit. I couldn't go back and had to go on. I was thirsty and soaked with sweat and thinking of my backyard at home, wondering how I'd come to be on the edge of this mountain, following a virtual stranger in a land that was so terribly beautiful that I was attracted to the idea of a death that was instant and blissful and eternal, a state that would fuse the molecules of my corporal self forever to this man and his heavenly sky. I'm not a spiritual person, you see, Abby. You understand?"

I'm nodding.

"There was nothing but thin air, shrubs, and earth, and the moving body of another human being in front of me. We walked until I was ready to give everything up. I was exhausted, at an end. But then he stopped and said, 'Here.' We'd come to our destination—the mouth of a cave."

Court pauses again. This time, he desperately needs a deep breath of sea-level air before he can go on. I give him that moment. He's gazing at that distant point beyond my shoulder again, and I take this opportunity to study him. Just now, I'm startled to notice that he's in shirtsleeves rolled up at the wrists, no jacket, no tie. His chest rises into a huge "V" over the tabletop and slowly recedes again. He continues. "If the walk was the precursor to death, then the cave was death itself, a steady diminishment of light into the complete absence of light. It smelled moist and animal-like inside, sweating minerals and gasses from time gone by. I was overwhelmed by the need to control my panic. Cuyuchi said nothing as we walked. At first, I could hear him moving and breathing as I followed along, having no idea where my next footfall would land, in a rut, on a rock, over a cliff, into an underground river, on a rodent or a snake, or into the wall on the side of the cave. About a hundred yards in, I felt the hair on the top of my head brush up against the roof of the cave. After that, I stooped a bit as I walked. We were moving slower than we had on the face of the mountain. Even Cuyuchi, who was so sure of himself, couldn't maintain his earlier pace.

"I was living on his breath and existence. We crept on in silence. You'd think that the dark would heighten my senses, but my terror obliterated them. I could no longer hear or see my leader. It made no difference whether my eyes were open or closed. I kept them open only in the hope of seeing. My ears strained in the hope of hearing. My body was filled with the sounds of my own hammering heart and ragged breath. There was no room for anything else. I couldn't even detect Cuyuchi's smell—those distinct odors that always clued me in to his presence. I was suffocating on a new, overpowering perfume: a pungent mixture of the cave's unique aroma and the rancid sweat of my own fear.

"At last, when it seemed we'd walked to the center of the earth, Cuyuchi stopped and I pulled up short. In an eye blink, we came to a halt. I couldn't tell you exactly how I knew it was time to stop. There was a signal no greater than a slight stirring of the air over my cheek like a feather. It was an intuition or a sixth sense that developed out of my urgent need to find the meaning in this. To reach a conclusion.

"Maybe you remember, Abby," he looks at me, "how I toyed with that reckless and romantic impulse toward death on the face of the mountain—a freefall into the abyss? Well, inside the cave, things changed. I came full circle. Suddenly my life was priceless and infinitely precious to me. The absence of light erased our bodies, seizing me with a powerful need to find completion, to regain the external proof of my existence. I was attuned to the beating of my heart, the struggle for breath, the moisture on my skin and in my mouth and on the top of my head, the water crawling down through my hair along my scalp and onto my neck. I felt the burn of exercised muscle, the tingle of nerve endings, and the chemical power of fear. Most of all—and this is it, Abby! This is what I want to tell you!"

My heart is racing. Court's eyes are glistening.

"My drive to live, to survive, to see the light again, was tied to the man who was sharing the black hole with me. There was no perception, only belief. If he hadn't been there, the opposite desire would have overtaken me, I'm sure of it! The temptation toward annihilation. We stood silently for a minute, until my heart slowed and my breathing grew calmer and I gave up the fight. I just let it be.

"I don't know if I can explain it… Where there's no

light, there's no separation. When I let my defenses down, I was at once completely inside myself and dispersed into the blackness around me. Cuyuchi and I were both expanding, interlacing, and suffusing the void. Gradually, I began to hear. At first, only small things like the shifting of a toe in the dirt and the faint sound of his breathing. After that, I sensed the most surprising sound. I could hear the beating of his heart. Maybe it wasn't a sound at all but the impact of heart muscle against his chest, causing a subtle, rhythmic pressure into the air around us. I began to perceive the smell I had grown so accustomed to, Cuyuchi's smell. Time stood still. Seconds or minutes passed, and at the end of it, we'd reclaimed our bodies.

"Only then did he speak. Again, it might not have been sound, but his thoughts, projected as speech. Now, so many years later, I'm convinced of it. He thought and I heard. 'You see it now, don't you, my son?' I responded with a word or a nod or a thought. 'Yes.' His point was clear without articulation. In a place where the world disappears, where everything tangible and external is removed, where intellectual needs are stripped and survival remains, the ego shrivels to a speck of dust. The only thing left is communication in its purest form. I read Cuyuchi's thoughts: 'Now you can truly listen. Remember what it feels like.'"

Court stops. I've stopped. His eyes meet mine. "I stepped to the side and allowed Cuyuchi to lead me out of the cave, moving toward the light."

He's at the end. We remain still, eyes locked, oxygen deprived, spent, enclosed in the darkness of the tunnel, a black oval surrounding us. I've been clutching the white cloth napkin in my lap and bring it up to throw on the table, twisted and damp. My fingers crawl toward his along the surface of the table and stop just short. All around us, near silence. Everyone has gone. At the other end of the room comes a clatter of dishes and silverware, a few barked orders, an occasional laugh. The wait staff is cleaning up.

Wordlessly, we stand. I tip precariously and right myself. Our tunnel opens into a wavy mirage of white light, glass, and silver. Tall, curtained windows block us from the outside world. There's a pause, a small communication of sorts, before we make our way down the aisle between the tables in the dining hall. I feel his height and breadth at my side and fall back, a half step behind. We enter the main corridor, as wide as the mountain path is narrow, as secure as the cliff edge is exposed and treacherous. Eggshell walls and patterned carpet contrast with green slopes. Recycled air doesn't satisfy like the sharp, biting intake of mountain air.

In the West Salon, four panelists sit in a row, their egos on display, the microphones, water glasses and pencils at each spot on the white tablecloth. A sea of gleaming, well-washed heads populates the audience. What is this? A conference of professionals and experts and luminaries in a field that has nothing to do with anything I've just heard—nothing to do with Court's idea for a "paper." Deep inside me is the embryonic anger that hasn't bloomed, a reaction to his treachery and deception. A false idea, for there was none.

We take seats in the back, connected to the others merely at their boundary. There *is* no connection because the tunnel has expanded and brightened to expose every surface in sharp relief. Surfaces only.

The sole female panelist is speaking: "My findings were startling. If you'll turn to my article at page fifty-seven of your materials…" Court's thigh touches mine as we sit, side-by-side in the straight-backed chairs. I can feel the intensity of his concentration, his laser focus on the speaker as he absorbs and internalizes every word. A slight movement to the right, and now my shoulder touches his. These points of contact—highlighting the absence of fusion—effectively stir up my terror.

Day after tomorrow I will be home again with my speechless Nathan. The thought seizes me with panic. I sit through the panel discussion in this panicked state, scarcely a word of it penetrating the surface. I'm waiting for it to end, when we will stand and turn to each other, and perhaps Court will have another secret to impart, the clue to what we've just learned, or should have learned, during the hour in our straight-backed chairs.

But this is what happens. A warm touch on my shoulder and the inevitable goodbye.

I've enjoyed meeting you, Abby. I've enjoyed listening to you.

Spoken word, or thought? On my part, there's a mixture of both: "The pleasure was all mine, Courtney." *Don't go, don't go, don't go…*

In the swirl of departing conferees, I stand alone in the West Salon. A figure emerges on a deliberate path toward me. It's that man I met before dinner, the one whose name I've forgotten. He comes up to me with a big smile on his face and says, "Interesting, wasn't it?" There's a hideous twinkle in his eyes. He winks at me and steps away.

At midnight, safely in my hotel room, I lie in bed, looking up into the imperfect darkness, every detail recalled. I see the gentle eyes, the slow blink, the hands resting on the table, palms up. After his story, we lock into silence, resisting the moment of separation. It's time to break away from each other, to join the others. He stands. I stand. He steps away from the table and passes me to lead the way. Frozen to the spot, I turn to watch him go. His back is broad, glistening with sweat, kissed by The Sun.

He stops and looks back over his shoulder. "Come," he says.

₪ *Searching for Earwax*

LUCILLE REPEATS THE ritual, inspects, smells, and palpates. The skin is smooth and the flesh firm, but oh, here's a soft spot. She replaces the apple and picks up another. There's a presence, an annoyance… Glancing up, she meets the eyes of a woman whose face is set in a sort of grimace-smile. "Ma'am," the woman says.

It's the second time the woman has spoken, Lucy realizes now. The raised tone confirms it. Lucy offers a blink and stands mute. People always in your business.

"Is that your…grandchild?" Not quite sure. They never are. "Over there?" The unwanted Good Samaritan points. Little Amineh is on tippy-toe, reaching for a bunch of bananas. The girl's mother wouldn't approve—those bananas aren't organic. And there's something else the mother wouldn't like. Piles of oranges, cantaloupes, peaches, honeydew melons, and two shoppers separate Lucy from her charge.

Lucy's grip on the nonorganic, red apple tightens. "Thank you," she says to the woman, no admissions implied. Independence is admirable, especially at age four. On their first day together, Amineh declared, "My name

69

means trustworthy," channeling her mother.

The interloper, satisfied to have redirected Lucy's attention, vanishes into the ever-shifting stream. It's a warm September Saturday, and pedestrians jam this Upper West Side sidewalk near the outdoor produce display. Bumped and jostled, Lucy plants her eyes on the child, the milk chocolate hand against the waxy yellow fruit. A bunch dangles precariously over the edge. She navigates around the shoppers and puts a clamp on the birdlike wrist. "Come. I've got a beautiful Rome apple for you."

An attractive lure, but now the child is impatient for it. "Hold your horses," says Lucy. "I have to pay." And figure out how to wash it.

On the way to the park, Lucy withholds the treat until they're settled on a bench and the apple is properly polished with a paper towel she pulled from a pocket. Five minutes later, after three huge bites are masticated and sent down the tiny gullet, the girl says, "You're just like my Grandma."

"Which Grandma?"

"*My* Grandma."

Lucy nods thoughtfully. On the downward bob, she notices the hands folded in her lap—an artist's pallet of brown spots and blue veins in crinkled white skin. Must be the mother's mother. "Why do I remind you of her?"

"She's always looking way over there. Or over there." With each "there," the girl flings her apple-holding hand, right and left, and then the apple flies through the air and rolls in the dirt.

With a limp cluck of disapproval, Lucy attempts a

stern look into the liquid brown eyes, but she can't hold it. "Now the apple's no good," she says, casting her gaze higher, above the girl's African braids. Better.

"See," Amineh says. "Just like Grandma." She jumps up and runs for the dirt-caked fruit.

Amineh Larousse-Jakande was a late baby. Her mother, Dorine Larousse, is forty-four. After the child's birth, the mother took a three-year leave of absence from her public-sector career to give her daughter a proper launch into the world. Ms. Larousse ("Call me Dorine") is a practitioner of elimination communication, a believer in organic farming, solar power, and vegetarianism, and a shunner of antibiotics and pediatrician visits, except in dire emergencies. The child hasn't been immunized against any of the major diseases. Or any of the minor ones. Immunizations cause autism, the mother says.

"But my children were never autistic," Lucy remarked with a little laugh during the initial interview.

"Oh, this is all new," Dorine explained. "A cumulative effect over generations."

The point did not seem credible. Nevertheless, Lucy affirmed, "I'm a staunch believer in science." She thought of that raised circle of skin on her left shoulder from an ancient smallpox vaccination. *Could I catch measles or whooping cough from this child?* Despite the risk, she accepted the job: four and a half hours every weekday afternoon, one o'clock to five thirty, after preschool.

At the end of the interview, when their oral contract was confirmed, Dorine asked: "Do you like to be called Lucille or Lucy?" Choice C, "Mrs. Steadman," was not offered.

Unaccountably, a naughty desire surfaced. "Either one is fine," she said with a little smile. The woman seemed entirely too vested in certainty.

It's been a week on the job, and Lucy now understands what Dorine means by "EC." Luckily, the elimination communication is water under the bridge. Amineh exhibits perfect control, with only occasional accidents at naptime. Liberality may be to blame for those. Lucy's own children never had accidents once they were trained. As she recalls.

The EC training and non-immunization make Amineh a walking sponge for germs—all the good ones, Dorine would argue. And the child is emotionally strong as well. "Of course, we're always on the lookout for narrow-minded people," the mother warned. "Those nasty looks and comments can damage her self-esteem."

As yet, there've been no such encounters to guard against—if guarding is even necessary. As far as Lucy can discern, Amineh has no self-esteem issues whatsoever.

Amineh grabs the handrail and climbs the plastic steps of the play structure. Plenty of healthy germs there. The apple is in a trash can, long forgotten. The child jumps down to the wood chips, latches onto another little girl her age, and wrestles her into a bear hug.

When Lucy's children were Amineh's age, they were climbing rickety metal ladders and placing their bottoms on searing hot steel slides. The see-saw was wooden, its dangers well-known: splinters and a jolt to the tailbone from a partner's abrupt dismount. Lucy's daughter Kathy is now thirty-five, and Marc is thirty-two. They have spouses and careers in cities from which it is always a big production number to arrange a trip of any length to New York.

Eyeing Amineh from the park bench, Lucy floats in a haze of possible regret. She's living what she asked for, and it's too late now, so she might as well enjoy it. This choice of hers. Go find another family and do some good.

Her gaze drifts lazily. It's a pleasant day, sunny, about seventy-five degrees, the leaves just starting to color, the quickening of autumn in the air. A time for endings and change, but this doesn't feel like a new beginning. Out of nowhere, Lucy's eyes start to sting and fill to the brims. She takes off her glasses and presses a palm to one, then the other. No reason for it, except the children. So many of them in a blur, darting in and out of the play structure. Life. Brand-new human beings.

She puts the glasses back on her nose, but the last bit of moisture still smudges her vision. Another sunny afternoon, thirty years ago, comes to mind. A suburban playground, dozens of children on the equipment, two of them hers, a chat with a neighbor mom about a news story: *Just one look away, that's all it took...*

Children are screaming. Lucy scans the playground, her heart notched up a tick. Where has Amineh gone? Not there, but...there, on the other side! The girl is thoroughly glued to her new friend, a cherubic blonde with an identifiable, contrasting nanny standing nearby. Amineh has made a good choice in a friend, and why wouldn't she? Little Miss Trustworthy is a miniature adult, even more mature than Charles ever was. In some ways. At least that's how it seems, looking back to the time, years ago, when thoughts of flight jumped up to surprise her. Lucy was in her early fifties then, at the onset of an unbearable freeze and burn. Each episode would arise with a subtle announcement, like a breeze over the deep whispering glacier within, followed by a flick of the ignition, fueling a slow burn in the gut, radiating, building, up from her abdomen into her chest and neck and extremities, flaming up into her head, red hot and fit to burst. *Go away.*

The hot decade, she calls it now. At low moments, she applauds herself for persevering so long. A full decade of tolerance beating back a steadily ascending repugnance. In the end, a person can take only so much and has to look out for herself. This self-validation is useful for soothing the roughest edges, not much more. A hundred repetitions fail to define "only so much," the gradual piling on of things that ultimately became intolerable. Now, in the evening, she clears the single plate and fork from her kitchen table and says to the air, "That was dinner."

"Grandma Lucy!" Amineh has a new name for her.

"Coming, sweetheart." With a hand on the bench, she pushes up and walks over. "Is this your new friend?" Amineh has throttled the fair child with another bear hug. Lucy glances at the nanny. "Hello."

"Grandma, Grandma! This is Curley."

"Kirby," says the little girl from inside the death grip.

"She your grandchild," the nanny declares in a questioning tone, nodding at Amineh.

"I'm the babysitter," Lucy says with a little laugh. "Nanny" doesn't seem quite the term for what Lucy does, not compared to this woman. "My name is Lucille," she says, as if that will explain everything. Why she needs to explain anything to this woman, as compared to that busybody at the market, she couldn't say.

"First time I seen you here."

"Yes, maybe it is."

"Bernadette!" the little blonde calls out. It's a screech, really, because Amineh has tackled her to the ground. Amineh is giggling, and it's all in play, but Kirby starts to cry. A weak child. Amineh is the dominant force in this duo, and Kirby doesn't like it, and now Bernadette doesn't like it either. The nanny grabs the child's arm and pulls her up off the ground. "Come on, now. Stop that cryin'."

Without a goodbye, Bernadette leads the towhead away from nothing and no one. The new friend and her "Grandma" simply never existed.

Amineh has already forgotten about Kirby. She runs off to climb the play structure and, perhaps, to find another friend. A dime a dozen.

No self-esteem problems whatsoever.

At five o'clock, they sit side-by-side on the Larousse-Jakande living room couch with a screen in Lucy's lap. She reads the story, increasingly annoyed at the interruptions. Amineh keeps reaching over, and her hand covers the screen. For the tenth time, a chubby fingertip touches a word, and for the tenth time, a bespectacled owl with a mortarboard on its head appears. "Game, g – a

– m – e, something to play, game," it says. Progress is slow, if the objective of this exercise is to read the story. Progress is just as slow, if the objective is education. Amineh has touched some of these words more than once.

"Why don't I go get us a book?"

"But I want this one."

"This isn't a real book. Surely you have a book somewhere."

Lucy gets up to take a look for something tangible. Something she can control. These days, she lives in a dream where nothing works. She developed a fear of the television set in 2003. Not that she'd want to return to 1960, when her father had to massage the screen of their new color set with his fingertips to enhance the "chrome." She accepts that today's devices have their uses, but she'd like to know how to get by without calling Marc for help. Her home laptop can be counted on only to crash. Before retiring in 2015, she thought of herself as a computer whiz—a faulty self-image propped up by the invisible, topnotch corporate IT department.

The living room in this spacious apartment does have a bookcase, but all the titles are for the adults, that is to say, for Dorine. New age childcare, natural remedies, chakras, and self-visualization. Behind her back, the robotic voice of the owl speaks for the eleventh time. When did children turn into automatons? When did it become impossible to distinguish normal people from the mentally ill, strolling city streets in conversation with invisible friends?

She walks into Amineh's room and finds a few real

books. When she returns to the living room, the child is standing on the arm of the couch, reaching up to the top leaf of a tree that grows in a pot of dirt. An actual tree grows in the living room. "It went up there." Lucy directs her focus but sees nothing on the tree. The girl totters on the edge of the arm and falls, without crying.

Just then, Amineh's father walks in the front door. Wednesdays are his "early" evenings by agreement with Dorine.

"Daddy!" the girl cries. He sweeps her up in his arms and laughs in a deep baritone. This is where the resemblance more closely lies, cheek to cheek. With her legs clamped around his middle, the girl puts the palm of her hand on his broad nose, presses it, and says, "Honk!"

Lucy's children never did that. Perhaps their daddy's nose—thin and hooked—was not an attractive target for this game.

"How'd the afternoon go?" asks Charles Jakande, ignoring the inference to be drawn from Amineh's twisted position on the floor when he walked in. Although Lucy has been invited to call the parents by their first names, she has difficulty with Mr. Jakande's, for obvious reasons. So she usually doesn't call him by any name at all. "Just fine," she says. Should she mention the attack on that little blonde girl? "Amineh is quite something else."

"She is, isn't she?" The father tickles his daughter under the chin and sets her down.

"We went to the store and got an apple and went to the park. And Grandma Lucy doesn't like Mr. Owl."

Lucy is taken aback. She's quite sure she never said

any such thing. What else does Amineh know about her and plan to report?

"Not Mr. Owl!" Another booming laugh. Mr. Jakande winks at Lucy over Amineh's head. *Can't say that I blame you*, his eyes seem to say.

When Lucy gets home, the red number "1" is blinking on her answering machine, a nineties relic she took with her when she left. Charles kept the unfathomable television set, and she hasn't bought another. It seemed only fair that the person leaving should take the insignificant things and voluntarily downsize to an apartment.

"Mom, it's Kathy. Hope you're doing well. When you get a chance, give me a call. I have some news." Click.

Lucy plays the message a second time, just for the sound of her daughter's voice, and decides not to erase the message. The miniature cassette tape is nearly full. These little cassettes are no longer manufactured, so Lucy periodically goes through the old tapes, deciding which ones to tape over. An infrequent chore, since she receives so few messages, but it's an activity fraught with anxiety. She's thought of asking Marc to search the Internet for answering machine cassettes, sold as collector's items.

In her message, Kathy uses the neutral voice she's learned to assume for their telephone conversations. This is the news. This is the news I ought to tell Mom. Kathy has lived in Seattle since she graduated from college. A very long time. Visits and phone calls abruptly stopped in 2014 for more than a year, but Kathy claims she's over it now. Her behavior tells a different story.

Hearing the message causes Lucy's heart to swell with emotion, and she needs a measure of self-control before making the return call. It doesn't seem fair to award Kathy a superficial nick in her responsibility belt merely for leaving a message on an answering machine tape. The onus is shifted to Lucy to afford Kathy an opportunity for the complete fulfillment of her daughterly duty. This little bit of anger pushes Lucy out of the realm of weepy emotion, onto neutral ground. As additional fortification, she remains standing while dialing Kathy's number.

"Hello, Kathy. How's everything? I just received your message." Actually, it's been a full quarter of an hour since she played it for the second time.

"Hi Mom. Everything's great. Thanks for calling back." There's an awkward silence because the opening lines have become difficult. One misstep could send them careening into a cauldron of incivility.

"Hope I haven't interrupted dinner," Lucy says.

"It's three thirty."

"Oh, sorry, that's right." Six thirty in New York means three thirty in Seattle. Why is Kathy home in the middle of a workday? "Anyway, sounds like you have some news to tell me!" Lucy makes it chipper.

Another pause. "Right, Mom. I have some exciting news." Still, that neutral tone, holding back. "But maybe you've heard."

There it is—a little reminder. "Well, no, honey." A bit of sarcasm can't be contained. "I don't think I've heard your news." And I don't want to know when you told Charles or how many times you've discussed it with him.

"I'm going to have a baby."

The room tilts into another dimension and Lucy drops onto the couch. She recovers swiftly but imperfectly. "That *is* exciting news. Just…just wonderful. Congratulations."

On the other end, her daughter's breathing becomes audible and irregular, revealing a shattered hope for something more. Lucy is adept at picking up these clues to Kathy's internal plane. As a young child, whenever Kathy prepared to deliver important news, she would walk up to Lucy, hang her head, and fidget in place while her mind worked hard to formulate the words that could evoke the desired response. When she finally spoke, if an absent Lucy merely said, "Nice, honey," Kathy's features would take on an expression of grotesque angst, and her breathing became labored and irregular, a slow buildup to an ear-splitting wail.

She doesn't wail now.

Toward the end of the hot decade, Lucy used to tell Charles that she would retire when the first grandchild came. In those days, Marc wasn't married yet, and Kathy was married but fully absorbed in building her career. The years went by. And then circumstances changed.

After a few of her audible breaths, Kathy says, "Thank you."

"How are you feeling?"

"Pretty well, actually."

"No morning sickness?"

"Not at all…"

Lucy still remembers the incapacitating nausea during

the first four months of her pregnancies. Surely Kathy has inherited some of those hormones? "You're lucky…"

"…not anymore anyway. I'm well over it."

"Oh. That's good. When is the baby due?"

"October twelfth."

A long pause. The silence divides them, because they both know the extent of Kathy's deceit. "I didn't want to jinx it," she says finally. The baby is due in two weeks.

"Well, I'm glad you're healthy and happy."

"You'll be a Grandma. Just like you wanted."

"For the second time," Lucy says with a little laugh. Only an hour has passed since Amineh called her "Grandma Lucy."

"What do you mean, second time?"

"Oh, nothing. It's a private joke I have with someone. Never mind." It's too complicated to explain her new position, especially since she might be angry with herself for having accepted the job in a state of ignorance about her own family. And where does the blame lie for her ignorance? She's not quite sure how she feels about Kathy not telling her. Actually, she *is* fairly certain, and it's not a good feeling. Lucy is a working woman again, with a responsibility toward a new employer. She clears her throat. "I'm very happy for you. Are you feeling ready for the big change?"

"Yes, I'm more than ready, but I'm glad I waited. There's no risk to my career now. They're giving me a six-month leave of absence, and this is my first week. I just couldn't go into the office anymore. I'm huge as a house." She hesitates before the last part. Lucy, who didn't restart her own career until Marc was in kindergarten, knows what Kathy is about to say before the words leave her mouth. "When I go back to work, Paul's mom is going to take care of the baby."

Of course. Paul's parents live in Seattle. "Well, that's nice of her." The weepiness is threatening again.

"Dad says he's coming out...he'd like to be here for the birth. Maybe you want to coordinate with him?"

An invitation, of sorts. "Mm-hmm. Yes, we will." Lucy can barely manage that many words. Her lips are trembling, and she wipes away a tear. She covers the receiver with her hand, sits up taller, and pulls in a deep, deep breath.

"Mom."

"It's okay, it's okay. That's wonderful news, honey, and I'm so happy for you, but I have to go now. I put something in the oven and I think it's..." Her voice wobbles into nothingness as her daughter fills the gap with parting words that float into her ear from a distance on a fragile wavelength.

Amineh usually does better in the afternoon when she takes a nap after lunch. Lucy always brings a novel to read, but she finds it difficult to concentrate. The living room is full of framed photographs. She makes the rounds, starting with a large one on the mantelpiece, depicting Dorine Larousse and Charles Jakande on their wedding day. The bride wore a black, full-length dress, and the groom wore everything in pure white: tux jacket, buttonhole rose, shirt, cummerbund, pants, shoes. Their images form a checkerboard of sorts, two squares and two rectangles in alternating black and white.

It's October fifth, one week to go, if doctors are to be believed. Lucy recalls that Kathy arrived two weeks after her due date, while Marc was eight days early.

Lucy is holding the framed wedding photo when Amineh wanders into the living room, hugging a book to her chest. "That's my daddy and mommy," she says in a husky voice.

"Yes, that's them." Lucy replaces the photo on the mantle.

"Why did you look at that?"

"They look very nice together, don't you think?" Perhaps Dorine would approve of the self-esteem-building nature of this observation.

"They were getting married. But now they have to go to the office so they're not at home."

"I used to work in an office too. I was an executive assistant to a corporate CEO."

Amineh's face is tilted up, still sleepy soft. She stares at Lucy, blinks, and furls her brow. "That doesn't spell any word." She walks over to the couch and sits down. "I know some of the words in this book. Mr. Owl showed me."

Lucy sits next to Amineh, thinking that, maybe, she should have checked for wetness first. But there was only that one accident at naptime during the first week. Having reevaluated, she now believes that the cause of it might have been the anxiety of getting used to a new babysitter. Lucy doesn't detect any odor, and then Amineh crawls up into her lap. Certainly dry. It's the first time they've been this close. Lucy wraps her arms around the girl and opens the book in her lap. Amineh points and says, "Dog, d – o

– g. A nice furry animal that barks and is your friend that you can pet. Dog."

Lucy smiles at Amineh's unique version of Mr. Owl. "Very good!" Her chin touches the top of the child's head. The braids are perfectly symmetrical and tightly woven, even after naptime. Lucy isn't quite sure how this hairstyle stays intact and fresh for so long, day after day, even now, the third week she's been caring for the child. A nice scent from a hair product rises from her scalp. Apricot.

Halfway through the story, Amineh twists at the waist, flings her arms around Lucy's neck, and plants a sloppy kiss on her cheek. The book falls to the floor. "I love you, Grandma Lucy!" She jumps down and runs toward the front door where her shoes are lined up, waiting. "Let's go to the park!"

On Saturday, Lucy takes the train from Grand Central, north to Pelham. The house is a twenty-minute walk from the station. When she lived here, she used to drive to the station in the morning and park in the lot for her commute to the city. Now that she's used to walking everywhere, she wonders why a car was ever necessary.

Charles may have already flown to Seattle. Or not. She hasn't checked, hasn't called or e-mailed. This morning she awoke with a touch of queasiness, heralding a difficult day. All morning long, and on the way up in the train, the feeling has been building. As she enters the walkway to the front door, she's not prepared for the all-consuming, shuddering nervous shock that grips her body. She's afraid that she could double over at any minute.

The house is the same, a little shabbier. A modest house with tiny rooms on a postage-stamp lot, a "starter" from which they never graduated. It's very quiet and apparently unlit inside, although electric lights wouldn't be necessary at noon on a sunny day. His car could be here or not, inside the closed, detached garage.

She rings the doorbell, something she did no more than once or twice in her married life when she inadvertently locked herself out. The sound of the doorbell is distinct and louder than she anticipated, magnified a hundredfold. The soundwaves emanate from the tip of her index finger and bounce from wall to wall in the foyer and enter every sad little room of the house, the living room, kitchen, dining room, bedrooms, and bathrooms. At last, the interminable reverberation comes to a complete halt in utter silence.

She stands at the front door and waits a decent amount of time before walking around to the backyard. Nothing to prevent her, no locks on the gate. The yard is overgrown with balding flowerbeds offering a few brown stalks and leaves. The swing set was removed twenty years ago, but the rectangle of lawn underneath has never recovered.

"Hello."

"Oh!" She jumps forward and turns around. "You startled me!"

Charles is standing at the back door. "No one ever rings the doorbell unexpectedly, so I didn't answer."

She might have guessed as much. Her husband is timid, a quality that forms part of the "only so much"—a liability that holds him back. Women with domineering husbands might long for gentleness and restraint, but these qualities in Charles simply come across as weakness. At least they did then. To Lucy.

Like the house, Charles is shabbier too. Perhaps he's looking at her and thinking the same thing. Her antennae fail to detect another woman, a replacement. She wonders if she emits the same empty aroma.

"I'm sorry I didn't call first," she says. It's not that they haven't been in contact these three years. There've been phone calls and e-mails and financial arrangements, an amicable aftermath. No court proceedings, no divorce. But the contacts have dwindled, and she can't remember the last time they spoke.

"I don't mind," he says. "But what are you here for? You might have missed me."

"Are you about to leave?"

"No. Not until tomorrow."

A ridiculous exchange. They're both nervous, and he's more than shabby, she notices now. His skin has a gray, oxygen-deprived hue and his eyes sag like an elephant's. He's gained at least ten pounds, shuffles slowly, and probably eats only high-salt, fatty foods, defying the doctor. Who knows if he's taking his blood pressure medication? These were a few of her premonitions, fifteen years ago.

What do two people say to each other when one of them left the other for no discernable reason, no reason at all except the daily tick of time, the boredom and inertia, the little judgments of their every difference, the gradual suspicion of things to come—veiled panic about the inevitable—and the self-deceit of reason over emotion?

"Lucille. We're having a grandchild. For God sakes, Kathy is giving birth, and we can't even go together, to be with our little girl!"

On Monday, Lucy is back on the park bench, watching Amineh. The air is cooler, and soon, maybe sooner than she'd like, their trips to the park will have to cease. Months of cold, dark days lie ahead, with many indoor afternoons.

Her internal theater is running the images and sounds from Saturday afternoon. Charles agrees to call her, to let her know when the baby arrives. If it's this week, she'll ask Dorine for Friday off. She can fly to Seattle early Friday, be there Friday night and Saturday, fly home on Sunday, be at work again on Monday. One day of work missed. Dorine will just have to grant her the one day. It's a long trip that can't be squeezed into a weekend, and Lucy doesn't want to leave anyone without permission.

When she says this—or something like this—to Charles, he calls her a "hypocrite." Not right away. He leads up to it first: "You need permission from everyone except the people you should care about the most." These are the strongest words he's ever said to her. She doesn't respond, just stands there silently, taking it. He's right. She's wrong. He's stronger, an indication of change. Where is the evidence that *she* has changed?

After that, he simmers down and they say a few nice things to each other. Charles is a pleasant, goodhearted man, and the negative words have cost him. She sees the shame in his face. When they part, she has an urgent desire to hug him. She comes up close but stops herself. He turns his head to the side, looks down, and turns back again, daring to look at her. She understands that any belated sign of affection from her could be taken as insincere, glib, and patronizing. An insult. But for just a moment, she stands very close to him and says a soft "goodbye." It's then that she notices a few things that haven't changed. The attractive stretch of his lips across his overbite when he smiles. And the earwax. Charles still has an awful lot of it, maybe even more.

"Grandma Lucy!" Amineh waves from the top of the play structure. Lucy smiles and waves back. "Watch me, watch me!" she cries. Amineh grabs the hanging rope and plants her feet on the plastic backboard to brace herself. She descends in four, hand-over-hand grips down the length of the rope and jumps to the ground with a proud smile.

"Bravo!" Lucy yells.

Amineh bows and starts to run, dodging errant boys and girls, disappearing behind the structure.

In such a short meeting, it's impossible to see every little change. Could there be more? During the hot decade, there were so many annoyances. Bodily functions and noises and smells and textures and quirks that are lovable to young adults when they're newlyweds in the middle of all that touching and sniffing and rubbing of each other but, with time, gradually reveal themselves under inspection, especially after the children are gone. The two long hairs that curl out of his nose when he doesn't have time to use the little snippers. The rattling of the bag of cheese popcorn when he digs to the bottom for the last kernels. The smell of unwashed feet inside the sheets of the bed they share.

Certain scenes are continually replayed. In the kitchen at breakfast, the start of another workday, her eyes go directly to an ear, whether it's right or left. A thought spins in her head incessantly, never surfacing to her tongue: How can he leave the house looking like that? What do his coworkers think? Ten years ago she mentioned it more than once. Never again. She sips her coffee and the flashing is intolerable, enough to make her head *explode*. It's time to go to the office.

"What is it, Lucy?"

"Nothing." Time to leave.

"It's something. You're mad at me, and I don't even know why."

"I'm not mad." The walls are closing in. Don't touch me.

He displays his usual, puzzled look, the insipid slant of his eyebrows. She leaves the room and *must* leave the house. But when she returns to him, she searches for it again, and there it is.

The children are squealing with delight. "Olly olly oxen free!" Funny to think that children still play such games. "Come and get me!" She tries but can't bring to mind any memories of Kathy and Marc playing in the backyard. The Steadman home videos are in a box at the house in Pelham. A tear trickles down her cheek and she wipes it away.

There were delightful days with the children, she's

sure of it, but they're buried under the scenes that turn her stomach. Days of planning, arrangements made, possessions shipped, careful, careful, so he won't notice, because how can she say anything? What is there to say? How can she explain it? The final version of a letter, rewritten a dozen times, is left on the kitchen table. It's a sunny Friday when he's at work, a day before a weekend when nothing is planned, no dinner dates with family friends or neighborhood couples. It will be awkward with these people. Going forward. Impossible, really. But she steps out the door anyway.

In the first weeks, she's not lonely because there's another man in her life, Norman Bradley. It's nothing sexual, purely work, a close, professional relationship. She keeps Mr. Bradley's calendar and knows the intimate details of his schedule, writes his correspondence and purchases birthday gifts for his wife. He's an articulate man who knows his capabilities and gets what he wants. Impeccably groomed, forceful without arrogance. At the top of the corporate ladder, he got there with Lucy by his side for almost thirty years. Along the way, she's rewarded with modest raises and promotions, from clerk typist to secretary to administrative assistant to executive assistant. Every year there's a single day of flowers and thanks. In the new millennium, national secretaries' day becomes administrative professionals' day. It's not that Mr. Bradley wasn't appreciative, but all she can remember now is the abrupt ending, the incompleteness. Barely a year into her new life, the bottom drops out. On one of his weekend jaunts in his private airplane, alone, Mr. Bradley nosedives into the Hudson River. Awful, awful. There's nothing left for her to do except help with the funeral arrangements and retire at the age of sixty-five. In the wake of the tragedy, her retirement is recognized with a three-hundred-dollar gift card and a sheet cake with "Good Luck Lucy!" artfully written in pink icing. The children won't speak to her, Charles barely speaks to her, and now this. Lucille Steadman fades into the sunset and starts collecting her pension, unsure if those years ever existed.

"Bernadette!" Lucy startles. Is that little towhead in the park? Bringing her eyes into focus, she sees Kirby, struggling anew under the domination of a playmate as the nanny stands ready to rescue her from imminent humiliation. This time, Amineh isn't the cause of it.

Lucy smiles to think of her first grandchild, Little Miss Trustworthy. With glazed eyes, she scans the playground. Where is she now?

Pushing herself up from the bench, Lucy props a stiff hand atop her eyeglasses to use as a visor. Where is that girl? She takes a few steps toward the play structure, cutting a stolid figure in the midst of gleeful, ricocheting children. Bernadette is holding Kirby's hand. The little girl looks up at Lucy with unseeing eyes. The nonexistent grandma.

Lucy walks right and left and around the play structure. "Amineh," she calls tentatively, bending stiffly to look underneath. Dozens of children, nannies and mothers, are oblivious to the rising panic in her chest.

"Amineh!" she cries, walking faster now, swiveling around, changing course. The playground is surrounded by trees, a hundred places to hide, convenient cover for anyone, anyone… "Oh my God, what have I done!" she mutters.

Lucy turns to find Bernadette close at hand. "You lost her?" The concern in her voice overshadows the judgment, the inner-city timbre. Centuries of pain fill her compassionate, knowing eyes.

"Well, I don't know…" Lucy can't look at the nanny. Simply can't look. She circles aimlessly, shuffling, clucking, retreating, calling out, "Amineh!" over and over again, but all she can hear, plowing through the dense thicket of her crimes, is this:

I love you, Grandma Lucy! I love you, I love you!

crime stories

✝ *Journal Entry, Franklin DeWitt*

January 24, 2015

GOD OR THE DEVIL awaits me. On March thirteenth I'll be eighty-nine, if the earth hasn't claimed me first. It's time to write about Maya.

Alexis encourages me. "Write, Grandpa. Write everything about your life. People want to know." My lively firebird, a promising ballerina. She says she wants to transcribe and publish *The Memoirs of a Ballet Critic*. I won't disappoint her, although I doubt that anyone is interested in the recollections of a teary-eyed man sitting alone in the dark, rapt and spellbound by the beauty he beholds on stage. People would rather know about the private lives of the dancers.

I've known many, but Maya soars above them all. I can't take her story with me and must release it to the world.

Alexis has delivered my lunch on a tray and I'm alone again, without much appetite except for thoughts of Maya.

On Monday, June 5, 1972, New York caught its first

glimpse of Maya Volosova and Dmitri Guryev. In that era of famous Soviet defectors—Nureyev (1961), Makarova (1970), Baryshnikov (1974)—Maya and Dmitri fascinated the public more than any others. They were striking and exquisite together. She, twenty-four, he, twenty-five. They were inseparable. They were lovers.

That first day, I was invited to observe the spectacle. We stood awkwardly in a wide semicircle, fifty members of the press corps and theater critics, enthralled like children around a monkey cage at the zoo. Location: New York Ballet Theatre on Broadway, the grand rehearsal studio, wood floored, mirror lined. The defectors, Maya and Dmitri, were performing their tricks for the media. It was silly and beneath them. Their new ballet master had put them up to it. I was awestruck, pen and pad forgotten in my hand.

In moments of rest, the Russians glanced dazedly around the room, shell-shocked and disoriented. An irrevocable decision had placed them in this strange land, their proclaimed kingdom of artistic freedom, never to return home. They performed admirably under the circumstances. Maya took a few, quick running steps and was suddenly in the air with a light javelin thrust of her legs into a perfect split, torso arched backward. The gallant, muscular Dmitri effortlessly held her overhead. Cameras clicked and whirred. Gently, she alighted, executed a few *piqué* turns, found her lover's forearm, and held it to balance. *Sur la pointe* of one foot, she extended her free leg up behind her in *arabesque.*

Standard steps, nothing new, but Maya had a singular manner of execution, infused with nuance and the illusion of trifling ease, like breathing. Her countenance was relaxed in the sort of aloof loveliness that doesn't even know it exists.

Ballet master Colin Welby, the instigator of this pageant, stood on the sidelines. What great press for him! NYBT had signed the new stars within a day of their setting foot in New York, less than a week after their dramatic leap to freedom during a Kirov tour in Paris.

They finished their partnering stunts, and Colin got them each to improvise a few solo movements. Maya skimmed floatingly on her *pointes*, an ethereal being, waiflike, tiny as a child, a sprite one minute, a goddess the next. When it was Dmitri's turn, our impressions of him died fast. Of course, in 1972, we hadn't yet seen Baryshnikov—the moving picture of the dance—but even then, we knew the difference between greatness and mere competence.

"Did you see that?" I asked Laura Kensington, the arts columnist standing next to me.

"Four *pirouettes*."

"Only four. And a small stumble."

"Ever so slight. Give him a chance. We'll see…" Clearly, he was nothing special, but Laura was willing to wait!

I was already convinced that Maya couldn't be in love with Dmitri, a mere prop standing in the shadow of a ninety-five-pound *prima assoluta*. If anything, he was her ticket to the West. This was my hunch. This I would find out.

It's Saturday, my three-meal day with Alexis. Here for

breakfast and lunch, she'll return at dinnertime, after another ballet class and rehearsal. Alexis is my son's greatest gift, a living angel who attends to me in every free moment. Last year, when it was easier to get out of bed, I sat once again in a darkened theater, this time beholding my lovely granddaughter. Only fourteen then, fifteen now. Already, she's a true artist.

Alexis pores over my scrawl, the only person who understands it. She's convinced that the old ballet critic is a personage of some importance. I won't dissuade her, but I don't kid myself. She wants to know about the famous dancers, not me. If my wife were here, she'd have better stories to tell, but she's been gone now these many years. Her life was harder on account of me, and she died of cancer when Alexis was only a toddler.

"Let me get your laptop, Grandpa," Alexis insists. "I'll set it up for you on the tray." She thinks this will get the words out of me faster. Not anymore, not with these eyes. Though my hand shakes, I can only put pen to paper. A keypad would be useless.

When she returned to pick up my lunch tray, she was surprised to see my plate nearly full. I'd been writing, as she wanted, not eating, as she also wanted. She gave up on feeding me and got me out of bed. A strong girl, she effortlessly supports her old grandpa as he shuffles around the house and back to the bedroom. Before she left she asked me: "I know you've been writing—may I see it?"

"Not yet, my dear girl."

"Are you writing about *her*?" Alexis urgently awaits the full story of Maya, but I won't show her these pages until I'm near the end.

I've had a moment of shut eye, when the vision of the first performance came vividly to mind. Friday, June 9, 1972, *Swan Lake*.

The timing of their defection was good for Dmitri and Maya, not so good for others in the company. Colin signed them for the two weeks that remained in NYBT's spring season. Their lawyers (already the defectors had them!) advised against signing away any further rights, leaving them free to perform elsewhere if they wished. Among the several ballets on the daily schedule, three performances remained of the full-length classic, *Swan Lake*. Colin bounced the leads, Suzanne Violette and Timothy Jordan, and replaced them with his new darlings of the dance.

A few days of hurried rehearsals were enough to get the Soviets in shape. They intimately knew the choreography of Petipa and Ivanov, which had been their bread and butter growing up at the Kirov. This was not the artistic ideal that Maya and Dmitri had been dreaming of, the abstract, contemporary American ballets that were verboten behind the Iron Curtain. But there was no time for anything else, and it was only fair to make them pay their dues, if only briefly, before casting them in new roles.

That first night, there was a heavy police presence at Lincoln Center. The tension was palpable, a rumbling, wavy mix of ecstatic anticipation and intrigue. As I took my seat inside the Met, I spotted, scattered along the periphery, several unlikely ballet aficionados: single men, strong-jawed and square-shouldered. Each one scanned the wide hall as he stood with his arms crossed or hands clasped in front, fig-leaf style. I feared for Maya without understanding why. These were the good guys, right? Security guards. But I couldn't decide if they were all in the same camp, if their faces were foreign or domestic, if their occasional, telepathic eye contact with each other conveyed affinity or enmity. One of them stared me down briefly as he made his visual rounds—it was enough to turn my gaze unwaveringly to the stage.

I sat precisely in the middle of the orchestra section, my usual seat, far enough from the stage to appreciate the full panorama, close enough to see the dancers' feet and facial expressions. The defectors injected this classic with a life that Timothy and Suzanne had never achieved. They brought Russian drama to it, a passion and inflection that were so exciting.

Especially Maya, playing the dual role of white swan/black swan. In the second act, as Odette, she was chaste and alluring, trapped and desperate, fated to turn into a white swan by morning, under a spell cast by the evil sorcerer Von Rothbart. In the third act, as Von Rothbart's daughter Odile, she was fiery, devious, and seductive. A temptress in black, transformed by the sorcerer to appear identical to Odette. Maya's rendering of these opposites was astonishing.

Dmitri, the handsome coatrack, did admirably well supporting her as Prince Siegfried, but when the time came for his solo, the mediocre technique and dead eyes lacked the power to inspire. It was just as I'd thought.

Afterward, I joined the company at a private party to

welcome the newcomers. You're right, Alexis, maybe I *was* important. Only certain people were allowed into these company events. Big money patrons were always invited along with a few "inside" reporters and critics. I'd paid *my* dues with two decades of cutting-edge reviews that could make or break careers. Over those years, I'd gotten to know the dance celebrities, and in a way, they included me in their set while I remained an island, authoritatively apart. I couldn't be bought. A good review had to be deserved.

At the party, Maya entered the room on Dmitri's arm. He wore a fashionable sort of dressed-down tux, and she wore a white, watery gown. The clothing was supplied by NYBT. The defectors had arrived in the country without anything except practice clothes.

I was drawn to Maya. I was already in love. Forgive me darling Zanni, but we weren't married yet. Still single, I was already an old man of forty-six. Far too old for the new object of my desire. She stood at a distance with Dmitri and Colin on either side of her. How was I to edge in between them?

Surprisingly, Timothy and Suzanne were also in attendance, stewing in a corner. Suzanne's redhead was difficult to ignore. Although my destination was Maya, I stopped along the way to converse with the outcasts.

"Did you watch the performance?" I asked Suzanne.

"What else was there to do?" With artistic delicacy, she flung a handful of her ample tresses over a bare shoulder. She was a beautiful, outgoing woman, almost too big and luscious to be a ballerina, about five foot seven, 115 pounds. I'd known Suzanne for sixteen years, from the time she joined the company at the age of eighteen and as she worked her way up from corps member to principal. Socially, her manner was tart but full of fun. That night, she was all acid.

"I thought you might have avoided it," I suggested.

"Colin wants me to 'learn from her.'"

"Hmm. He couldn't want my all-American girl to become a Russian hot-blood."

"Hah! You should see him lathering at the mouth over his new foundling. Artistically, of course." Suzanne's green eyes flashed. "She *is* an interesting little thing, though."

I turned to her ballet partner. "What say you, Tim? Anything to learn from Dmitri Guryev?"

"Not much that I can see," he retorted.

"I would have preferred to see *you* as the prince tonight," I told him.

Suzanne sputtered into the emptiness where I should have deposited a compliment for her.

"You know how he got here, don't you?" Timothy was on the verge of confirming the rumors then circulating in the media.

"Tell me." I already knew the story, but wanted to hear it from Tim.

He lowered both his brow and his voice, for my hearing only. "Guryev was the one with the connection. Volosova was the one everyone wanted."

"Not surprising."

"You heard about Claude Fournier?"

"The impresario who arranged their escape through the back alleys of Paris."

"*And* paid their way to New York. Don't worry. He got his kickback. A year ago, that Frenchman made a trip to Leningrad and became acquainted with Dmitri. They conversed quite easily in French. Dmitri doesn't know a word of English, by the way." Tim smirked. "Dmitri whispered his secret desire to defect, and Claude suggested he could help—he's a very close friend of Colin's. But Claude was no fool. He told Dmitri he needed a Kirov prima ballerina thrown into the deal to sweeten the pot."

"And how am I to believe you know all of this?"

"Claude was also…a friend."

"Of yours."

The male liaisons in the dance world were multi-layered. Colin and Tim, despite their age difference, were also rumored to be an occasional couple. To my credit, Tim must have perceived me as "safe," otherwise he wouldn't have confided such intimate details. Or, maybe he just needed to vent—he was noticeably incensed to have lost his starring role in *Swan Lake* to a second-rate Russian.

"You must be angry at your old friend Claude for making this casting switcheroo possible."

"Let's just say that Claude and I didn't part so nicely. He and Colin are better friends."

"Unlucky for you." But I was already bored with Tim's grumblings and wanted to hear about Maya. It was clear that the Soviet "lovers" were less than that, or something else. Each was the passport for the other. Dmitri needed someone with real talent, and Maya needed a connection. My heart began to pound the seconds until their inevitable breakup. "So, you're saying that Dmitri started up his affair with Maya…"

"…to offer Claude a prize in exchange for his help. But Dmitri didn't need to do much coaxing. It was obvious that Maya was also looking for a window to the West."

At my side, Suzanne was sniffing for attention. "Now that the Kirov has lost their Odette," she said prettily, "maybe I should defect to the Soviet Union."

I laughed. "Yes, darling, you do that. Just like Lee Harvey Oswald." But I stroked her head to show it was all in fun. She had such luxurious hair, I can feel it now.

With a few words of condolence, I quickly parted from the disgruntled stars. An opportunity presented itself. Just then, I glimpsed Maya stepping away from Colin and Dmitri, making her way along one of two intersecting lines. I took up the second line and met her about twenty yards away from her male escorts.

"Miss Volosova, let me introduce myself. Franklin DeWitt, columnist. You may have seen my reviews."

"Yes, yes, of course, I read all the time." What a lovely sound! Her voice was rich and deep for such a petite woman. I expressed my admiration for her command of the English language, and this was her reply: "Many years study. In private. Secret. I know I must come, you see."

"To the United States."

"Yes, this is the home for my art."

"Your art is everything to you?"

"Everything." *Effrytink.*

"You danced beautifully tonight."

Her head dipped slightly. Trite expressions of praise wouldn't impress her; she'd heard these words often enough. If I didn't act quickly, the opportunity would be lost. Behind her, Colin was exuding fatherly anxiety, casting a protective shadow. "When can we meet again? I'd like to interview you."

She looked up at me for what seemed a long time. In her very high heels, she came only to my shoulder. Almond brown hair, an aristocratic face like a czarina's, unafraid, naked, washed clean of stage makeup. Her eyes were gray with flecks of yellow.

Before she answered, her gaze darted to the side in a little show of terror at what might be lurking at her back. Both Dmitri and Colin were behind her, but so were a lot of other people.

"Yes," she said after a long pause. And then—how can I forget?—she put her hand on my arm. "We should meet." She was looking into my eyes when Colin came up alongside.

I smiled at him and staked my claim. "Miss Volosova has graciously consented to an interview."

"Really now?" Colin threw back his head with those artistically longish locks, everlastingly salon blond to cover the gray. I was forced to look up his nose for an instant before he lowered his head and directed his eyes at Maya, then me. Having demonstrated his authority to withhold consent, he granted it. "I suppose I can arrange that."

My hand threatens to spasm. The pen is laid to rest.

That Sunday, my review appeared in the *Times* on a full

page of the arts section devoted to the defectors. Laura Kensington was a contributor. Nestled inside her prose were photographs, including a close-up of Volosova's face in the role of Odette, full stage makeup and white-feathered headdress. The caption beneath it read: "The lovely Soviet defector prepares to go on stage at the Met." So, Laura and her photographer had gotten to Maya first! Or was this a mock-up with fabricated content, embellished with a smuggled file photo from the Kirov? I examined Maya's image for details. The photo could have been taken anywhere.

The next day, I had my interview. Colin gave us the use of a small office at the NYBT studios. I arrived early and was nervously reviewing my questions when Colin's young boy assistant escorted the ballerina into the room. Maya was dramatically attired in layers of dance sweaters and leg warmers, a long scarf wound multiple times around her neck. "A cold," she said.

For the first ten minutes, while we talked about Maya's training at the Vaganova Ballet Academy, Colin's assistant examined and picked at a hangnail, refusing to budge from his seat. Eventually he left us alone.

I tested the waters obliquely: "That article in the *Times* yesterday, I imagine it was distracting to be inter-viewed right before going on stage."

"That woman, she arrive in my dressing room. I don't know how."

"Did she say her name?"

"Laura Kenzingk. And a photographer. They bring me some letters."

"Letters?"

She leveled an intense look. "*This* is why we must talk."

We? My love for her swelled magnificently—she'd chosen me for a secret! The subject was obviously delicate. Her eyes grew moist with emotion, although it could have been a symptom of her cold virus.

"That woman give me letters from my mother and my brother! 'Heartbroken,' they say. Why did I leave them? Why this…this 'betrayal' of my teachers at the Kirov, my family and the motherland?"

"Did she say where she'd gotten those letters?"

"She didn't!"

"Do you suppose—?" I stopped myself. A KGB connection to Laura Kensington? Unthinkable. But there'd been stories like this about other defectors. Attempts to sabotage their performances, backstage "accidents" with falling props, faked or coerced emotional letters from family members. The object was to crush any chance of success in the West, or to instill enough guilt that the defector would return home and be charged with treason, stripped of any further life as an artist. Defection was an intolerable insult to the Soviet delusion of cultural supremacy.

"It was their handwriting, but it was not them."

"How was it 'not them'?"

"My mother and brother—they want for me what is the best. They never write these things. Oh, Franklin," the tears started to fall, "tell this woman to stay away!"

"You want me to tell Laura…"

"You know her, yes?"

"I do."

"Tell her do not come! Never try to see me again!"

Uncertainty fueled her torment. Either the KGB had forced the hands of her mother and brother, or her family members had, on their own, penned their sorrow and arranged for its delivery. Either possibility was unbearable. Maya needed protection from Laura Kensington and any other would-be messengers. I gladly accepted the challenge, even though I feared that Maya had no other use for me. Perhaps, with time, her feelings would run deeper than mere gratitude.

Maya gave me the address where she and Dmitri were staying—a carefully guarded secret—and warned me of heavy security. I promised to visit her the following night, to give her an update of my efforts. She promised to hold her bodyguards at bay.

I couldn't sleep all night, thinking of her. The next morning, I sought out two people. First, Laura. On the way to her office, I was jittery with fatigue and had the sense of being followed, even without any overt signs of it. When I arrived, Laura's secretary was in the anteroom. No one else was around. I entered Laura's office and closed the door behind me, feeling nervous and slightly silly. No one could hear us, but I imagined a bug.

Assuming the role of FBI agent, I interrogated her rapid fire, bait and trap. I was woefully inept. She gave me this explanation: "A little man with a Russian accent came up to me outside the theater and handed me those letters. 'Gee-ef dees to Volosova. Letters from family.'"

"A stranger?"

"Of course a stranger. You think I run around with types like that?"

"How on earth did he know who you were and where you were going?"

"I have no idea. It was a little creepy, I admit."

"And you didn't think it through. Anything could have been inside those envelopes! What was written on the outside?"

"Her name, that's all. Come on, Franklin. Cut out the Dick Tracy. It would have been cruel to hold back letters from her family. What would *you* have done?"

"Gone to the police."

"Not when the best interview of your career is waiting. You would have done the same."

"Maybe, but…"

"Your envy is showing. I got to her first, plain and simple. Got past the gatekeepers before you did. So there. Accept it."

I accepted it and didn't mind so much that Laura got the first interview because I'd been given something far better. Maya had made me her trusted confidant and protector. But I wasn't about to reveal this. "Your visit upset her greatly, that's all I can say." I turned to go. "I suggest you stay away from Maya to avoid causing her any further distress." It was a pitifully weak demand with nothing to back it up. Laura only smiled at me with shining eyes.

Feeling put down and inadequate as a detective, I went back to my office to await my second appointment of the day: Suzanne. I wasn't sure how, but I wanted to use her as my informant. She was the person I knew best in the company and the only one I could approach. She was also likely to be in daily contact with Maya, since they were at similar levels of virtuosity, and Colin had told Suzanne to "learn from her." There was resentment, to be sure, but I figured that Suzanne would get over it. She had a heart of gold, could see the business logic behind Colin's decision, and was confident enough to know that he hadn't replaced her. At thirty-four, she was an exciting, mature dancer at the height of her career.

I asked Suzanne how Maya was doing, and immediately, she sensed my interest and concern.

"Ah, you have a little crush!" She mocked me. "You have nothing to worry about. Maya is perfectly happy, except for that worm of a boyfriend, Dmitri."

"What's he up to?"

"Every time I see those two together they're spouting off in hot Russian, 'nyet' this and that. Nothing at all like their on-stage love affair."

I was heartened to hear this. A breakup in the works! In my obsessive state, I was sure this meant a chance for me. "Nothing violent, is there?"

"I saw him grab her arm once. She pulled away and cursed wildly in Russian."

"Your interpretive skills are amazing."

"Anyone could figure it out."

"Have you spoken to her?"

"Not much. But this morning, before class, we were in the studio together, sitting on the floor, banging out our new *pointes*. Her only complaint about defecting is that she has to get used to another maker. She claims her new shoes are inferior."

I thought nothing of this. Professional ballerinas need two or three pairs of *pointe* shoes every day and love to complain about them. A ballerina's "maker" is a cobbler who knows her foot intimately and handcrafts each shoe to unique specifications. The stiff toe box is created from layers of cardboard, glue, and fabric, stitched and nailed to a leather sole. Each ballerina has her own ritual for molding the shoes to her liking by hammering, floor banging, or mashing the toe boxes between sensitive hands. After a few hours of wear, the shoes are "dead." Limp and useless.

"Who's her new maker?"

"Stanley Graven. Sign of the cross." Graven's unique symbol was a Maltese cross, which he impressed on the bottom of every sole.

"Who's the old maker?"

"Don't know. The imprint is"—she deepened her voice—"a hammer and sickle."

I shuddered. "Comrade ballerina!"

"She still has about a dozen pairs from her old maker," Suzanne continued. "The box just arrived by air freight—a friend of hers in the Kirov smuggled them out of her dressing room in Paris. They're in the storage room reserved for the principal dancers. It's under lock and key, but she seems nervous to let them out of her sight. She puts on a pair only when she's feeling especially insecure."

"The great ballerina feels insecure?"

"You know. Homesick. And I think she's missing someone she left behind."

"Her mom and brother."

"Nope. I'm guessing it's a boyfriend. We all know Dmitri is just a cover."

"Well, sure, we all know about Dmitri, but how do you know there's someone else?" I tried to remove the adolescent squeakiness from my voice.

"I just know it. She hasn't said anything. It's intuition. That's something we women have, Franklin. Intuition."

In that moment I admired Suzanne enormously. She was compassionate and magnanimous toward her little sister, a girl ten years younger, who should have been regarded as a rival in the company. I asked Suzanne to look after Maya, to protect her from harm, to report back to me what was going on inside the studios and the theater.

But this was asking too much, and she resisted. "Why should I, Franklin? She's a big girl. She doesn't need a mama." Her eyes were on fire. She was vivacious and even more redheaded in her rage. But there was mockery in her emotion. She knew me too well. Why should she humor a man driven by lust? "Maybe she's homesick and lonely," said Suzanne, "but she made her decision and will have to live with it."

I enjoyed her honesty and was beginning to see, maybe a little bit, how I really felt about her. I squared my shoulders and acted the grownup. "Suzanne. I've known you half your life. You're the only real friend I have on the inside. I can't reveal all the details, but there've been some threats. You have to believe me. She needs someone to look out for her."

After further arm-twisting, she came around to the idea. I was grateful and thanked her with an embrace before we parted. Alone with Suzanne's perfume on my collar, I counted the minutes until nine p.m., the appointed hour for my visit to Maya's apartment.

NYBT was housing the Russians in a luxury high rise on the Upper East Side. When I arrived that evening, the uniformed doorman told me to wait in the vestibule while he summoned a scary-looking fellow in the lobby. I gave that man my name and purpose and showed him identification. Maya had preapproved my visit, and he waved me ahead. Another such man was standing outside her apartment door on the twelfth floor, and I repeated my demonstration.

Maya came to the door wearing a purple dressing gown, her feet bare. Behind her, on the living room floor, she'd left a basin of Epsom salt water and a towel.

Stripped of their pink satin adornment, a ballerina's feet are not always a pretty sight. Corns, calluses, blisters, bunions, and blood. If a shoe suffers a premature death in the middle of a performance, or if something else isn't quite right with it—a hard bulge, a broken arch, the tip of a nail protruding from the insole—the dancer must stay on her toes, maintaining the illusion of ease.

Maya's feet were no exception. I caught a glimpse of them before averting my eyes to the couch, where Dmitri was sitting. He stood. In reply to my greeting he said, "Hello," and gave me a blank look when I asked, "How are you enjoying your new home?" He nodded and said, "Yes." In the awkward silence that followed, he said, "Pardon," like a Frenchman and left the room. Timothy was right. The man didn't understand a word of English.

"Come and sit," said Maya, gesturing toward the couch. It was long and plush, with white cushions. I took one end and she took the other, tucking her battered feet beneath her. There were dark circles under her eyes. She gave me a wan smile, her vitality expended and left behind in the NYBT studios, where she'd had a grueling day of class and rehearsal. Sitting on the couch in the intimacy of her home, I didn't feel quite inside my own body as I regarded her tiny form across from me, a presence so diminutive yet momentous that she appeared translucent, of another world.

The goddess spoke: "Tell me that you talk to her. That woman."

I assured her that Laura Kensington would no longer be a bother. It was a bold statement at odds with reality, something I couldn't vouch for. I said nothing about my agreement with Suzanne.

"This is not interview," Maya said, waving her hand in a circle. "None of this, about the letters. You print nothing."

"I wouldn't dream of it." But how could she trust me? Even today, it astounds me that a defector from the Soviet Union, a person conditioned for a life of wariness and vigilance, would assign such a sensitive mission to a relative stranger. But I still had a boyish, innocent face, well into middle age. I'm sorry you wouldn't know it now, Alexis. I can't bear to look at myself in the mirror.

I told Maya: "I will do everything in my power to ensure your safety and your ability to concentrate on your art."

"Thank you. I am grateful."

We talked for an hour or so, more about her life than mine. Her words and gestures were veiled in a mood of profound sadness. With Dmitri nowhere to be seen, hidden away in another room, our discussion was free. Toward the end I remarked, "I've heard you're disappointed with your new maker."

"Pfft! Shoes are terrible. Pavel is the only one knows my feet." She looked off into the distance. Instantly, I knew there was something under the surface. Perhaps some of Suzanne's feminine intuition had rubbed off on me. "Pavel?"

"Yes, Pavel Shirokov. My 'maker' is how you say it. He knows my feet, the high instep, the short baby toe, the spreading metatarsal. He knows this. No one else." Her eyes had grown misty.

"I hear that Stanley Graven is excellent. If you give him some time, he'll get to know your feet just as well."

"I doubt very seriously." She jumped up from the couch. It was my signal to go. I had, of course, botched this meeting very badly. By mentioning Stanley Graven, I'd given away my connection to Suzanne. How else would I have known this detail?

Near the front door, she found the energy to come out of her funk momentarily. Charmingly, she rose up on tiptoe and kissed my cheek. "Thank you for that Laura person."

I was in heaven. "May I come backstage after your performance tomorrow?"

"If they let you. They watch the door now. Very careful. After that other time, I tell them no one."

"Let no one in?"

"No one."

My heart sank again. I should have been elated to

know that she was taking control of the situation. It was her assertion of that control against *me* that was so disappointing.

As I walked out the door, I didn't know it was the last time I would see her alone.

I hear a key turn in the lock.

Alexis has just gone, and I've gained a second wind. I ate a bit of dinner, had another stroll on her arm, and can face the night, alone. A single beam of lamplight falls upon this page.

In the dark again, I sit. Wednesday, June 14, and Sunday, June 18, 1972, the final performances of *Swan Lake*.

Don't think that I didn't try to see her again. After Wednesday's performance, I sought entry at the usual backstage door but was cut off, all my goodwill and insider status of no value. The following night, and the night after that, I went to her apartment building. The bodyguards were under strict orders to turn me away. A few times, in broad daylight, I visited the NYBT studios. Colin was not available. Neither was Maya. I took these rejections personally, although there was no reason to doubt that her instructions pertained to the world at large.

Twice daily, I contacted Suzanne for a report. "You worry for nothing," she said every time. On Sunday afternoon, the day of the last performance, she said, "Thanks to you, we're now the best of friends. She's a fascinating little thing! Doing just fine and so happy to be here. Maybe a little tired and stressed, but no sign of any goons on her trail."

"Are you *sure* she would tell you if there were any threats?"

"How would I know? We've been friendly for such a short time. But I do know this—she's on to you, Franklin!"

"On to me?"

"She knows you've been trying to see her. Every day. She mentioned it before class this morning. 'You know this man Franklin? Should I be worry for him?'"

"Worried about *me*?"

"You, sweetheart. I told her you're harmless as a kitten. Still, I would bug off if I were you."

Her advice fell on deaf ears. I was certain to keep trying, *if* I'd had the chance.

In the dark then and now, I see and feel everything again. At the Met, as the lights dim and programs rustle, the overture begins, and I wait impatiently for Maya to take the stage. For the last time.

In the third act of *Swan Lake*, Prince Siegfried is tricked into declaring his love for Odile, the deceptive double conjured by Von Rothbart. In the fourth act, the Prince returns at midnight to the *lac des cygnes* where he begs for, and receives, Odette's forgiveness. But they're powerless to overcome the sorcerer's spell. The Prince's betrayal has sealed Odette's fate. Come morning, she'll turn into a white swan again, this time forever. The despairing lovers cast themselves into the lake.

In the moments before her stage suicide, Maya's portrayal of Odette transcends the boundaries of despair. Her swanlike arms flail limply, her knees buckle. I'm transfixed, in shock. This isn't the choreography. With a tripping run instead of a soaring leap, she casts herself into the lake and disappears. Dmitri follows with a *grande jeté*.

The apotheosis. In the final moments of the ballet, the lovers glide into the afterlife on a gentle, uplifting theme. As the strings beat out their quiet strokes, the stage remains empty except for the lake—rippling sheets of midnight blue fabric catching a moon beam. Behind a transparent backdrop, the lovers rise into the sky on a heavenly cloud.

Something is wrong. I choke out a cry. Around me, people are gasping. Dmitri is struggling to support Maya, holding her by the waist with one arm, his free arm overhead in fifth position. His face is stricken with panic. Limp and feeble, Maya is folded nearly in half over his arm, her torso arched back and arms flung behind her, *arabesque* drooping, *pointes* collapsed. With a final effort to lift herself up, she falls backward onto his arm with an audible rasp and a catlike screech.

My eyes are a blur of tears. Help me, dear God!

The grandfather clock strikes twelve. I've fallen asleep briefly, wanting to forget.

We were in the dark. The house lights were off when the curtain fell on a scene of panic. An army of police officers swarmed into the audience, taking us hostage. The lights flicked on, revealing pure chaos. Later, I learned the details.

In full costume, Maya's lifeless body was transported by ambulance to the hospital. Colin and Dmitri were fast behind in a taxi. As soon as they arrived, death was pronounced. Was Dmitri heartbroken? He'd just lost his meal ticket. Without Maya, the plum roles were no longer guaranteed. Was Colin heartbroken? Businesswise, he'd lost nothing. The contract was fulfilled, and Maya hadn't promised to sign another. Colin made sure he had the white swan costume and toe shoes in hand before leaving the hospital. These artifacts would fetch thousands at auction, and the company needed the cash.

Maya's death stunned the world and grew to mythical proportions with the discovery of a note on her dressing room table. "Pavel, this performance is for you. I'm wearing the last pair." Hasty translations of her Russian distorted the message into a suicide note. Her last performance. The last pair of shoes she would ever wear. Torn from her lover, ruing her mistake, Maya had publicly committed the ultimate act. She had gone to meet her maker.

But how? Rumors abounded. Depression and unrelenting physical demands beat her down to a wisp, making her susceptible to a hidden weakness. A brain aneurysm. A congenital heart defect. She'd starved herself and collapsed from pure exhaustion and dehydration. She had willed herself to die.

Several days later, the autopsy revealed the cause: cyanide poisoning. A horrible death by chemical asphyxia, its climax marked by the "death scream," an involuntary response to the internal collapse of her lungs. Questions were answered and others were raised by the medical examiner's strange findings. Not ingested or inhaled, the poison was injected into her left foot, the lateral plantar artery. Who would devise such a bizarre method of suicide?

The district attorney opened an investigation. Search warrants were executed at the Met, the NYBT studios, and Maya's apartment. No syringes were found, but already a week had passed—plenty of time to destroy evidence. Sharp minds said, "The left shoe!" Colin was forced to relinquish the *pointes*, and here they discovered the instrument of her death: a tiny, hollow nail, designed to work its way through the insole and act as a syringe with the pressure of a well-placed *plié-relevé*. To Maya, the prick of pain would have been a small annoyance not unlike any other indignity a ballerina must endure from a negligently crafted shoe. The potent poison gradually worked its way through her body as her heart pumped, delivering death in the final moments of the ballet.

The mystery deepened when the soles of the deadly *pointes* were examined. They bore no symbol at all, neither Maltese cross, nor hammer and sickle.

The shoes were sent for analysis to uncover their maker, and the search for conspirators began. Someone had placed those shoes in the box, and someone had made sure that she wore them. No one was exempt from interrogation. Dozens of people were hauled into police headquarters. In France, depositions were conducted of Claude Fournier and others involved in the Paris "leap to freedom."

Immediately, I came forward with everything I knew, the names of the makers and their marks, and Laura Kensington's delivery of the letters. Laura was the person of greatest interest to the police. Repeatedly, they questioned her about the little Russian man we supposed was a KGB agent. A sketch artist made a drawing of the suspect, and it was printed on the front page of every newspaper in the country and across Europe.

Ultimately, Laura wasn't detained because she clearly had no motive to harm Maya. Nor did any of the other key figures. Not Dmitri (he needed Maya), or Colin (he hoped for a long-term contract), or Claude (he'd received his finder's fee), or Stanley Graven (he was pleased with the new, lucrative toe shoe account), or Pavel Shirokov (he loved her).

Or me or Suzanne.

Forgive me, Alexis, I must stop here.

This story is not about Maya. No, it is not.

How can I say this? You've seen the old newspaper stories and your father and I have explained some of it. I won't be guilty of another sugarcoating.

I go on.

A month after the murder, the public was aching for a culprit, someone to string up. Anonymous tips flooded in. Innocent men were detained on the basis of their slightest resemblance to the sketch in the newspaper. By then we knew that the shoes were made in the USSR, as confirmed by the inferior quality of the pink satin and other materials which were identical to those in the hammer and sickle shoes, a few "dead" ones that Maya had left behind. No question, Pavel was the maker, though his mark was missing. A motive was easily con-trived. Heartbroken and angry at Maya for leaving him behind, Pavel became a willing participant in a KGB plot. A cry went out for his arrest, but it was impossible. The only extradition treaty on the books was of questionable validity, signed by the leaders of the U.S. and tsarist Russia in 1893. Even so, Article IV of that treaty relieved the parties of any requirement "to deliver up their own citizens or subjects." Pavel was safe.

I cannot remember the name of the detective who interviewed me. I've blocked it from my mind. He was scarlet faced, dogged, and persistent. I was afraid, I remember that. Afraid for my own sorry self, convinced that I was one of a handful of suspects who'd been allowed entry into Maya's private residence.

I told him: "Miss Volosova granted me a single interview at the NYBT studios. We ran out of time that day, and she permitted me a short visit to her apartment the next night to complete the interview." I indulged in a silent sigh of relief, having confessed the most damning fact.

"Do you have the clipping?"

At this, I balked and shivered. "Clipping?" In my gut, the emotion and guilty knowledge roiled: my shameful desire for a woman half my age, my promise not to print our interview, my belief in a secret mission to protect her. I felt childish and ineffectual. How could I claim the status of protector when I hadn't protected her? "I was still working on the article when she died. It was never printed."

The detective smirked. "How long does it take to write an article?"

"I was working on a special column, a long retrospective, a life story."

He didn't look convinced, so I kept blathering. "I needed to do more research on defectors and artistic freedom, perhaps add some details comparing the daily routines of dancers in the two countries. For instance, Maya—Miss Volosova—made an interesting observation to another ballerina in the company, a complaint about the feel of her American *pointe* shoes. It was only a pet peeve because, really, she was ecstatic about being in this country. She told Suzanne as much on the day she died."

"That would be Suzanne Violette?"

"Yes."

"She was the ballerina who told you about Volosova's *pointe* shoe complaint?"

I didn't answer, but my face must have said it all.

"She was the one with the victim before she died?"

"Well, yes, they were friends."

"Friends? But Volosova took her place in the company."

"Not exactly. Just a few performances."

I froze up, fearing that I'd said too much already, and I said nothing to explain, nothing to help her.

In the following days, I badgered other company members into telling me what they'd said to the police. The floodgates were open: many had seen the two balle-rinas together, giggling, sipping tea, banging out their *pointes*, making trips to the locked storage room where they both kept their toe shoes. Someone even claimed to have glimpsed Suzanne in the company of a funny little man who looked very much like the sketch published in the newspaper.

Early one morning, I picked up the ringing phone and heard this: "Franklin! I've been arrested!" Suzanne was allowed a single phone call, and I was the person she called. I was that person because she loved me, and at that moment I knew that I loved her.

Shame enveloped me. Yet I said nothing to her about my slip during the interview with the detective, and I said nothing to the authorities about her innocence. The front page of the newspaper had a photograph of my beautiful Suzanne in police escort beneath the headline, "Ballerina Accused of Conspiracy to Murder."

I found a lawyer for her. But I said nothing.

I visited her in jail. But I said nothing.

A grand jury was empaneled to hear the evidence and hand up an indictment. My brave Suzanne exercised her right to testify. Although the proceedings were secret, I imagined her testimony from everything she told me later:

Prosecutor: "Ms. Violette, tell us about the last time you spoke with the victim."

Zanni: "I visited her dressing room about fifteen minutes before curtain. I wished her good luck and a beautiful performance."

Prosecutor: "Was she wearing her *pointe* shoes?"

Zanni: "Yes, but they wouldn't be the ones…the poisoned ones."

Prosecutor (snidely I imagined, with a wink to the foreperson of the grand jury): "And how would you know that?"

Zanni: "She was wearing the shoes for the second act, when she makes her first appearance. She had different shoes for the third and the fourth acts."

Prosecutor: "And why is that?"

Zanni: "The shoes are pale pink for the second and fourth acts. They're black for the third act."

Prosecutor: "So, when you saw her last, she was wearing the pale pink shoes for the second and the fourth acts?"

Zanni: "No, just the second act. The shoes are dead after a single act and can't be worn again."

An unfortunate choice of words.

In all of this, Suzanne uttered not a word about my part in forcing her closeness to Maya, how I put her up to all of it. She said nothing about my obsession, my repeated attempts to get to Maya. Wouldn't *that* have been a pretty motive for murder? The leering stalker failed to get the girl. But Suzanne, with her pure heart, knew that my desire was mere folly, a middle-aged man's last fantasy before he finally grew up. She did not betray me, unaware that I had betrayed her.

The prosecutor put the conspiracy charge to the twenty-three grand jurors for a vote. We won't blame them. They were ignorant of everything discovered twenty years later, after the fall of the Soviet Union. They didn't know about the memorandum between the First and the Second Chief Directorates of the KGB, outlining "The State's Problem of Defectors in the Arts." They didn't know about the design of the death shoe, like Sputnik, a glorious achievement of Soviet science, developed after Makarova's defection in 1970. By 1972 the design was perfected, just waiting for the next defector. While Maya was on tour in Europe, Pavel was innocently making a pile of her shoes, looking forward to her return. Immediately after Maya's defection, the Soviet authorities confiscated the lot as "property of the People," found a pair to which Pavel had not yet affixed his imprint, and inserted the lethal nail. An agent planted the pair in Maya's box of shoes in Paris, and during the days after her defection, made sure that a "friend" in the Kirov shipped the box to her in New York.

The rest of the plot relied on her love for Pavel's shoes and the certainty that she would eventually wear them all. It was mere chance—or was it?—that she happened to pick the fatal pair for the fourth act of the final performance of the season. Did she notice the difference in these shoes, the lack of a mark? After her death, the crooked scheme claimed another victim. Pavel heard the news and guessed that his shoes had been the instrument of her death. He committed suicide by hanging.

None of this was known at the time the grand jury voted to indict Suzanne of conspiracy to murder. And none of it was known to the judge (bless him!) who reviewed the grand jury testimony and threw out the indictment. In a packed courtroom, the judge proclaimed the investigation to be a witch hunt and the indictment a product of prosecutorial overreaching. The charge rested on the flimsiest of evidence that wouldn't hold up in court. Suzanne was released, but she was traumatized, unable to dance for two years. A career at its height was left in ruins from the humiliation of a cruel notoriety. When she returned, it was only to dance supporting roles for a few years before an early retirement.

Oh, how I loved her! Weak as I am, cowardly as I am, I loved her. We were blessed with a son, your father. I love you both. Alexis, you must believe that.

Instead of *Memoirs*, shall we call this book *The*

Confessions of a Ballet Critic? Does it lessen my guilt to pretend that my sins were of no consequence? Zanni, kind soul, would have befriended Maya anyway. She was just as fascinated by her as we all were. On the day Suzanne was released into my arms, this is what she said to me: "After everything, I'm saddest of all that Maya is gone. She was pretty and funny and so exquisite to watch. She was a tigress and a homeless orphan. She was the real victim here."

And still, I said nothing. How I betrayed you, how I made you suffer, Zanni! Did you know of my cowardice? Did you find me out all those years ago when I breathed not a word?

My hand aches, but my heart aches more.

I must write.

But I haven't the strength.

God take me! I'm ready to meet m…

January 25, 2015

A ray of light passes through the opening in the curtain.

With every new day, I grow weaker. It's time to write about Suzanne Violette, the most stunning ballerina the world has ever known.

✝ *Pure Kill*

INVESTIGATOR PETE SQUIRES, Internal Affairs, propped his lanky frame upright in a dark corner of the tiny interrogation room. There was an empty chair nearby if he wanted it. Glancing at the one-way window, he gave an invisible nod to the officers on the other side. An hour ago they'd handed him the target, veteran cop John Mangrove.

Assistant District Attorney Marilyn Holmes was conducting the "interview." Mangrove and Holmes sat in straight-backed chairs on opposite sides of the unsteady wooden desk. Dead center over their heads, a naked bulb in a metal cone spilled a pool of brilliance.

Squires had been the first to handle Mangrove before ADA Holmes arrived. In those moments, he'd seen the shallow breathing and fast pounding heart in the thick artery on his neck. Mangrove was all swagger, even as the flicker of eyelids betrayed his fear. He hadn't been charged—yet. But he wasn't free to go. Squires recited his rights, receiving a quick and flippant waiver in return. The suspect didn't need a lawyer, everything could be explained. This is what Squires had been hoping for.

But he'd waited another quarter of an hour for the ADA to arrive, and he let her repeat the ritual. She was careful, and it was right to be careful because she would decide what they could prove and how to make the charges stick. Squires gave her the room she needed. Let them say what they would. He didn't see why Holmes shouldn't be given the respect she was due.

A pioneer, the only woman to enter the DA's office in 1958, Holmes was already well-seasoned by 1971, entrusted with high-profile cases. It had to be tough entering a man's world, the smoky corridors of the criminal courthouse. Squires admired her guts and her accomplishment—from afar. His admiration was not something he would admit out loud, or perhaps, even to himself.

Still, when it came to comments about women in law enforcement, he couldn't stomach listening to a foul mouth. John Mangrove sat there spewing blatant dis-respect, not for Holmes but worse, for his former partner Wanda Rivera, another female groundbreaker. Twenty-two and fresh out of the academy in 1970, Wanda had entered a force that bragged a two-percent female presence. Bravery served a beat cop well, and Rivera had the moxie. She proved it every day, just getting into the radio car with the likes of John Mangrove.

"It was all Wanda's fault he got off in the first place," Mangrove was telling the ADA. "Blasted everything to hell."

"We know the story," said Holmes. "And we know otherwise." Squires could tell she was baiting him. That was the beauty of it. Mangrove was too caught up in himself to see it. Despite the size difference between the combatants at the table—John's muscular six feet to her sturdy five and a quarter—Holmes had the skill to gain the upper hand in any standoff.

"Well, let me tell you the parts maybe you don't know," said Mangrove, turning his blue eyes toward a distant point. "The Corsican. We'd been onto his smack mill for a year, an apartment on the Lower East Side. He walked around untouchable, but we had him. The stakeout was planned for the last day in April. With backup outside, we went in. I was in the lead, then Gunderson, Sprague, and Wanda."

Squires noted the choice of name for the female. Wanda, not Rivera.

"Lucky for me you had Rivera along," the prosecutor said.

"You like to throw all your cases into the crapper?"

"I like a solid case. I like the truth." Holmes crossed her arms over a mannish, white business shirt. Spoken like that, with her square-edged appeal and owlish deep-set eyes, no one could contradict her.

"With all due respect, counselor, you've never been on a stakeout." Mangrove flexed his jaw muscles and strained for a semblance of deference. "We took a risk going in. They were armed. The Corsican and his main distributor were inside. We broke in and got them easy in the living room. A little blood would've been all right by me, but it was no muss, no fuss. They almost held their hands out for the cuffs. The dope was another story. We knew about the fresh delivery, five kilos pure."

"Five? Sure about that now, are you?"

"*Five* was the word, and the informant was reliable. A 'handful,' he said. Don't know too many people with six fingers, do you? It had to be in the apartment somewhere. I was heading for the bedroom when Wanda starts having a hissy fit, 'You can't go in there!'"

If Mangrove's impersonation could be credited, Wanda screeched like a cat in heat. But in the next breath he took it all back, lowering his brow and directing a slightly abashed look at his female inquisitor, the woman who held his life in her hands.

"Problem was, John, you forgot the search warrant," Holmes reminded him. "The arrest was okay under the home arrest statute, but you can't search a man's castle without a warrant."

"Castle! It was a place of business, not a home! But let's say it was the Corsican's castle. We're already in the castle, and who's gonna say the five kilos isn't there on the coffee table, right where he can grab it? I know the law. We can seize anything in his reach at the time of arrest. Wanda knew the sucker would walk if we came out empty-handed, but she's screaming, 'don't go in there!' 'Zip it, Wanda,' I said. 'Go change your panties. You don't have to testify.' Senior officer on the team *always* testifies. And that would be me."

"Didn't work out that way, did it?" asked Holmes. "A little problem at home got in the way."

In his obscure corner, Squires recalled the day he'd been brought in to investigate the missing kilo, in May of this year. Mangrove was fighting a hostile alimony war against his soon-to-be ex. As luck would have it, he couldn't get out of his own deposition in *Mangrove versus*

Mangrove on the day of the suppression hearing in *People versus Lisandru Olivari*. Mangrove spent the day facing off against his snarling wife and her downtown attorney instead of the refined, well-mannered Corsican and his diamond cuff-linked counsel.

At the criminal hearing, ADA Holmes called Wanda Rivera to testify. The truth came out. No heroin in the living room, no contraband within reach, no search warrant. Lead officer John Mangrove went into the bedroom alone while the others held the suspects. Officer Mangrove came out of the bedroom alone, carrying "five" kilos in a black plastic bag.

The judge ruled the search unconstitutional and suppressed the evidence. It was a Friday, May 28, and the Corsican had been locked up for a month, remanded without bail. The gavel came down and he blew out of the courtroom like the wind, undisturbed by the huge hit to his pocket, taking a loss on five kilos—or was it six? Next day, he was back to business as usual.

These memories added heat to the oven. Squires felt a drop of perspiration slowly descend his temple and trace the long, flaring length of his dull-brown sideburn down to his jawbone. *Must be eighty-eight degrees in here.* This wasn't the place to be on a sweltering August night, enclosed and cut off from the rattling window units on the outer walls of the precinct. Squires was wearing a suit, as required, but he'd loosened his fat tie, removed his suit jacket, and draped the wide lapels around the back of the empty chair. Wasn't much else he could take off.

It was tough keeping his mouth shut, but Holmes didn't need a foil. Mangrove was talking, and the assistant

DA was guiding him there, seamlessly.

On the other side of the window, Police Officers Manuel Torres and Steve Gunderson watched the interrogation. John Mangrove was sweating bullets, and Manny was enjoying the sight.

Manny and John had been partners since the beginning of May when, a week after Olivari's arrest, Wanda finally succeeded in getting the transfer she'd been requesting from the start. It was rumored that she'd considered filing a sex discrimination complaint but decided against it. The top brass "encouraged" the filing of these complaints, but Wanda, like every woman on the force, knew they didn't remain anonymous and she'd be open to retaliation. The best and only option was to transfer out with hopes for better luck on the next partner.

It took her a year to get her wish, a transfer to the Upper West Side, as far away from John Mangrove as possible. Still, she couldn't shake the memory of her daily humiliation, his disgusting foul mouth and demeaning remarks, his roaming eyes making their nasty exploration of her face and body. Without a doubt, the man liked women, but he liked them only in a certain way.

Manny was the heir to the driver's seat in John's radio car. Assigned to the narcotics squad, they spent their first month together stumbling over bodies. It was a rough time. A wave of near pure smack had hit the streets, and junkies were dropping dead with needles in their arms. An amateur or a sadist was at work. In any case he was a fool, wasting half his profit by sending it out on the street so pure, killing off his customers.

With each new body, Manny got an earful of John's railing against Olivari, even though he was still locked up tight.

"How could it be the Corsican?" Manny would ask. "He's out of the picture."

"Couldn't be anyone else. He owns the Lower East Side. You think he puts it on the street himself? He's got people."

"But his operation knows how to cut it. They're in it for the profit."

"One of his flunkies screwed up. It happens. We should be looking for a body in the river."

"I'm just saying it doesn't make sense."

A few weeks later, when the Corsican walked, Manny got another earful of John's railing, this time against Wanda. If she hadn't been "on her monthlies that day," the Corsican wouldn't be out on the street again, spreading death.

By that time, the body count dropped, but they still hadn't traced the source. The problem simply went away. Wanda, now far removed from John, privately sought out Investigator Pete Squires, Internal Affairs. Afterward, Manny heard how it went.

"I put two and two together," Wanda told Squires. "It's John Mangrove you want."

She was proud, smart, and tough. Diminutive, no more than five feet, and inexperienced. Squires wanted to believe her, but why should he? "Five kilos were vouchered," he told her. "The informant checked out."

"The word was 'handful,' not 'five.' John went into the bedroom alone, and he had time for a little sleight of hand before Steve Gunderson helped him voucher the evidence. Maybe John figured out how to hide a kilo in the radio car, or maybe he left it in the apartment and went back for it. A week later he's making a killing, laying out the junkies and paying off the ex."

"That's a lot of sleight of hand."

"You don't know the prick like I do."

"That's the problem I'm having."

"What problem?"

"Your attitude. Your, shall we say, vendetta against him."

"Look. I'm calling it like it is. I'm through with him. I got out from under. He's a lowlife, sure, but the facts are the facts. And here's another possibility."

"Another?"

"John isn't just a rogue operator who saw his chance. He's working for the Corsican."

"How so?" Squires was starting to get hooked on Wanda's dark-eyed intensity.

"I hate to say it, but John was too smart to mess up that arrest. He threw the case. Maybe he couldn't stop the surveillance, but he could tip off the Corsican. He warned him before we went in, and the arrest turned out nice and easy. He got his payment in drugs and let me do the testifying."

"You're saying he could count on you."

"I'm saying if it wasn't me, he'd've done it himself. He knew the law. His testimony could keep Lisandru Olivari locked up or not, his choice. I'm betting he would've testified to the truth and thrown the case."

Wanda Rivera was giving Squires a lot to think about.

"Go talk to Manuel Torres," she added. After leaving Squires, she warned Manny to expect a call.

Manny had a few things to tell Squires about his new partner. Late nights in a radio car, personal details tend to leak. John's nonstop complaints about the ex and the alimony suddenly vanished as he turned his attention to other women. He seemed to own them all, the way he constantly ordered Manny to slow the car or stop whenever he spied a looker on the street. And another thing. He was bragging about a new purchase—his brand new, sleek black 1971 Corvette.

Squires was very interested. He wanted to test the truth in Wanda's accusations and started to concoct ways that Manny could help. But even before a plan was hatched, Manny was working on his own agenda. As much as it turned his stomach, he started to cozy up to John.

Sylvia, the Corsican's lady, entered the NYPD's radar in 1969. She was desired in more ways than one, but just like her darling Lisandru, she was untouchable.

In addition to her status as the Corsican's lover, she played a role in the business akin to director of human resources. There were occasions when, a day or two after a visit from Sylvia, an employee might end up with a bullet in the temple. She used her beauty and skillful deceit to infiltrate the ranks, reporting back to the boss if she discovered anyone less than loyal.

Things changed when Lisandru was doing his short stint in jail. Two days before his release, Sylvia found herself locked up. She'd been pinching small amounts of her boyfriend's goods, hoping to make a little money of her own. Being super cautious, she worked an area uptown, far from Lisandru's neighborhood. But her ignorance of the new territory cost her. The client turned out to be an undercover officer working a buy and bust operation.

At first, Sylvia was a logical suspect for the wave of overdoses. She wasn't a sadist but possibly an amateur who'd never paid much attention to the nitty-gritty of the drug business. Still, it didn't match up. When the lab came back, the amount she'd sold to the undercover was properly cut, not pure kill. John Mangrove remained the prime suspect.

The day the Corsican walked, Mangrove's superiors saw their chance. Sylvia could be turned and made a valuable asset in their renewed investigation of her bad boyfriend. The timing was perfect. Sylvia was still incarcerated, unable to make bail, and she was more fearful of Lisandru than the penal system. With plenty of ears on the street, he surely knew of her arrest, and she needed a good explanation. Already, she bore a faint scar under her right eye, where his fist had broken the skin a year ago.

But, would Sylvia go this far? Would she sign on for something this dangerous, working with the police against the Corsican?

ADA Holmes was called in.

"Why this little stuff, Sylvia? What were you going to tell him when he found out?"

A tear spilled from the corner of her eye and ran over the patch of stippled skin underneath. "I...you wouldn't understand."

"Try me," said Holmes. Although the prosecutor's personal life was a mystery to her colleagues, she seemed to have an uncanny feel for human relationships. The owlish eyes were aloof and watchful, not revealing whether she believed in the tears or believed merely in Sylvia's acting abilities.

"He's...I love him, but..."

"I don't buy that."

"He gives me everything I want."

"But not your freedom."

"I have no money. It's all his."

"And if you complain..." Holmes moved closer and did what she'd never done in her many years as an assistant DA. She touched the arrestee. On the cheek. Fleetingly, her middle and index fingers brushed the scar tissue.

The gesture ripped a seam, releasing a torrential gush of tears. In a gasping shudder, Sylvia cried out, "I have to get away from him!"

In that moment, Holmes knew that Sylvia would turn. This beautiful, battered woman was looking for a new life, a way to break free from her jailer, and her little side business uptown had been part of the escape plan. Her natural talents could be used by law enforcement to send her boyfriend up the river for a very long time. And, if there was anything to Wanda's theory, Sylvia might have something to offer up on John Mangrove as well.

ADA Holmes wrote the cooperation agreement and kept it under seal. The case against Sylvia would be dismissed in exchange for useful information. In open court, Holmes announced that the cops had made a mistake. In the wrong place at the wrong time, Sylvia had been swept up in a raid and was being released with the NYPD's apologies. With this convenient excuse in hand, Sylvia returned home.

"CI No. 9" was born. Manuel Torres was assigned as Sylvia's handler.

After an hour in the chair, John Mangrove was asking for water, and Squires left the room to get it. On the other side of the one-way window, Manny Torres and Steve Gunderson had been watching, rapt. They looked up as Squires walked by.

"So far," said Squires, "it doesn't look like he knew about the IA investigation."

"As far as I could tell," said Manny, "he didn't find out."

"When I called him in to talk, it was about a missing kilo. That's as far as it went."

"He assumed it was Wanda who accused him."

"That's what he told me too," added Steve. "It was Wanda."

"We never reveal names," said Squires.

"I'm just saying," said Manny. "I had to hear about it every day, how 'that bitch Wanda' had it in for him. And he's still worried about it."

"Good. I want him worried. We never officially cleared him. It's an open case."

Manny shook his head and chuckled. "Tonight, when we brought him in and he saw you—that was a charm!"

"'Why is *he* here?'" Steve aped.

"That's the point," said Squires. "I want him to think

we're still interested in the missing dope. We don't want him knowing about the other thing. Not yet, not while we're still talking."

"You're okay on that," Manny assured him. "He doesn't know Wanda accused him of throwing the case or working for the Corsican."

"Never mentioned anything to me," said Steve.

"And no way you two ever let on about Sylvia?" asked Squires.

"He's clueless," said Manny.

"You should've seen him sniffing after that tail," said Steve with a laugh.

"Well," said Squires, "let's see what the prosecutor gets out of him."

He went to the water cooler, drank an icy cupful, and tossed the paper cup. Then he got a glass of warm, rusty tap water from the bathroom sink and returned to the interrogation room.

Mangrove took a gulp, made a face, and downed the rest of the glass. "Manny was a big improvement over Wanda, all right," he continued. "We had half a chance of making a new case against Olivari. Two months we worked it, all of June and July, watching the new apartment and the people coming in and out. Especially his girl."

"Lady Sylvia. She caught your eye."

"We always had our eye on her. But things different. She became a key player."

ADA Holmes lifted her brow over round, unadorned eyes. Mangrove squirmed. *Beautiful*, thought Squires as he watched Holmes at work.

"It was obvious what was going on, the way she carried that huge handbag in and out of the building. Sometimes she was with the Corsican, other times on her own or with other people in the operation. She was involved in the business on a daily basis."

"And not just as a bed partner."

"Partner in crime. Ask any of the others. We all saw it. Gunderson and Sprague usually worked swing, and Torres and I were on graveyard. Sometimes another team would cover days, but we didn't need it. That's when Lisandru and Sylvia slept, eight to four. Late afternoon they had breakfast and got to work."

"Graveyard was most active?" asked ADA Holmes.

"Hopping."

"But the four of you couldn't handle it all. You weren't on the job seven days a week."

"No, but..." Mangrove's voice trailed and he averted his eyes.

Just beautiful, thought Squires.

Mangrove bucked up and faced off again. "I had to get that scumbag this time. I wasn't about to miss the chance for a take down. So I started working overtime, volunteering my nights off."

"How generous of you. Extra nights following Sylvia?"

"That was part of it."

"Or most of it."

Mangrove scowled and wiped his wet forehead with the back of his hand.

"Need some more water?"

"Nah," he snarled. "Nasty stuff."

"Sure you're okay to go on?"

He writhed in his seat, becoming testy. "You think you know the whole story. Why don't *you* tell it?"

"But I *don't* know the story, John. Not like you."

Manny cast the rod with immediate results. Sylvia was the perfect bait.

They were set up in a van across the street, conducting surveillance. "Check this out," John said. Already his tongue was hanging.

Manny didn't need to tell CI No. 9 how to dress to get the job done. It was summertime, and she wore the sheerest, skimpiest layer from shoulder to thigh, her legs even longer in three-inch heels.

"You've seen her before," said Manny.

"Sure, but not like this. Lisandru should get the leash. I wouldn't let her out of the house looking like that."

"What's in that huge shoulder bag you think? More than just lipstick."

"We can guess. Or I can find out." John had taken the bait.

With all the ingredients of his plan in place, Manny decided to go all out. He started working double shifts seven days a week, one with John, one with the CI.

He liked to laugh about it with Sprague and Gunderson, whenever John wasn't around. "I should've been a talent scout," he liked to say. "I'd *really* make a killing." Sylvia's acting abilities were awe inspiring. The scar helped, and the full, trembling lips and incandescent eyes that picked up the rays in streetlights. She had a way of tossing her black hair, proud one moment, vulnerable and moist-eyed the next.

Were the tears fake or real? Manny didn't doubt that Sylvia needed to be rid of the Corsican. She had her reasons, and Manny had his own.

After their first sighting of Sylvia, John called the shots. He assigned himself the job of following her whenever she appeared on the scene, alone.

"You need backup?" Manny would ask, giving himself an internal wink.

"Nah, I got this one," John said. "She's mine."

Manny would wait five minutes before stepping out of the van, knowing where to find them. He could have waited until daylight to get the CI's report, but it was foolish to trust her completely. He watched from a distance, reading their body language, unable to hear what they were saying. Sylvia didn't wear a wire. She couldn't risk it because of her daily intimacy with the Corsican. But Manny was looking for an opportunity. A recording would be the sure way to erase loose ends and reasonable doubts.

Manny's first tail was in early June, so easy it was almost a joke. John caught up with Sylvia as she slowed her delicate click-clacking on the sidewalk, a couple of blocks from the Corsican's apartment. It was two in the morning, but the streets were still plenty active. Manny dipped into a dark driveway, diagonally across from the serendipitous encounter. Sylvia moved like a dancer in a slow rumba, and John heeled before making his move, brushing her arm as he walked past. He turned and did a double take, so sure that Sylvia, like every female on earth, lived and breathed for his attention.

Even from a distance, Manny could see the virile chest puffing and the cock of the head. The rest he could imagine. There was a stupid grin and a trite pickup line. Sylvia dutifully responded with coy interest and a wide, submissive smile.

John was hooked. From that day forward, he waited like a panting dog poised at the ready for the next time she stepped out alone, without the Corsican by her side.

Meanwhile, the partners were becoming fast "friends." Manny got into the habit of dropping by John's apartment at ten or eleven o'clock before their graveyard shift. John would open the door to Manny with an expectant look, a brief show of neediness. No one else seemed to have an interest in visiting him. But his loneliness had to be ignored if Manny was to succeed. There was no room for sympathy in the plan.

John's bachelor pad was conceived for entertaining the ladies. The living room was furnished with soft leather furniture, a wet bar, and a four-speaker sound system. The bedroom was dominated by a king-size bed, draped and pillowed in tiger stripes. Still, Manny never once came upon a female visitor during his unannounced visits. Most times, John answered the door wearing a sweat-soaked muscle shirt, holding a pair of twenty-pound dumbbells. His pumping room was equipped with weights and lined with mirrors for a pleasing self-inspection of the glistening biceps.

Drinks would be offered. John usually had a belt or two before work. Manny tried to be sociable behind a scrim of illusion to divert John's attention from the liquid surreptitiously poured down the sink.

One evening, John sat on the couch, sipping from a glass of Jim Beam in his left hand, gazing at his off-duty piece in his right hand. Like a caveman with his favorite rock, he tossed the weapon playfully, feeling the weight of the Colt Python and its three-inch barrel. A popular handgun, small but powerful. Manny sat across from him on the leather easy chair, focused on the Beam he swirled inside his own tumbler. The amber smear was smooth and inviting. How he wished he could drink it down, blink twice, and wake up at the end of this caper, mission accomplished!

John had already met Sylvia for the second time. Manny pretended to be interested in his partner's appraisal of her physical attributes, emitting grunts and nods of approval. "Right about that," Manny laughed. "Sylvia's a real looker."

"Nothing I can't handle." John's laugh was low and guttural.

"You'd like to get a piece of that?"

"Who wouldn't?"

"You're crazy, man. The Corsican's woman? You're asking for a bullet in the head."

"Hah!" Still holding the gun, John swiped his hand through the air, a sign that all of it was just talk. But Manny saw the gleam of interest in his eyes. It was just like last night, when he'd watched them from a dark niche across the street and sensed the same gleam in John's eyes from the attentive tilt of his head toward the lady.

Just before their graveyard shift, John said, "Ready in a minute." He went to the bedroom, taking his handgun with him. Manny heard a drawer open, the Python deposited, the drawer closed. John emerged with a different gun, his service weapon in a shoulder holster.

Three weeks passed. After his fifth meeting with Sylvia, John came back to the van, full of his own exploits and smart detective work. He related most of it, holding back the best parts for himself, not guessing that Manny didn't need a full report. The untold details held the true source of John's excitement.

In a foul crevice between two city buildings, John had pressed up close to Sylvia, circling her waist with his arm. That huge shoulder bag got caught under his right forearm, and he felt a hard, distinctive shape, something a cop couldn't ignore.

"What's this, baby?"

She shrugged her shoulders.

Groping the outside of the bag, he felt the distinctive outline of a small handgun. He pretended to be startled, maybe even a little scared of her. "Packing heat? Should I be worried?"

She grabbed the top of his hand, gently pulling it away. "Johnny," she said, using her own special name for him. "It's protection—but not from you." She confessed that her interest in Johnny was growing, but cautioned that they had to keep their meetings a secret, relegated to dark corners or unknown bars and night spots, away from *him*. If he found out, she was dead.

She started to tremble, her mouth quivering and moisture pooling in her eyes. She told her story. Everything had gone from bad to worse for her—Johnny couldn't possibly imagine. Her days were filled with dread, every minute fearing the things her boyfriend would make her do, the people he forced her to meet, the expectations he held of her, his impossible desire. She was drawn to him but feared him intensely, the dreamy eyes that deceptively drew her in and suddenly, without warning, turned stone cold and murderous.

"Who *is* this charmer?" John asked innocently.

"His name is Lisandru."

"What kind of name is *that*?" He pulled her close, relishing the helplessness and the deep curves of her body. "Let me help you. Let me go after him."

"Stay away, Johnny! He'll kill you."

"You don't know what I can handle."

"He's a murderer."

"I'm worried about you, baby." He stroked her black hair from crown to nape.

"I'll find a way to leave him. I have to. It's just that..."

"Just what?"

"I might need some help."

"Anything, just say the word."

"You would do that?"

"Anything at all. But if he comes after you," John moved his lips close to her ear, "shoot the bastard."

"You're saying I should kill him?"

"I'm saying don't be afraid to protect yourself."

She broke down even harder then.

Back in the van, as he told bits and pieces of his story, John's excitement was palpable. He was getting close to Sylvia, and she was bringing him closer to his nemesis, the Corsican.

"Too bad her arrest uptown was no good," John said. He was aware only of the official story, the little speech ADA Holmes had given in court when she dismissed the case "with apologies." John shook his head. "Can you imagine if we had something on her? She could be flipped. What a prize that would be!"

"Imagine," Manny said.

"Maybe I can do the same thing with the gun. I have her on a weapons charge."

"Blow your cover?"

"Hmm."

"It could backfire and we'd get nothing from her. The Corsican would be tipped off that we had his lady."

John shrugged. "I didn't think it would work any-way," he said, not willing to give his junior partner any credit. But there was something more behind it, the real reason he didn't want to blow his cover. It was the girl he wanted. A chance with the girl.

What a prize, Manny thought.

"So, I followed her and bumped into her. I was just a guy on the street expressing an interest, you could say. The plan was to get something going between us. I'd get close enough to find out what I could about the Corsican."

"Pretty sure she'd go for you?" asked Holmes.

"The ladies like me. Something *you* wouldn't know about." *Ouch*, thought Squires. Mangrove was skating the line.

But Holmes just let out a belly laugh. "A ladies' man, are you?"

"I've been told... But it doesn't matter. The only one

that mattered was Sylvia, and she went for it. She was crazy for me." Squires noted the tension in Mangrove's throat. The Adam's apple bobbed in a dry swallow. *More like he was crazy for her.*

"So, how many times did you meet at your apartment?"

"Hah, hah," Mangrove intoned sarcastically. "None. What do you think, counselor? I'm gonna tell a target where I live? This was business. This was detective work."

"You kept it on the streets?"

"And a few dives on the Lower East Side. I'd treat her to a drink now and then."

"All very chaste."

"There was a little bit of the other thing." The Adam's apple bobbed again.

Holmes raised her eyebrows over those owlish eyes.

"But not a full score, if that's what you're getting at. She needed something else, and I stepped in at the right time. She was desperate, looking for a way to get out of the business and away from her boyfriend. He'd gone too far with her. She started carrying a gun."

"What kind?"

"A small handgun. Short barrel, that's all I knew at the time. I felt it in her purse."

"Felt it? That's all?"

"I wasn't about to blow my cover, taking too much interest. What does it matter? We all know what it is now. She was touchy about the whole subject. I'd gotten this close to her because she was scared and needed protection. It made her feel better to have me around."

"You were the big savior. That's just about where we found you tonight, isn't it?"

"Not what you think…"

"Makes complete sense—"

"Maybe you'd like to know the facts?"

"Excuse me, John. Go right ahead."

"Thank you very much," he said like a schoolboy. "Sylvia told me the Corsican was a changed man after he got out of jail. Convinced he was being watched every minute. He found a new apartment, but he also started doing more of his business on the street. Sylvia said he was dragging her around with him to all his meets, mostly in back alleys, negotiating business with his suppliers and distributors. What she was saying matched up with our surveillances. The coward was using her as a buffer."

"You're saying a man like that doesn't have male firepower to back him up?"

"Sure, but Sylvia was…you don't know her like I do."

"No, I don't."

"She's a distraction. That's what the Corsican told her. With Sylvia around, he was less likely to get swindled or shot. She was better protection than two armed body-guards. Even vicious animals think twice before shooting someone in front of a lady. And he was making these deals on his own terms. He'd be naming his price, and Sylvia would be working those eyes and hips. It's impossible not to look."

Impossible for you, thought Squires.

"So, tell me about tonight's meet," said Holmes.

"Ronny Geld was demanding a one-on-one with

Olivari, just to negotiate price. Ronny's a big supplier, a dangerous and greedy bastard. A few of his competitors have been 'eliminated' under suspicious circumstances. But the Corsican was a potential customer, and this was supposed to be just talk, away from anyone who might overhear. No bodyguards, no weapons, no money, no dope. Sylvia was scared because the Corsican wanted her to be there, to help drive down the price. He came up with a plan. Sylvia would hold back for five minutes, enough time for him to make an offer. Then she'd show up, acting like she'd been following him. She was supposed to walk in on the meeting, acting pissed as hell like they just had a lovers' spat. An element of surprise. Ronny would be distracted and rattled."

"Because it's impossible not to look."

"Impossible."

In his obscure corner, Squires gave a virtual shake of the head. With Mangrove at the scene of this meeting, Wanda's conspiracy theory made some sense. Was Mangrove the Corsican's bodyguard? Why hadn't CI No. 9 given him up to her handler? The cooperation agreement required it. Maybe, just maybe, Sylvia had some feelings for this creep. But that was just too hard to believe.

Mangrove thinks we're falling for this? A lovers' spat? What kind of drug dealer conducts business like that?

A man in lust would fall for it. That's what Manny was counting on, and he was proven right. John related Sylvia's story with genuine belief in his eyes and the expectation of big results. He and Manny would be witnessing a meet between two powerful kingpins in the heroin business.

Manny offered to ghost while maintaining radio contact with a backup unit. John didn't go for it. As usual, he called the shots. No other officers. Manny would follow but had to hang back, pulling in closer only on John's signal, as soon as he had a clear view and adequate cover. They couldn't allow the Corsican to suspect watchful eyes.

At 1:20 A.M., John left the van to meet Sylvia a few blocks from the spot where the negotiations were to take place in ten minutes. It was too hot to wear any more than a T-shirt, so he tucked his service revolver into his waistband, under the loose shirt end.

Manny took five minutes to check his own weapon and other equipment, the receiver, recording device, and earphone. For the first time, CI No. 9 was willing to take the risk of wearing a wire. She hadn't seen the Corsican all day. He believed she was miles away, visiting her sister in the Bronx.

Earphone in place, Manny started out, a few blocks behind the other two. He heard Sylvia's breathless voice in his ear. "Johnny!"

"Hey, baby."

There was a rustling and scratching and boom of body contact as their clothing pressed and shifted over the mike.

"I'm so glad you're here, Johnny! I couldn't have gone alone. Hey, what's this?"

"My piece. You have yours?"

"Right here, but Johnny, I'm not going to use it."

"Just in case. Don't be afraid to protect yourself."

"But I've got *you* for protection."

Over the mike came the faint sound of Sylvia's high heels on pavement. John wore soundless sneakers. Manny was a block away, still out of view.

"Wait here, Johnny," she whispered audibly. "I don't want him to see you."

"He can't see. Go ahead. I'm right here."

Manny entered the block and saw John, his back pressed against the building that bordered the alleyway. His right hand gripped the bulge at his waistband. He twisted back and looked at Manny but held his left arm straight out with a flexed hand, signaling him to hold back. Sylvia had gone around the corner, into the dark.

Manny heard her breathing in his ear.

Manny heard the click-clack of her heels.

Manny heard, "No, Johnny, don't! Don't shoot!"

Four gunshots sounded like fast popping fire-crackers.

John pulled his service revolver and took off around the corner. Manny was fast behind, with Sylvia's clacking heels in his earphone.

Squeezed by tall buildings, the alley was narrow, long and dim, lit only by the glow from a few windows in apartments several stories up. A few steps in, a junkie sat on the pavement in a slump against a wall, nodding out. At the far end of the alley, John's caveman form was hunkered low in the shadows, near a dumpster.

Manny fled past the junkie and slowed up, wanting to watch. The bodies were heaped next to the dumpster, but John didn't touch or look at them. He was a few yards away from them, in a squat, inspecting the pavement as he shoved his service revolver into the back of his waistband. Gingerly, he extended a hand and hooked an object with his pinky finger.

Sylvia was breathing hard in Manny's ear. "How's it look?" she asked, laughing big. This time, she was speaking directly to Manny. Quietly, he reveled in the sound of her voice with nothing to fear. He'd instructed her to turn off the recorder after the shots were fired. Now he turned off his receiver and shoved the earphone into a pocket before John could see it.

With a few heavy footfalls, Manny came up fast and panted, "Where's Sylvia?" He stepped toward the bodies and exclaimed, "Jesus, God!" Crouching near the first body, he felt for pulse or breath, and did the same with the second one. Nothing. In the dim light, he could just make out the spreading circles of blood on chest wounds in each. The hours in target practice with CI No. 9 had paid off.

"Dead," Manny announced. "Come on! We'll call it in and look for Sylvia."

Stunned into silence, John rose to his feet unsteadily, a small handgun dangling from his pinky finger by the trigger. He stared at the gun for a full ten seconds. "No," he said.

"Wha'd'ya mean 'no'? She can't get very far in those heels."

John emitted a laugh, shaking his head. "My girl has good taste in weapons! Bought herself a Colt Python!"

"Come on, let's go," Manny urged again.

"No," John repeated, turning to look at the bodies.

"We're not chasing her down. It was self-defense. I heard her yelling 'don't shoot!' before she fired. Check for weapons." He dazedly glanced around at his feet while Manny checked the bodies. Nothing in their hands. The Corsican had a small pistol tucked into his boot. Geld's handgun was tight down in his waistband. So much for coming to the meet unarmed.

"I don't see anything," Manny fibbed. He couldn't risk John messing with the evidence. "I'll call it in."

"Wait a minute—"

"I didn't bring the two-way," Manny cut in, annoyed by the pathetic sound of John's broken heart. "Wait here. I'll go back to the van and put out the APB for Sylvia."

Manny headed back toward the light. He wasn't gone for long. A patrol car, the one he'd arranged, was waiting nearby on the street. At the mouth of the cave, he made a show of flagging it down. Within a minute, the place was swarming with homicide detectives and half the narcotics squad, including Sprague and Gunderson. They didn't mind doing a double shift for this one.

"When you catch up with Sylvia, don't go hard on her. It was darker than a tomb in there. She thought she saw a gun. It was self-defense. I heard her screaming my name, calling for help. She was yelling, 'Johnny'..."

"She called you 'Johnny'?" Holmes looked amused.

Another detail confirmed, thought Squires.

"Sure, why not. That was her nickname for me. She was in danger. She was yelling for me. Then, right before she fired, she yelled, 'don't shoot, don't shoot!' Someone pulled a gun on her, or else she thought she saw one. I swear it and I'll testify to it."

"Just like you were going to testify that the Corsican had six kilos within his reach? Sorry, I meant *five* kilos."

"I'm sick of hearing about Wanda!" Mangrove's eyes shifted to Squires. "You've got nothing on me!"

Squires and Holmes exchanged a look. At last, it was his turn to speak. "You're right on that one, John. We're not charging you with sale or possession of narcotics." Squires found it difficult to concede this, because something still didn't feel right. He had a gut belief in Mangrove's guilt of narcotics crimes, but his intuition wasn't going to pass for evidence in court.

"Like I said. You've got nothing on me. And you've got nothing on Sylvia either. Put me on the witness stand for this one! No one could lie about something like this. She was yelling 'don't shoot'! She was in trouble. Someone pulled a gun on her—"

"That's not quite…"

"—it was self-defense—"

"…how it sounded to us."

"So, go light on her." John's eyes popped wide. "Sounded like what?"

"Don't you worry, John." Holmes gave him a big smile. "When we see Sylvia, we'll be going light on her."

It was close to six A.M. when Holmes and Squires wrapped up the Q and A with John Mangrove. Manny Torres was liking the way things were coming out. Quietly in his own world, he was having pretty thoughts about where he'd be later in the day after he and Steve finished up their paperwork on the murders of Lisandru

Olivari and Ronny Geld. He'd been up for the past twenty-four hours but was still operating on adrenaline, ready to go another twenty-four.

So many times he'd imagined this, the culmination of months of hard work. In a few hours he'd be on his way uptown. He'd knock on the door of his secret love, sweep her up in his arms, and deliver the good news. He couldn't wait to see the shine in Wanda's eyes when he told her they'd done it. Together, with the help of CI No. 9, they'd ruined John Mangrove. And no one suspected. Not Squires, not Sprague or Gunderson. Not…Holmes?

There was still room for worry.

Holmes and Squires shut and locked the door of the interrogation room on Mangrove, who'd just been told he was under arrest for double homicide. Soon, he'd be taken to the lock up at the courthouse for his arraignment. In the meantime, he was knocking himself out, banging on the table and screaming at the top of his lungs, "It's a set up!"

The prosecutor needed to finalize a few details with Torres and Gunderson. Squires tagged along. The four of them walked away from the unpleasant, muffled sounds of the ranting prisoner, out into the reception area of the precinct, where it was cooler.

"Where do you have Sylvia?"

"In a room down the hall," said Gunderson.

"I'll be speaking to her next," said Holmes. "For the grand jury, I'll need copies of the wire transcript and the registration and serial number on Mangrove's Python. When will we get ballistics and fingerprints?"

"I put a rush on the reports," said Manny. "Should

be about forty-eight hours. I don't expect any surprises. From the look of the wounds, those were .357 magnum bullets, a fit with Mangrove's gun."

"Not to put a wrench in," said Squires, "but what if Sylvia's prints are on the gun?"

"Under the law, it doesn't matter who pulled the trigger. Whether he gave his gun to her or he pulled the trigger himself, they went down that alley together and acted with the same intent, isn't that right, Manny?"

"Right."

"And that bit about her carrying a gun too? What was that about?"

"She'll tell you. She carried a starter pistol in her shoulder bag. She'll show you. The only piece at the scene was Mangrove's Python, other than the victims' weapons, and they were still tight to their bodies."

"Okay. And Sylvia doesn't have anything to say about the kilo and the slew of dead junkies?"

"She wasn't there when Mangrove arrested her boyfriend. She just doesn't know."

There was a short silence, each one of their expressions saying, *Mangrove stole that dope and sold it*. They all just knew it.

"How about Mangrove's involvement with the Corsican's business?"

"I've asked her a hundred times. Sylvia doesn't have a word on that."

Holmes smiled wryly and shook her head. "It was pure folly then. He was smitten with her. Protecting her from the big bad boyfriend. It's as good a motive as any." Holmes caught Manny's eye for just a second too long.

The awkward pause was there and gone. "So that's it for now," Holmes continued, looking at each of them in turn. "Heat of passion. If intentional murder doesn't stick, we've got him for manslaughter. Good work, men. I like a solid case." She pointedly looked at Manny again, their eyes locking. "And...," her eyelid, just one of them, slowly lowered over a wise, round eye, "I like justice."

With the arrival of morning light, Manny received the message. In this case, justice was better than the truth.

The prosecutor turned, and Gunderson escorted her to the interview room where Sylvia waited to tell her tale.

✝ Day Three

WHEN THE SPACE is eight by ten, concrete and metal bars, a man clings to his little rituals. That's all he has. Sanity is that fragile.

Hour after hour, Spiegel sits on the cot, elbows on knees, head hung low as he taps a nameless tune with his heels, alternating right and left. It's a tricky rhythm, made intimate by the spongy thud of his soft-soled shoes. Lyrics are written and rewritten in his head, momentary inspirations just as easily forgotten.

If the cage won't kill him, the waiting will. He wants this to be the day, doesn't want it to be the day. His bargain-basement lawyer tells him that time is on their side. It's day three and the jury is struggling. They have a doubt.

The lyrics help but can't erase the parade of setbacks in his case. Very little has gone right for Spiegel, starting with the pre-dawn raid of his apartment, handcuffs slapped on as neighbors gawked. Stationhouse inter-rogation. Lineups. Demand for a lawyer. His modest salary as a bartender at Sixties can't buy him anything better than a squeaky-voiced kitten by the name of Phil

Curtis. First thing his counsel said to him was, "Cut that hair."

"I won't."

"Looks bad. Bound to be someone on the jury won't like it."

"Short hair looks worse. It'll be a lie." Spiegel wears it long for his job. Sixties is a retro establishment with pictures of Woodstock and Buffalo Springfield on the walls. His compromise for trial is a clean ponytail.

Eyes on the floor, he loops a wayward strand behind an ear while tapping out his rhythm, cooling the boil to a simmer. A high-priced lawyer would've gotten the lineup evidence thrown out. Would've convinced the judge to allow expert testimony about unreliable eyewitness identifications. Everything is an act in that courtroom. The jury ignores Curtis and listens to the prosecutor, Damion Vasco, a taller man with a deeper voice and broader shoulders. A man who looks like he knows what he's doing.

Spiegel beats down the failed tactics, opening a window in his mind to a vision of his only true supporters. In the courtroom, his mother and sister wipe their glistening cheeks and offer their trembling smiles. When he testified, their eyes shone brightly from the hostile sea of faces, beaming an unconditional belief in him.

A better lawyer would've prepped him for testifying instead of making him fight for his rights, then leaving him out in the cold. One tap right, three left, one right—a new rap. *It's...* Midtrial, with the jury out on a coffee break. "It's my only chance," he told Curtis. Tap, t-tap,

tap, tap.

"You'll hang yourself. Happens every time. You don't know what you look like."

Spiegel doesn't need reminding that most people cringe at the sight of his mug. "You want me to sit here and do nothing?"

"I'm lookin' out for you, man. We have a better chance arguing reasonable doubt."

"I can't just sit here. I have to tell them—"

"Don't say it! I don't wanna know what you did or didn't do—"

"But—"

"—if you wanna testify, that is. I can't put you on the stand if you tell me anything. I'll lose my license."

What kind of lawyer is that? Spiegel ignored the "advice" and took the oath. He sang for his life while Curtis dipped his head and looked at the floor on direct examination, made no objections on cross.

What're the chances that the jury is talking about his testimony right now?

Two rows, twelve faces, but he sees only the girl, the one sitting in the front, just right of center. Eleven neutral faces, at times interested, bored, sleepy, or guarded—but the twelfth is a stealth drone on target. Focused and relentless. She could be the one to send him to Folsom, dogged enough to badger any holdout until they come to a unanimous "guilty."

Marlena, Marlena… The name rolls easily off the prosecutor's tongue, shaping his lips like a kiss. The way Vasco talks, the victim could've been his little sister. With shining eyes, Vasco pounces. *That man* got her drunk. He points. *That man* did those things to her. Photographs. Here she is alive, Ladies and Gentlemen. Here she is dead. Curtis remains mute, ignoring Spiegel's elbow in his ribs while the girl in the front row of the jury spotlights those photographs with her saucer-like eyes. She sucks in the evidence and turns to the defense table, staring at Spiegel openly, puzzled one minute, squint-eyed the next.

A better lawyer would've seen her coming and knocked her off the jury. Curtis botched it, used up all their challenges and was left with a pathetic objection. "Challenge for cause, Your Honor. She's the same age as the victim. Every time she looks at my client, she's gonna see an attacker."

Motion denied.

Spiegel can't rid himself of her eyes. He sees them day and night, in the courtroom, in his sleep, three hours ago, during the read back of his testimony. Especially then. But her face did something different. There was the usual, intense stare, and then…her expression changed. It relaxed and settled around a thought. *Yes, now I know.*

Tap. *Yes.* Three slow taps. *Now I know.*

A shout breaks his rhythm. "Spiegel! The jury's coming in."

He looks up, trying for a blank face, but the fear has nowhere to hide.

Day One

Denise Beaumont will be glad when this is over, but that doesn't mean she's tempted into cutting corners. Something is bothering her more than the stolen time.

Sure, this isn't the way she planned to begin her

summer of freedom. In the midst of celebrating—graduation and her twenty-second birthday—she received the jury summons. It was a mild annoyance, a single day to be lived through and written off. What a shock to find herself on a jury in a two-week murder trial!

With her brand-new bachelor's degree in humanities from San Francisco State, Denise isn't quite sure where she'll find work. Meanwhile, it isn't so terrible being back home again, across the Bay. Her parents say they're okay with a short "vacation" before the all-out job search begins, but now she isn't quite so sure. Dad smiles like the Cheshire Cat when she walks out the door every morning for jury service. "Couldn't have come at a better time. Doing your civic duty!" *Cut me a break, Dad—it wasn't so easy ranking number three in my class!*

In the jury room, Denise scans the faces of the other eleven, some of them here willingly, others not. She can't say that she's one of the willing, but she can't deny her pride in doing her "civic duty," as Dad puts it. She understands and appreciates her responsibility, unlike those people who weaseled out of serving with their tales of hardship and prejudice. A bunch of complainers—maybe even out-and-out liars—but Judge Shirley Creighton let them all off. Denise has no excuses, and she's incapable of fabricating any. No schoolwork, no exams coming up, no money for travel, no job.

So here she is, having passed the screening process and proved she's a blank slate. She answered all Judge Creighton's questions truthfully during voir dire. She's never met the attorneys or witnesses and doesn't know the defendant, Dexter Spiegel, a man only a few years older than she is. He's a strange mixture, sitting there in a gray suit and cranberry tie with his ponytail and sullen expression. Denise has never been to a bar called Sixties, a popular haunt of UC Berkeley students on the north side of town, and she isn't familiar with the crime scene, the eucalyptus grove on the west side of campus. Her answers to the judge's questions might have been different if UC Berkeley hadn't rejected her under-graduate application. Maybe she's resentful about that? If so, it's no excuse for begging off a murder trial. A campus murder. Judge Creighton asked if anyone would find it difficult to sit on a murder case. Silence, heads shaking. "Has anyone here ever been the victim of a crime?" The judge scanned their faces, looking for likely victims. A few raised their hands. Not Denise, although an un-pleasant thought was playing at the back of her mind. She blinked hard and stared at the judge, a woman of patience and wisdom. Honestly, Denise couldn't say that she'd ever been the victim of a crime.

Not everyone who was picked for the jury answered "no" to that question. Some of them had been pick-pocketed or burglarized but still assured the judge that their verdict would be based only on the evidence in this case. Now, Denise wonders. After two weeks of shared coffee and lunch breaks, she's gotten to know many of these people—and she can guess just as much about the others.

The twelve are locked in together, escape impossible. Of course, the door literally isn't locked. Two court officers stand on the other side, protecting them, ready to relay their messages to the judge. The room is airless, windowless, prisonlike for Denise, who's slightly claustrophobic.

She predicts, based on the way things get started, that they're in for a long haul. "Let's take a straw vote to begin," says the foreperson, an unemployed actor who calls himself Tanner Breedlove. ("Between roles," is what he said during voir dire.) An obvious stage name. He has a controlling, pug-nosed air, the kind of person who likes to be the center of attention. "We're just seeing where we are," Tanner explains. "Raise your hands. How many of you say—"

"Wait a minute," Denise protests. "Can we do this on paper ballots or…?"

"Right," says the boy directly across from her. "A secret vote is better."

She likes that boy, Joe Antomarchi, the only juror younger than she is. Joe is twenty-one, never went to college, and paints cars at his father's auto body shop. Not intellectual or analytical but with plain good sense. The next youngest to them is Tanner, who's maybe thirty-five, trying to look twenty-nine. The rest of the people in the room are middle-aged or senior citizens.

Denise, for one, doesn't want everyone to know that her vote is "not guilty." They haven't discussed anything yet, and isn't that what the judge told them to do? Denise also has a four-year academic habit of scrutinizing every situation for its deeper meaning. She wants to review *all* the evidence. In detail. Methodically. Only then will she know if the tickle of her conscience is a reasonable doubt or something closer to cowardice. She supposes that some murderers don't take kindly to the people who lock them away.

Tanner signals his surrender. "All right." He counts out twelve small squares of paper from the supply they've been given. "Pass these out. Don't think about it. Vote your instincts. We just want to see where we are."

Don't think! Some foreperson! Denise grabs one of the stubby, well-sharpened pencils and cups her left hand around the paper as she writes. They place their ballots face down and shove them toward Tanner, who makes a big deal out of swirling them around before turning them over and counting. Nine to three for conviction. Who are the other two? Denise guesses her friend Joe and Charlotte O'Reilly, a retired high school teacher who has two grown sons, a few years older than the defendant.

"Okay, looks like we need to convince only three of you before we can get out of here." Tanner is making no secret of his desire to get back to his audition schedule.

"Let's go through the evidence," Denise says.

"Yes, let's," says Charlotte. "We can start with those three eyewitnesses."

"They'd been drinking," says a man at the far end of the table. His name is Robert Stiller, a phlebotomist at Alameda Medical. "I think we should consider whether their judgment was impaired," he says. Maybe Robert was one of the "not guilty" votes.

"A few beers is all," says Tanner.

"Michael had five," retorts the phlebotomist. "Do you know what that makes your blood alcohol level?"

"Augie said he had only two beers, and Leona wasn't drinking at all. She had club soda. And who served them? That bartender at Sixties. The defendant. They've been there a couple of times, and they know his face. Half an hour after they left, they saw him again, in the eucalyptus grove. They all identified him in lineups. Independently. You can't get any better evidence than that! *Three* eyewitnesses, all graduate students, the cream of the university, smart people, and they know the guy. What more do you want?"

"Yeah," says Joe. "Three people are saying the same thing. What is there to talk about?"

The overbearing Tanner has now convinced Joe. Or maybe Denise has been wrong about Joe. Anyway, this is not the systematic analysis she had in mind. "Let's go through the witnesses one by one," she suggests. "There were a lot of people in the bar that could have followed her. Maybe the witnesses identified the defendant in the lineups because they'd just seen him at Sixties. His face was on their minds. People can be mistaken."

"Especially when they're traumatized," adds Charlotte. "Just think about what they saw! Can you imagine the *guilt* they must be feeling? I mean, if they hadn't interrupted him…"

Silence grips the room until Robert whispers into it. "She might still be alive."

After a moment, the actor makes an entrance. "So— now you're ready to string up the witnesses. Hah! They aren't to blame for his savage act!"

Act, indeed! Tanner's booming theatrical voice doesn't impress or intimidate Denise. "Mr. Curtis pointed out that there wasn't any physical evidence found on the victim. Spiegel's blood or hairs or skin or…or anything else. And the weapon wasn't found. So, we have to really be sure about the identifications."

"You're one of the 'not guilty' votes, I can tell," says Tanner. "I know what *I'm* sure of. Phil Curtis needs a remedial acting class. He's so phony, calling the defendant 'Dexter' and patting him on the back every chance he gets!"

Oh, this man makes her livid! Denise fairly yells, "We're sending someone to prison! We have to—" Her voice cracks unexpectedly, but she regains it. "We have to be sure."

"I agree," says a man named George, a middle-aged CPA who also has no excuses for avoiding jury duty, now that it's two months after April 15. "We have to be sure. We should go through the evidence step by step." His voice is steady and businesslike. Denise looks around the table and picks up signs of agreement, some people nodding, others saying, "Yes," or, "We should." Brad, Henry, Cynthia, Otis, Kerri, Amanda, and that woman with the impossible-to-pronounce name. Robert at one end, Tanner at the other, Joe directly across from Denise.

They spend the rest of the day reviewing the testimony of the three eyewitnesses. There's little to debate about what happened *before* the crime, the facts that are merely ordinary and unremarkable. Michael Headley, Augie Delorio, and Leona Clairborne are Ph.D. candidates in the department of molecular and cell biology of UC Berkeley, friends who've become close after endless hours together in the lab and lecture hall. On a Saturday night in the fall of last year they went out to dinner, and afterward, to Sixties for drinks. It was still early in the semester, and the heaviest academic pressures were not yet upon them. They grabbed three stools at the far end of the long, wraparound bar, where they drank and laughed until closing time. The defendant, Dexter Spiegel, was serving drinks along their half of the bar. Another bartender served patrons on the other side, and a couple of servers shuttled between the bar and the tables, delivering drinks to customers.

How much did the three friends drink? Not a matter of dispute. Leona, who drank only two club sodas with lime, remembers what her friends drank, and they confirmed it in their testimony. Michael admitted that he had a weakness for a particular brand of craft beer, and he drank one after another. If Leona and Augie said he had five, then it was five. Augie sipped slowly and had only two.

The prosecutor asked them, in turn, "Did you know the victim, Marlena Glinkowska?"

"No," three times.

Each was shown a photograph. "Did you see this woman at Sixties that night?" None could recall. The place was crowded, and they weren't paying much attention to anyone else. Another witness, a server named Tanya, confirmed that Marlena sat with a girlfriend at the small table closest to the bar. She was drinking Cosmopolitans. Spiegel was mixing them.

"The elusive girlfriend," Tanner says. Marlena's companion didn't testify at the trial.

"Judge Creighton told us not to speculate as to her whereabouts," says George.

"I'll tell you 'whereabouts' she is! She skipped town. Why would she want to admit under oath that she abandoned her drunk friend to walk home alone, to be stalked by a murderer?"

Denise can't blame Tanner for saying what everyone's thinking but, oddly, his words throw her into another place and time. A flash of an image, felt like a sting, jumps to mind. Sophomore year at SF State, a party, a few too many drinks, a girlfriend who left her stranded, no one to drive her home, a boy who offered a ride… She shakes the thought away and says, "There could be other reasons she didn't testify—"

"—but it doesn't matter," Tanner continues. "What difference would her testimony make? She wasn't in the eucalyptus grove, that much we know."

"It *would* have made a difference," says reasonable George. "She could have told us whether Marlena knew the defendant or talked to him that night and agreed to leave with him."

"One way or another, we know he killed her. That's all that matters here."

"Excuse me," says a quieter voice. Otis, a freelance photographer. "I don't think Marlena knew him. I think he followed her after the bar closed. He was eyeing her."

"Yes, that cocktail waitress…," starts Henry, an affable octogenarian.

"The table server, you mean," corrects Charlotte, gently. "Tanya."

"Yes, that's her. I remember Tanya saying that Spiegel was looking at the girl in a way that wasn't very nice. 'Leering,' I think she said…"

"The judge struck that testimony," says Denise.

Henry cups his ear with a hand. "She strugged it?"

"Struck. We can't consider it. Judge Creighton sustained Mr. Curtis's objection and said the testimony is stricken from the record."

"Oh," says Henry, settling back into his chair.

Tanner laughs dramatically. "I'm *so* glad we aren't considering it! For my part, Spiegel's leering was *completely* stricken from *my* mind before I voted 'guilty'!"

They decide to move on to a proper subject—the testimony about what happened after the bar closed at two in the morning. Augie, Leona, and Michael lingered outside, sitting on a bench in the small courtyard between Sixties and a neighboring restaurant. Tipsy, boisterous customers strolled or stumbled past them, but the three friends paid no heed. They were too busy laughing about a clueless undergraduate in the small seminar on DNA that Augie was leading as an assistant to Professor Petrie. After that, their conversation turned to their plans for the rest of the night. Leona wanted to go home to sleep. A long Sunday of analysis and writing lay ahead. Augie, the night owl, wanted to go out for coffee before going home, so he could pull an all-nighter on his thesis. Michael, the happiest of the three, was game for anything. Finally, most of the lights flicked off in the courtyard, not a soul in sight. With that, Augie and Michael agreed to walk Leona home. The men would decide from there whether to go out again.

The quickest route to Leona's apartment was through the campus. They entered at North Gate, walked past Haviland Hall, Moffitt Undergraduate Library, the Life Sciences Building, and onto the path through the eucalyptus grove.

Here is where the jury's difficulties really begin, where decorum completely breaks down. Several people are talking at once, ratcheting up the volume. A court officer opens the door just as Denise yells, "Stop!" They freeze in stunned silence, Denise the most surprised of all. She lowers her voice and says, "Let's go around the table, one at a time." With order restored, the court officer retreats and closes the door.

They start with Robert. As he relates what he remembers, heads are shaking. The next two jurors give completely inconsistent accounts. The fourth adds new details missed by the others. Were these people sleeping during the trial? Denise remembers every word. She thinks. But now she isn't so sure.

After going around the table, they decide to send out a note. "We, the jury, would like to hear the testimony of the three eyewitnesses about what they saw in the eucalyptus grove." But it's five o'clock by the time they assemble in the courtroom. Judge Creighton excuses them for the night with a promise to have the testimony ready in the morning.

Day Two

It's horrible to sit through the testimony again, even with the sterilizing voice of the court stenographer reading from the screen of her steno machine. To Denise, the words of each witness evoke a hologram in the empty box, a face and a voice recalled to mind.

This part of the testimony is the most graphic, the most important. Why do they need to hear it again? These are the key facts. Shouldn't they be embedded in memory? Or does the mind bend under the weight of a grievous duty? The need for certainty, the consequence of mistake. If that's true for the jurors, isn't it more so for the eyewitnesses?

Dexter Spiegel sits impassively next to his lawyer, staring straight ahead. The jitters are evident, heels tapping soundlessly. Denise tries hard not to stare at him, but her eyes keep coming back. There's something about him she doesn't like. It's a visceral reaction, a feeling she's had from the moment she first saw him. Is it because he committed—*may* have committed—a heinous act? Or is it something about his face? She fights the revulsion with self-directed, internal lectures. She admires Judge Creighton terribly. The judge has instructed them to discuss, to weigh, to analyze, to convict only if they're convinced beyond a "reasonable" doubt. Denise clings to reason like a magnet to steel, even suspecting that it's an overreaction, an overcompensation for impulse. She resists the urge to jump to judgment. She shouldn't vote "guilty" just because his face fascinates and repulses her.

The stenographer is reading Michael Headley's testimony under questioning by the prosecutor. The story begins slowly, setting the scene, the route Michael and his friends took through the campus. The path is lit intermittently by overhead lamps, casting filtered rays into the aromatic grove of strip-barked tree trunks.

"Mr. Headley: 'There was a noise in the grove, and we turned to look. I could see two people halfway behind one of the largest tree trunks. We stopped right there, because it didn't look right. The woman was facing the tree, the man was standing behind her, almost like he was pushing her into the tree. The woman was…'

"Mr. Vasco: 'Please go on. What did you see?'

"Mr. Headley: 'It looked like her skirt was hiked up around her waist. The man was in profile to us. He was holding her by the throat with his left hand. His right hand was lower, on the belt of his pants. He must have heard us, because he turned to look. I don't know why, but it seemed to last forever…'

"Mr. Vasco: 'What seemed to last forever?'

"Mr. Headley: 'The look. We stared at each other. It was probably just a few seconds, but it was frozen in time. He'd been caught, and everyone knew it.'"

Again, Denise is drawn to Spiegel. He has a face she wouldn't like to meet in a lonely spot in the middle of the night.

"Mr. Vasco: 'Describe the face of the man you saw.'"

His forehead is high and wide, with invisibly sparse eyebrows on the ledge that overhangs his eye sockets. The eyes are dark, deep-set little pebbles. At times during the trial the eyelids have been red-rimmed—whether a sign of anger, sadness, or sleeplessness, Denise can't tell. Maybe madness.

"Mr. Headley: 'He had a very prominent forehead and his eyes just looked like dark depressions. I couldn't see much of his hair, so it was probably close to his head, pulled back in a ponytail…'

"Mr. Curtis: 'Objection.'

"Judge Creighton: 'Sustained. Mr. Headley, please do not speculate. Just tell us what you saw.'

"Mr. Headley: 'Okay. The other thing I remember, he had a thick neck, even though his face was thin and almost bony, with sharp cheekbones, like the shape of a skull.'"

His nose is disproportionately small, almost non-existent. The cheeks are partially hollowed out above the long, thin ridge of his pursed lips. As he sits next to Curtis, the mouth rarely opens, except to whisper something in his attorney's ear. It wasn't until he testified that Denise noticed the teeth. Even then, his mouth didn't open very wide. One of the canines is larger than its mate, dagger-like and noticeable before the mouth expands to expose the entire row. The mud-brown hair is evenly combed and banded at the nape of his tree-stump neck. There's a slightly shorter strand that refuses to stay in the tail. He drapes it over his right ear. The ears are petite, well-formed, and tight to his head.

Denise listens carefully to all the testimony. The three witnesses have trouble describing his hair, as if it didn't exist or wasn't noticed. No one remembers a ponytail, and on cross-examination, Mr. Curtis gets them all to admit that they can't remember if Spiegel's hair was loose or tied back when he was bartending at Sixties. Each witness remembers a detail the others do not. Michael is the only one to notice the thickness of the neck, and Augie is the only one to remember the flatness where his nose should be. In the middle of her description, Leona mentions the ears. "He turned toward me, and I could see the shape of his face. His ears stuck out on either side. He was staring at me, but I couldn't see his eyes. They were like black holes."

Michael, Augie, and Leona are consistent about one thing: they all say that the man in the eucalyptus grove was the bartender from Sixties. And they have no difficulty identifying him in the courtroom. In turn, each witness points unwaveringly at Spiegel and says, "He's the one I saw by the tree," or "in the grove."

They also agree on what met their eyes after the man turned to look at them. The woman screamed and struggled in his grip. Her head twisted grotesquely toward them. Her eyes made a frantic appeal to the three people who'd come to save her! But the ambient light caught what they'd missed—a sharp flash of silver at her neck. The thrust was deep and quick. Her eyes opened wide and she crumpled, clutching her neck. The man darted away through the grove.

The three friends stood aghast, their eyes riveted to the victim for a shocked second until they found their limbs and ran to her. Already there was nothing that could be done. Marlena's life was pumping efficiently out of her neck, a hot, spurting geyser that no amount of pressure or blood-drenched clothing could stanch.

The reading takes all morning. Lunch has been ordered for them. When they return to the jury room, a cardboard box on the table holds twelve sandwiches wrapped in white paper, bags of chips, cookies, and cans of soda.

"I'll be taking my lunch to go," says Tanner. "Let's get this over with now." He reaches for the diminished pile of blank paper slips.

Joe eyes the contents of the box hungrily. "I thought that would never end. I'm starving." He dives in and starts to rummage. "Good, they're marked." The court officers know their preferences. Joe finds the sandwich he wants and shoves the box to the next person.

"Come on and vote," says Tanner impatiently, walking around the table, distributing the papers.

Random comments are circulating along with the lunch box. "Why did he have to do it? Why didn't he just run?"

"Marlena would have identified him."

"But three people were looking right at him!"

"*He* didn't know if they could identify him. The lighting wasn't the best."

"We don't have to decide *why* he did it."

"The knife was already at her throat. It was a knee-jerk reaction."

"Yeah. Could've been a reflex when he was taken by surprise."

"You're saying he didn't *intend* to kill her?"

"No! Not that. If the knife is out, you intend to use it."

"We can't get inside his head."

"We're not supposed to. The judge said to look at the natural consequence of his act."

Denise picks a sandwich but isn't hungry. The comments float into her ears and find a pocket of memory. A sharp flint of anger breaks loose. She isn't asking, like the others, "why did he kill her?" but "why didn't Marlena get away?" She's baffled by the unknowable power that chooses one girl and lets the other one go, leaving the boy with no piece of her but a fistful of ripped muslin. Leaving *her* with a ruined peasant blouse and mud ground into the seat of her jeans where she huddles and shudders in a dark backyard behind a sleeping house, her wildly beating heart burning on alcohol fumes. A heart still beating. A living body, retching.

"Eleven guilty, one not guilty," Tanner announces, his lunch still neatly wrapped, ready to leave the courthouse with him.

Denise is disappointed in her hoped-for allies, Joe, Charlotte, George, and Robert. She drops her head and inspects her hands.

"Okay, out with it, whoever you are!" She looks up to see Tanner's eyes boring into her. Most of the others are staring at her too. They all know she's the one, and they aren't happy about it.

Across the table, chewing voraciously, Joe tilts his head to a cockeyed angle and examines her face. They've been lunch buddies for two weeks now, but that's pretty much shot to hell. "Denise," he says after swallowing, "if you keep voting 'not guilty' you have to explain why."

"There were some problems with their testimony."

"They got a good look at him. That's all we need to know. It's facial recognition. One of them even said it was 'frozen in time.'"

"That was Michael, the drunk one." She looks at Robert for agreement, but the phlebotomist lends no support. She turns again to Joe. "And there were other inconsistencies."

"Like what?"

"Yeah, like what?" demands Otis in his loudest voice yet. The vibe in the room is bordering on scary. Her thoughts are a jumble of black holes and hollow cheeks and thick necks and the slice of hair that Spiegel constantly flips behind his right ear. Ears that "stick out," says Leona, but they don't. In a wavy hologram, Leona's eyes skate toward Spiegel as she mentions the ears. A bit of a frown on her mouth—subliminal recognition of the problem.

"They aren't even sure about his hair," Denise says. "Or his ears."

"Ears? What are you talking about? There's nothing about his ears."

Denise sinks into a deep mistrust. Joe wasn't listening! By the time the stenographer got to Leona's testimony it was past noon, and Joe's stomach was already growling.

The afternoon drags on painfully, contentiously, noisily. By three thirty, in partial surrender, Tanner has eaten half of his sandwich. Itching for action, he proposes a note to the judge, reciting as he writes. "We, the jury...no, we the *eleven* members of the jury would like Judge Creighton to talk to the *one* juror who's being unreasonable. What's your number, Denise?"

Joe supplies it: "She's number four."

"Juror number four. No, better yet, I'm including your name, Denise Bow-something. How do you spell your last name?"

Tears sting her eyes as she sits mute, angry at them, furious with herself. Why *should* they listen to her? Every word out of her mouth sounds like the crass triviality of a dimwit.

Charlotte takes pity. "We don't need to say who it is. The judge's instructions apply to all of us. Denise, you have to have a *reasonable* doubt. That's the key word here!"

George adds, in a fatherly tone, "Let's give her a little more time. I think Denise will come around." Mr. Forty-Seven to Miss Twenty-Two. "You'll listen to reason, won't you Denise?"

She's reached a high pitch of uncertainty. *It's him. It isn't him. It's him. But what if it isn't him?* What if it isn't? "'I didn't kill anyone,'" she quotes out loud.

"Well, we all know *that*, honey," says Tanner, with a feminine flip of the hand.

"I mean, that's what Spiegel said."

"What *else* would he say?" scoffs Joe.

"But we haven't even talked about his testimony! The judge told us to discuss *everything*."

Voices bellow a mix of disdain and agreement. Her suggestion is enough to get them going again, to prevent Tanner from sending the note to the judge. They review Spiegel's testimony, simple and fairly short until Mr. Vasco dug into him on cross-examination, relentlessly chipping away at his credibility.

"He admitted he's been convicted of joy riding."

"As a teenager," says Denise. "How is that anything like murder?"

"He said he believes in giving the customers their 'money's worth.'" A few uncomfortable laughs.

"Strong drinks," says Denise. "How does that prove he followed her?"

The debate surges forward, helped by their elevated blood sugar—the chocolate chip cookies in the lunch box are rich and delicious. So many inconsistencies in his testimony! Was it two twenty or two thirty when he left

Sixties? Had he parked his car on Arch Street or Scenic Avenue? Did he go home immediately or stop for cigarettes first?

"It's the same problem," Denise says. "You can't even remember his testimony."

"Oh, we remember it all right," says Otis. "He couldn't keep his story straight! It shows he was lying!"

"Then you have to say the same thing about the eyewitnesses!" She starts to list every inconsistency she can remember.

Finally, she ekes out another compromise. Tanner writes a note to the judge, requesting a read back of Spiegel's testimony. It's already late, and they can guess that today will be a repeat of yesterday. They'll be sent home and asked to return in the morning.

Note in hand, Tanner gives her a smug look. "This is absolutely the last thing we're doing for you, Denise. The *last* thing." Even Tanner has grown to love her.

"You'll see," George says, addressing Denise in his paternal tone. "The man is lying."

Day Three

"Mr. Spiegel: 'I would never hurt anyone. I didn't follow anyone out of the bar. I didn't kill anyone. I didn't go to the eucalyptus grove that night.'"

This time, Denise doesn't need a hologram. He's twenty feet away, in the flesh, listening to his own words as the stenographer reads them. He studiously avoids looking at the jury. She stares at his profile. His right eyelid is red-rimmed, and she knows now what it means, the futility of disillusionment and distrust. Which one of them has the better claim to this feeling? In the end, Dexter will be living the consequences, the only one to know if this imperfect process ultimately arrived at a just result. Denise will go back to her life, not quite the same.

The stenographer reads. It was a busy night. Spiegel worked his shift and wore his hair loose, as usual.

Tanya confirmed this fact, Denise recalls.

Spiegel doesn't remember Marlena and doesn't recognize the person in the photograph shown to him. He has no specific memory of the graduate students who testified against him. So many customers were demanding his attention that night. He finished his shift at two, arranged his receipts in the drawer, collected his tips, and left at two twenty. Even if he wanted to, he couldn't have walked out of there with a customer at two o'clock. He had to reconcile his receipts, and then it was left to the manager to close the bar after him.

Much of this was confirmed by the manager, who also testified.

Denise wonders what the other witnesses might have missed. Did Marlena speak to Spiegel, arrange to meet him? Was she foolish enough, drunk enough? Or did he, by stealth or chance, catch up to her on campus, in the dark?

Spiegel recalls seeing a few people sitting in the courtyard when he left the bar. He can't say who they were. He walked past them and went to his car, parked several blocks away from the campus.

There's no witness to corroborate this.

He thinks he parked his car on Scenic, but it may have been Arch.

No one to corroborate.

And why is that? Denise wonders. Why is there never a witness when you need one?

She stares at his profile and puzzles over the revulsion she's felt and pushed down, only to resurface. Her mind is now open to it and takes her where it will. The profile, the intensity, the set of the mouth, the similarities, the differences. There's no one to verify Dexter's story, no one to verify hers—no one to believe her—if she were to say that the boy deliberately took a wrong turn into a street lined with dark houses at three in the morning. No one but Denise to say what she knows without any doubt—that the boy was going to do something horrible to her. Something unthinkable. The boy who looks like Dexter Spiegel.

"Mr. Spiegel: 'I drove straight home. It was a fifteen-minute drive.'"

No one to corroborate this.

Spiegel remembers stopping at a gas station along the way to pick up cigarettes but has no proof of purchase. He paid cash and didn't get a receipt.

No one to see this…

No one but Spiegel knows what he did that night, and no one but Denise knows what happened to her, two years ago. There could have been dozens of witnesses at that party, the swarm of undergraduates crammed into a rambling Victorian on a San Francisco hill. But no one noticed her, no one warned her as the boy roped her in and she listened and laughed and threw back another shot of tequila. He was a science major of some kind with plans to transfer to UC Berkeley. Not the best-looking young man, but his penetrating rawness attracted her on that wild night. He was daring and edgy and different, his words sharp and opinionated about important things.

As the stenographer drones on, Denise hears Dexter speaking, sees his gestures and eye movements—nothing like the boy's.

Details are fuzzy, but she remembers a few. He had small, deep-set eyes, short-short hair close to his skull, a wide and prominent forehead. His nose...she can't picture it now. She was drunk, and her girlfriend had disappeared. The girl with the car. Spinning around dizzily, she searched the rippling bodies and distorted voices, recognizing none of them. Her friend was gone, and suddenly, desperately, Denise wanted to go home. A minute later she was in his car, seated next to the profile in the dark. Not long into the ride, his edgy attractiveness morphed into a quiet stealth, steadily descending into hostile entitlement. A wrong turn. A dark street. *That's not the way...*

Denise no longer trusts Michael Headley's frozen moment in time. Her own drunken moment did not capture the face of her villain in memory. Bits of it are there, but they're overpowered by the glare of white shock...

The car slows. He's looking for a secluded spot, gripping her thigh over the bottom edge of her blouse. He turns to her, his head backlit by a pale light from a driveway. The eyes are dark holes of smoldering hate. The ears stick out in silhouette! Her hand goes to the door handle. He reaches and grabs but jinxes his own plan with a reflexive stomp on the brake. She bolts out of the lurching car, stumbles (*I'll come after you!*) and runs into a driveway. Crouches behind a house. Waits.

Blurry details remain, the rest of it overpowered, taken down by that frozen moment. *That's not the way...* The jolt of sickening discovery, a fatal mistake. Too late! When did that moment come for Marlena?

Denise stares at Dexter's profile and sees the bits and pieces. Hair can change. Ears don't. She fingers the hem of her shirt, remembering the missing edge of her muslin peasant blouse that went unnoticed until the next morning. She wants Dexter to turn to her now, to give her a sign that he didn't kill Marlena. She can't stop looking at him. She senses him feeling her attention. She wants to know the truth and fears she never will.

It's day three and she wants this to be the day, doesn't want it to be the day. She needs more time, but maybe not. There's a choice to be made, despite the truth. Condemn him now or buy more time. Hang the jury with her vote, run to Mr. Vasco, tell him everything, let *him* decide if there will be another investigation, another trial.

The hammering cross-examination is coming to a close. Finally, the stenographer stops reading.

Dexter turns to her, and for the first time this morning, their eyes meet. His expression is at once shocking and reassuring, the eyes fiercer than she imagined, sparks of determination and despair.

Can't you see? I'm innocent!

She sees the humanity but still doesn't know the truth.

Their gaze holds for a long second that seems to last forever. At the deepest point of their communion, a warm cloak of calm embraces her. Helpless, she surrenders to the need for peace, allowing the tension to drain from her face and neck and shoulders, to drip from her fingertips. Hardly aware of herself, the corners of her mouth curl upward.

Does he know what she's thinking? Can he tell that she's made her decision, that she knows what she'll do when she returns to the jury room?

Her eyes tell him. *Yes, now I know.*

☦ Collector's Find

ROSALYN HEARD THE click as the outer door opened, a shudder of the glass panel as it closed. Soles of business oxfords sanded the floor and settled into place, hesitated, crossed the empty reception room toward her open inner door. A single breath, and the square edges of a man filled the frame. His immaculate presence made her see forgotten things: a jutting file drawer, folders teetering on the couch, a jagged pile of motions on the desk. Ancient cases from bygone years surrounded her, a mess that wanted elimination.

Her eyes skimmed the chaos, found the man's face, and quickly brushed past him to a framed diploma on the wall, noticeably askew. She lifted a lipstick-stained paper cup, raised an eyebrow, and dared another look at him. Sipped. The coffee, mottled with powdered creamer, was cold.

"Miss Bleinstorter?"

She nodded, smiling inwardly. To a woman of forty-six, the word "Miss" was a bit of a joke.

"I'm in need of an attorney," he said, a ray of light finding the dust. Different.

"Come in," she invited, pointing.

Neatly erect in a fine tailored suit, he entered. Why wouldn't a man like this consult an attorney uptown? He took the seat indicated, sending a crackle of aging leather into the silence. "I understand you specialize in real estate?"

The question gave away his source. The yellow pages. After a five-year involuntary "leave of absence," Rosalyn had no choice but to advertise. "That's right," she agreed.

"I'm pursuing a real estate venture, some commercial properties. I need an attorney to look over the paperwork and attend the closings."

Rosalyn nodded, cleared a wad of phlegm in her throat, and pushed the coffee cup behind a stack of papers. "I can do all that," she said, panic rising. The man was too cool, his words gliding off a fresh pink tongue retracting smoothly into a full mouth. Not a whisker was visible on his gleaming jaw, although his hair was dark, the crisp edges recently snipped. Mercury eyes, deep like wells, were shadowed with a hint of sleeplessness. He was about her age or younger. Maybe older. She couldn't tell with men. Their lives weren't displayed on their faces the way Rosalyn's past had come to rest in hers.

"I'll need some information," she said, pulling out a yellow pad and letting it fall on the newspaper she'd been reading. She fished a pen from a jangle of paperclips and rubber bands in the top drawer. "Your name?"

He produced a business card: "Sergei Rankov, President, COLLECTOR'S FIND, DISTRIBUTORS."

"Collector's Find," she repeated, needlessly scribbling.

"We wholesale collectibles to souvenir shops, philatelic dealers, and five-and-dimes," explained Rankov. "Stamps, coins, dolls, decorative plates, porcelain figurines, ashtrays, bric-a-brac—"

"Bric-a-brac?"

"Odds and ends. You'd be surprised what people like to collect." Their eyes caught, and a corner of his mouth twisted upward, confirming that he'd come to the right place.

Even now, she often relived that day, six years ago, when Estrella walked into the offices of Spitts & Bleinstorter, PC. It was 1990, a year when things between Roz and Derrick had gone from bad to worse in love and the law. Within a month of each other they'd both turned forty, the number hitting Derrick hard. Overnight, his hair turned a shocking, jet black, and he replaced the Old Spice with patchouli, of all things. His eye started to roam, and Rosalyn, with her undying hopes, became the fool. She cast suspicious looks and spoke in veiled threats. "I never proposed," he liked to say whenever she curled her lip to bare the fangs.

Derrick's professional ethics, never the best, slipped into the gutter. Casual lies to the court, lapsed deadlines, and shoddy research defined his work. Not that Spitts & Bleinstorter didn't cut corners—even Roz herself in dire need—but the dereliction had risen to a new level. Judges, attorneys, and clients were becoming impatient and demanding while Derrick, oblivious, kept showing up late if he showed up at all, sporting his new clothes and deliberately tousled locks, unable to mask the jazzed look in his eyes and a tremor in his hands. Long nights with the ladies—or something worse? Roz suspected a return to the white powder, an old friend of theirs from those all-nighters in law school, fifteen years ago.

Derrick was mired in this questionable state midway between professional respectability and irrevocable demise on the day Estrella slithered in, clutching her little cocaine indictment. Released on bail, unhappy with her current counsel, she was out shopping for a new attorney, decked out for the purpose in one of her distinctive second skins, a fuchsia jersey and metallic-silver Capris. Derrick conducted the intake interview and claimed her, leaving Rosalyn with just a trace of Estrella's flowery scent as Derrick's office door shut behind them, sealing attorney and client inside for a very, very long time.

A week later the girl returned, claiming to have an appointment. Derrick was out of the office, God knew where. "He's in court," Roz declared, hoping it was so.

"Mr. Spitts, he want the information, some kind of thing about—what you call that?—to throw out the evidence." She patted the outside of her large shoulder bag, blinked scoops of dark lashes, and shifted her weight from right hip to left, pulling the taut, crimson material of her Capris high up into the V between her legs.

"A motion to suppress."

"Right, the suppress thing."

"Come with me." Rosalyn would take care of this.

Estrella followed, bringing along a pungent, tropical fruit scent, and lowered herself with a wiggle into the leather chair which, even then, had started to grow brittle. "Wait here," said Rosalyn.

She backtracked and went into Derrick's office to retrieve the file. Inside, she found what she suspected, more than enough information to prepare the standard motion papers. The police report and indictment told of a common undercover surveillance. A known dealer had given a package to Estrella, who'd placed it in the trunk of her car and driven off. The dealer was arrested, and Estrella was stopped some distance away, where officers seized a ten-kilo package and her car, a late model sedan, perfect for the forfeiture program.

Rosalyn knew the scenario well. Estrella was a courier in a narcotics ring. Her second "appointment" with Derrick—for another "legal" consultation—was pointless. He had enough information to generate the usual boilerplate motion with the canned argument on legal onionskin: *The officers lacked probable cause and violated the defendant's Fourth Amendment rights*.

Roz carried the file back to her office, propped her pillowed backside against the edge of her desk, and faced the girl with a quick stare-down. "Don't worry, honey." She slapped the manila folder against an open palm. "We'll fix you."

Sergei, on the other hand, was a person Roz looked forward to seeing. He was the perfect client to usher in her new law practice, 1996. After the first few appointments, he began dropping in at will to consult "my attorney." Any other unexpected visitor might receive Rosalyn's deep-throated grunt of dismissal or a closed door. With Sergei, she didn't wish so much to discourage as to impress him with her little shows of busyness and importance the moment he knocked on the doorjamb—a hastily scribbled note on a legal pad or a reluctantly lifted eye from a law book—the props always in reach in the event he called.

His visits were changing her habits. Mornings she awoke early now, spending extra time rummaging in the closet and dresser drawers, picking through stained and raveled undergarments, pushing aside dusty, outdated fashions, everything a size too small. Odors previously unnoticed seemed woven into the aging fabrics. She squinted hard at herself in the bathroom mirror, torn between needing and not wanting to see her face, just as willing to pretend something else in a fantasyland of dim lighting and failing vision. With alacrity she sponged on wet amounts of foundation, penciled in the eyebrows, crafted a fuller version of her mouth a centimeter beyond her lips and filled in the maroon outline with a lighter shade. Never did she allow this portal to fade. After coffee, after lunch, five times a day, the mirror and lipstick emerged from her purse.

Each time, he brought her something from his cache of collectibles. She cleared a bookshelf, even dusted it, to display her swelling collection—proof of the number of times he'd come. A miniature stained-glass window with the Lord's Prayer, a porcelain replica of Niagara Falls, a wind-up ballerina, a copper statuette of the United States Treasury cast from molten pennies. She accepted each gift with a thrill of gratitude, the corners of her painted mouth twitching upward, pushing at the encrusted layers of disappointment.

She had plenty of time for him. As yet, she had only

two paying clients, easy residential closings. Real estate was clean and uncomplicated, a pleasant relief from the messiness of criminals, but Sergei's interests were adding a new, challenging dimension. Several commercial deals were in negotiation: a fast-food franchise, renovation of a dated strip mall, a used car lot, a Victorian house converted into professional offices. Rosalyn found herself awash in zoning ordinances, construction bids, franchise agreements, leasebacks—concepts she'd never before encountered. Twenty years ago, fresh out of law school, Roz would tackle any new challenge with ease and enthusiasm. But the years with Derrick had chipped away at her native intelligence and integrity, no match for an endless stream of clients, all guilty of something, corralled and desperate. Her intellect had grown sluggish, but Sergei was providing the impetus for self-renewal. She fought to reclaim herself, not wanting to fail in his eyes.

"It's not even my car. I borrow it, you know. I never put any cocaine in there. This bags of white stuff could be powder sugar. You seen any lab study on this? Where's the proof?"

"You wouldn't be indicted without a lab report—"

"I don' believe it. Maybe they trying to set me up. You wanna know what those pigs do to me?"

"I've got what we need for the motion—"

"The big one pull me out of the car like that..." Estrella stood and violently tugged the arm of an invisible person. Herself apparently. "Then the sweaty guy come over here and grab my other arm, and I don' even know they cops, you see? No police car, no badge, no blue shirt.

They throw me on the car and pat, pat, pat, like this, you know, *like this!*" She demonstrated in every curve and niche of her body. "Here and there, and maybe a little rub," she massaged a buttock, "right there on the street and everyone walk back and forth, looking! So disgusting what they did, *esos cerdos!*"

While Estrella ranted, Rosalyn flipped through the meager file, searching for the retainer agreement or proof of payment. Nothing. When she looked up again, Estrella was shackled and jammed into the back of a police car. "'Lady, you going to the station,' they say and they laughing and the sweaty one show me this white packages from the trunk. That could be powder sugar, how do I know? It's not my car, I tell you!" Incensed, she made a miraculous escape from police custody and sashayed around the room in agitated fury.

"Sit down, Estrella. No...*sit down.*" Rosalyn had seen better playacting. "We've got enough for the papers. We'll ask the court to suppress the evidence and dismiss the indictment."

"And get these animals."

"But we can't do anything without a retainer. Didn't Mr. Spitts explain that to you?"

"Retainer?"

"Payment."

"Oh sure, I pay you. How much is it? I have the money. I make jewelry, you know. See these?" She touched her dangling earrings, hammered silver with turquoise stones. "You like it? I'm in the jewelry business. How much you need?"

"Well, it depends. More work, more expense." She

eyed the client, looking for signs of discomfort or resistance. Seeing none, she went for it. "You're innocent, right?"

"Of course. What I been telling you?"

"Then you'll be going to trial, and trials eat a lot of time and money."

"I don' care. Just keep me out of jail." Estrella fished inside her shoulder bag and extracted an inch stack of worn fifties, bundled with a rubber band.

Rosalyn worked for a poker face. "How much is that?" She'd seen her clients with money like this, so dirty it crawled with disease. Cash should be avoided in favor of a check, one step removed from the back alley to keep the state forfeiture hounds at bay.

"About five thousand."

Rosalyn hesitated, sensing more inside the shoulder bag.

"Not enough?" Estrella blinked, the bills a dead weight in her hand.

"Trials usually go higher than twenty grand. We'll need at least half as a down payment." Estrella didn't budge, merely blinked. "It's to your advantage," continued Rosalyn. "When things heat up, we don't have to stop work to come looking for money."

"But why they gonna have a trial about some powder sugar? And what about the suppress thing?"

"Sure, well." The girl was making her work for it. "As good as we are, there's no guarantee. Some of these judges...let's see." She glanced in the file. "You're assigned to Judge Weston. His brother's a police detective—you can't get anyone more in the DA's pocket."

She rolled her eyes and sucked in deeply, a little playacting of her own.

It was enough to send Estrella back into the handbag. She pulled out a second stack like the first, piled the two up and handed them over. "This is all I got right now."

Roz took it, fingering the grime.

"I'm an artist, you know. We don' make that much in the jewelry business. You pay me back if there's no trial?"

"Sure, don't worry, you'll get an itemized bill." She penciled "$10,000" into a form retainer agreement, and Estrella signed it without a glance. Roz pulled the client copy off the back and gave it to her.

Later that day when Derrick returned, he didn't mention Estrella, either forgetting or not wishing to admit the missed appointment. Rosalyn considered what she'd done but wasn't terribly worried. She knew the day would come when he'd open the file and see the retainer agreement inside, noting receipt of "$1,000." He would ask her about it then, but she'd been careful, and the alteration couldn't be detected.

With beating heart and sweating palms, Rosalyn divided the cash, immediately depositing one thousand into the Spitts & Bleinstorter account. She stuffed nine thousand into the toe of an old sneaker at home and waited several days before depositing half of it into her personal checking account. She waited another week and deposited the rest.

For a long while, everything was provisional, mere talk. One day, Sergei gave her a collector's edition of five

Princess Diana commemorative stamps displayed on blue foam in a plastic case. He presented the gift with an off-center smile. In his other hand, he held a sheaf of papers for her review. "They've accepted my offer on the professional building," he said. "Here's the contract. I'd like to close as soon as possible. Why don't we discuss it over lunch?"

Rosalyn accepted with a flutter in her rising chest and jammed the contract into her briefcase. Plunging under the desk, she retrieved her handbag and righted herself, flushed and heaving, with a little stumble on new heels.

What good fortune to be wearing, on the day of Sergei's unexpected lunch invitation, a new outfit made possible by his retainer, a cool two thousand dollars paid with an official Collector's Find company check. The navy suit, an optimistic size twelve, was a snug fit, and her patent pumps elevated her to an unthreatening height about two inches shy of his five-foot-ten. He held out a hand and let her pass through the door ahead of him as she felt the heat of his eyes pinned to her girdled backside.

Outside, Sergei suggested a restaurant uptown and flagged a cab. He opened the door for her. She ducked, inserted a foot, and tumbled onto the slippery seat, feeling resistance against her thighs. She was barely able to separate them in the tight skirt. He slid inside behind her, too soon. Their hips touched, untouched. Rosalyn scooched toward the window, her skirt riding up, and she tugged at it.

Using her briefcase as a shield between them, she pulled out the contract. As the cab pulled out into traffic, she scanned the document with a blasé look, becoming slightly nauseated with the sway and bump of the ride while trying to discern at least the headings above the blurry fine print. She would not put her reading glasses on.

"What do you think?" he asked as they neared their destination.

"Looks all right. Maybe a small problem here or there."

"Oh?" He looked away from her and out the window.

"Nothing I can't handle."

"Of course. I have faith in you." He turned back and roamed her profile with his gaze.

"Let's see…" she said, wanting to assume the dominant position now. She flipped a page and ran a red fingernail down its length. "Payment by bank check, certified check or attorney's escrow check…hmm… Which bank are you going with?"

"Bank?"

"Who's financing?"

Sergei waved a hand dismissively and glanced away. "Don't worry about the bank right now. Let's get past the inspections first."

She nodded, pointing an index finger in the air. "Right. Let's get past the inspections."

With this, all business aspects of their lunch meeting came to a close before they arrived at the restaurant, a four-star establishment. After "no" and "no" again, Sergei overcame her resistance to a cocktail, followed by a bottle of wine with the meal. The alcohol loosened her mind and brought back those Friday lunches of years past at the corner pub with Derrick, their ritual client-bashing sessions that often turned into real sloshers. Sergei started talking about Collector's Find and his business plans while his eyes strayed from hers, taking in her hair, her mouth, elsewhere. She said little. What would he think—what would he *really* think—if he knew everything about her?

When it was time to pay, a silver clip flashed, and he removed clean, straight bills. She had the fleeting thought, a fear really, that she should be the one to treat her best client, pick up the tab and take a business deduction. But, after taking the final red sip, her doubts easily evaporated with the vapors from her glass. He apologized for not having time for coffee and quickly insisted that they meet again the following day. He would pick her up at her office. There was something he'd been wanting to show her.

Every Monday, they would review their cases and discuss scheduling for the coming week. The Monday following Estrella's visit, Derrick pulled out the file and remarked, "So you got the retainer—"

"You forgot—"

"—in the Marquez case."

"—to get it the first time."

"She said she'd bring it in."

"Well—"

"She paid, didn't she? I'll get the motion out this week. And this one…" He tossed the folder aside and picked up another. His abrupt gesture gave Roz the proof she needed of his guilty conscience.

For weeks they'd been conducting business this way, just enough to avoid professional havoc. Speaking the fewest words possible, they exchanged a variable play of stony looks and averted eyes, silently acknowledging their discontinued intimacy. Rosalyn could barely remember their last "date," a fumbling collision and disengagement, a sigh, excuses, and leave-taking in the middle of the night. At work the next day he was sappily patronizing, as if entitled to take credit for honoring a distasteful obligation.

Despite their personal falling out, there hadn't been a professional dissolution. Rosalyn refused to initiate the break, unwilling to flog herself for Derrick's misbehavior. Despite his sliding performance, she convinced herself he was still useful to her as a backup attorney—dodging the real reason, her hidden fear of going solo after all these years. And so she tried not to care, distracting herself with the money. She bought some new furniture and a foxtail jacket.

How would Derrick react when he learned of the ten grand? Revenge could be sweet, both within and without the law. But the Derrick she knew, the man who seemed to lack a conscience, was still beholden to his partner and lover of fifteen years. Roz guessed that when he found out, he would vent and hurl insults and obscenities but then quietly let it go, justifying her little theft as an informal domestic settlement.

"I *am* impressed," said Rosalyn, surveying the outside of Sergei's enormous warehouse, a gray, tin-roofed structure in a desolate industrial sector. Sergei unlocked a massive padlock and slid the door open, revealing the vast contents, boxes stacked ten feet high in dozens of rows, neatly penetrated by a large aisle along the concrete floor, smaller aisles on either side.

He flicked a light switch, illuminating the central row of ceiling lamps, bare bulbs protected with wire mesh. Feeling like another speck of dust, Roz settled inside the threshold as he closed the door behind them, bolting it shut.

The huge vibration sent a shiver of excitement through her, not unlike the climactic vertigo that overcame her in high places, rooftops or cliffs. The thrill was familiar but long forgotten, connected with a different kind of event in a former life. "Your business is larger than I thought…"

"We have accounts with every outlet selling collectibles in the Tri-State Area, all the way into southern New Jersey and northern Connecticut."

"I had no idea there was so much demand…" She drifted along the center aisle, her hand grazing the outermost cartons. She stopped. "What's in here for instance?"

"You'd be amazed what people like to collect." Sergei took her elbow and directed her a few rows down to an open box. He dug inside and pulled out a three-inch wooden replica of a mallard duck, inserted the bill between parted lips and blew, sending a "quack" through cardboard canyons.

"These boxes here…all of them?"

"The entire row, all ducks. Here. You may have

this...duck." He kissed the mallard and placed it in her open palm, tenderly pressing her fingers around it, leaving behind the warmth of completion. "I hope I don't offend you by mentioning that this particular item retails for twenty-five dollars. I purchase them for about two dollars apiece." In his eager eye gleamed a boyish desire to impress.

"That's quite a markup," she said in a church whisper.

"People will pay extraordinary prices for these kinds of knick-knacks. The business has been extremely profitable. Now you can appreciate my need for investments and tax shelters."

"Yes, of course..."

"And I want you to be a part of this. All of it." He waved his arm in a semicircle, including the entire inventory. Vertigo surged again, sparks and tingling. She backed into a wall of boxes to steady herself.

A sound startled her, deliberate footsteps on concrete. Far down the row, a man approached. Sergei thrust a flat-palmed hand in the air, bringing the man to an abrupt halt. "Excuse me," he apologized cordially and went off to meet the interloper. A hundred yards distant, they conferred in low voices, heads bent into the space between them.

She regarded the men, their body language. Sergei was clearly in charge, his gestures vivid and purposeful, while the stranger nodded in subservience, absorbing his instructions until, with a final nod, he turned and disappeared into the stacks.

Taking long even strides, Sergei returned to her. As

he approached, she thought of what he'd said, how he needed her as a business associate. Maybe wanted her in another way. Her heart pounded high up into the squeeze of flesh between her jutting lapels, speeding recklessly into her fragile wall of caution, smashing it to bits.

There was a small miscalculation, an absurd impossibility. A week after Derrick filed the motion, the police lab admitted a rare mistake. The evidence samples from two cases, Estrella's and another, had been mislabeled and switched. As it turned out, Estrella's white powder wasn't cocaine at all but a mixture of sugar, baking soda and talc. The cartel had used her as a decoy to divert police attention from the real transaction, a bigger one, going down elsewhere in the city.

Quite likely, Estrella didn't even know she'd been used, and her ranting about powdered sugar had been exactly as it seemed, pure theater. She'd beaten the charges with simple luck, no thanks to Derrick's professional representation or his boilerplate motion.

Rosalyn reasoned away her fears. To the cartel, ten thousand was mere scratch from the petty cash account, and legal fees were a necessary cost of doing business. The Spitts & Bleinstorter receipt would satisfy Estrella's superiors, and the girl should be happy to walk away from a criminal indictment unscathed, in good stead with her boss. Instead, something unexpected happened. Estrella acted on her chance for a little personal profit.

"That client Estrella Marquez…" began Derrick one morning. "She's calling me, screaming about ten thousand dollars."

Seated behind her desk, Roz listened with her head bent over papers.

"Said you promised a refund."

She scanned the papers, riffled them.

"Where's the money? I don't see a deposit in the account."

Finally, slowly, she lifted her eyes. "You believe this girl? This lying coke dealer?"

"Let's just say it makes sense."

"A little whore makes sense to you."

"I don't care who she is, no one's gonna say a lawyer stole ten grand in cash unless there's something to it."

"I'm accused of stealing now?"

"You didn't put ten minutes into this case. I know I didn't."

"Oh, but you *did* spend a lot of time with her."

He laughed bitterly and raked the bottle-black hair from his forehead. She stole a look at him, the face a sickly bluish white, the hands he didn't know what to do with. "You think you're smart," he spat. "You haven't got a clue what you're into."

His tone was alarming, but she rolled her eyes in feigned disinterest. He saw her game and went for something deeper. "Pay or we're through."

"We're already through."

"Sure, well." Another laugh. "I'm talking about the business."

He turned as if to go, pausing just long enough to test the effect of his words, sensing her vulnerability. He swiveled around to face her once more. "She calls me again, I'm sending the call to you." He pointed and walked out.

When he'd gone, she remained unsettled by the lack of any obvious explanation for his vehemence. Another attorney might fear the grievance committee, a malpractice suit, or loss of reputation. But these things wouldn't concern Derrick in his current state of dissipation.

It didn't make sense, but in the end, his motives didn't matter. Rosalyn simply couldn't live with the thought that she'd become just like them, no better than the thieves she represented. Estrella's voice rang in her ear, racking up the proof. "Where's my money, bitch?" Call after call.

Roz would have returned all the money if she could, but only three thousand was left and she had no savings to speak of. She deposited the three thousand into the Spitts & Bleinstorter partnership account, gave herself a two thousand dollar "advance" on paper, and sent Estrella a partnership check for five thousand along with a padded bill for services covering the other five.

She waited, a day, two days, a week. Apparently it was enough, and the calls stopped.

The first closing, the professional building, was easy. No financing or bank attorney, no complicated forms. Collector's Find cash had been accumulating, ready for investment. "Why should I pay interest to a bank?" Sergei scoffed, and he was right, of course. The closing took all of fifteen minutes; the deed was exchanged for a check from Rosalyn's escrow account, which had recently been funded by a Collector's Find check.

Sergei, who never laughed and rarely smiled, seemed

ebullient. Over a glass of champagne at their celebratory dinner, he beamed with pleasure and reached across the white linen to touch her hand. "You were magnificent," he said, stroking the tops of her naked fingers with the smooth undersurface of his thumb.

Rosalyn tittered, sending a jellied spring of flesh upward. There was a small burst under her jacket. A button? "It was nothing, Sergei. You're the brains behind this, the one who made the deal."

"Without you, though, without you…" His thumb pressed a circular massage into the top of her ring finger, aided by the greasy lubrication of her gardenia hand lotion.

In the days that followed, the closings strung along in quick succession. The meetings with Sergei accelerated, stressing her shelf of collectibles with the weight of their intercourse. Money flew, escrow checks were written, Rosalyn tingled and hyperventilated. It became easier to give Sergei a set of deposit tickets, letting him stuff the escrow account directly with Collector's Find profits. Rosalyn simply confirmed her balance before showing up at the closing with her checkbook. After each transaction there was a special lunch or dinner, intimate handholding, watery gazes, and a sweet buss "goodbye" on the cheek.

Sergei was old-fashioned that way, leaving her flattered and confused. His chaste foreplay must be a sign of their age, she mused, proof of their respectability and careful compliance with the proper steps on the path to legal consummation.

After the sixth transaction, it came. Everything was from a dream, the wine and candlelight, Sergei's timid, off-center smile and quick blinking lashes as he produced and opened a ring box to reveal the unbelievable dazzle of an enormous gem, two or three karats, she couldn't guess.

"I've been looking for just the thing for you, Rosalyn," he stuttered, so quaint all of a sudden, abandoned by his usual command. In a nervous, speechless fumble, he removed the ring from the box, and her left hand rose to the occasion, ready to receive the magical coupling, a golden insertion into another world. A steady, secure, wanted, belonging world.

She gazed down and turned it here and there to catch the soft yellow light.

"What…" he cleared his throat, stumbling. "What do you think?"

What did she *think*? She didn't need to think at all, other than to marvel at his sudden shyness and uncharacteristic inability to frame the question directly. But still, she hesitated before answering, feeling acutely the moment of truth. Oh, she knew more than enough about *him* to make up her mind. He had revealed every aspect of his business, dreamed aloud, and included her in all his investment decisions. But what, really, had she told him about herself? He deserved to know the truth about the theft and its humiliating aftermath. If she told him, would he still want her? Maybe she could phrase it with certain, strategic omissions to soften the blow. She couldn't put it off any longer. Sooner or later he would find out.

"Sergei, thank you, it's so beautiful…" This being her first, she didn't quite know how to accept a marriage proposal, an implicit one at that. "I'm so thrilled, and I *do* accept, but there's just maybe a thing or two we have to discuss, things we should know about each other—"

"Tell me, what do you need to know about me? I'm an open book."

"You? Oh, no! I didn't mean…"

"You understand all there is to know about me, don't you? I can sense it." He bore into her, not unpleasantly.

"Yes, you've been very forthright. What I mean is, maybe you need to know a few things about *me*, about my past…"

"Now, what sort of a *past* could that be? You smoked marijuana in college; you've had a few lovers. Maybe even committed a professional indiscretion or two. Terrible things such as this? Perhaps?"

Professional indiscretion. She hiccupped uncomfortably on that one but was gratified to see, literally, the proverbial tongue in his cheek. He took her hand in both of his, lifted it to his lips, and kissed the middle segment of her ring finger, letting the diamond brush his lips on the way up. "I'm interested," he said breathlessly, "in the Rosalyn I see before me *now*. You don't need to drag the skeletons out. They're already preapproved."

He was making everything so easy, and why not? Didn't she deserve something good after all she'd been through? It was better to say nothing, to go forward and say nothing at all.

On the day they came for her, Derrick wasn't in the office. He wasn't in court either, and in fact, she hadn't seen him in three weeks. He'd disappeared the day after she paid Estrella, leaving behind a mess of unfinished cases.

Roz wasn't alarmed to see the men in her doorway, but in the moment between identifying themselves and explaining their presence, bewilderment seized her. Why would the FBI be interested in such a tiny thing, the theft of a few grand from a coke courier? The next moment, her street savvy self-image was shot to hell by their stunning announcement.

"Rosalyn Bleinstorter," said Special Agent Paul Bergin, the red-faced, beefy one, "you're under arrest for money laundering." The shorter skinny one just smiled.

They were very polite and allowed her to grope under the desk for her handbag before escorting her to the door, one in front, one behind. On the way outside to their waiting vehicle, dazed and sandwiched, she saw it like a movie on the skinny one's back, exactly the way things looked to them. Dirty cash in, clean attorney's check out. Estrella's stack of grimy bills changed for a PC check, "pay to the order of." In the back seat of their car with the lock clicked down, she laughed out loud, choking on bile and salty tears. How funny would it be if she told them the truth?

Later, S.A. Bergin laid everything out for her because he cared—said he cared and wanted to help. She believed him, a man with a lion cub's face, square forehead and scouring-pad bush of hair. He wanted to help her if she would only give him something in return. "You see, Rosalyn...may I call you by your first name?" She nodded in a fervent flush, thinking of him as "Paul." After only two hours alone with Paul in that little, single light bulb of a room, he was making her feel safe. "You're only one person, and you're not one of the group they're really after," he explained. The feds were building a multi-defendant case, politically big, against defense attorneys who laundered their clients' cash and hid behind confidentiality rules. Paul believed (was he right?) that Rosalyn, with her small-time take of only five thousand, was new at this, and maybe she'd been tempted just this once and would never, ever do it again.

"Am I right, Rosalyn?"

She began to swoon under the power of his direct gaze and the lull of his deep voice, so different from the manic edginess of that man who'd imprisoned her heart and career for too many years. Now she was safe, released into the care of Paul Bergin, a rock of strength and solid goodness. He would protect her. The lock on the door proved it. She listened. "These other attorneys, they were dealing in millions. If you work with me, Rosalyn, turn state's evidence, maybe I can cut you a deal, get it dropped to a misdemeanor and a few months. I could see you out again in no time."

Glassy-eyed, she nodded agreement. *I could see you*, he said.

She did then what she'd always advised her clients never to do—waived her right to an attorney and started talking on her slender faith in Bergin's promise. Her clients always buried themselves this way, getting caught in their own lies, but she was smart enough to beat the game. She didn't need to admit the theft to get out of money laundering. Her motives, the jealousy and base revenge, were too embarrassing, and what would Paul think of her then? She told him exactly what she'd told Estrella. It was a retainer, half of it refunded as unearned.

"But Rosalyn. *Cash*. You took cash from a cocaine dealer."

"What, a check's better? Credit card? Money order? It all comes from the same place. You'll put the entire defense bar out of business if we have to confirm a clean source before getting paid."

S.A. Bergin smiled, grew ruddier, impressed maybe by her argument. But suddenly he turned on her, ready to spar. She took it as part of an act, the tough inquisitor, and it thrilled her. "Nice, but no help," he jabbed. "All the Esquires are telling that story. You think I fall for it?"

She fluttered her eyelids in helpless confusion.

"A jury of Bowery drunks wouldn't buy it. I'll tell you what really happened. You changed street money for a law firm check and took a cut for your services."

"Yes. Legal services."

"Then why use your personal account?"

"I…"

He jumped into her hesitation. "No innocent explanation for that."

She lowered and shook her head. "This is embarrassing."

"I can't give you a deal if you lie."

She hesitated again, because now he was waiting. "The girl only had cash. I had to use my own account because of Derrick."

"Derrick?"

"He's a little bit like you on this—doesn't like street

cash. A dirty check is better." She dared to throw him a conspiratorial wink. "I was hiding it from him, that's all. It's not a federal offense, is it?"

Bergin's face resumed its pleasant, fleshy look, with the laughing gaze of a mild skeptic. "Sure you weren't hiding anything else from him?"

She arched her backbone and tried for spirited sassiness. "You can imagine what you like. I've told it straight. Go on and ask the girl."

"Estrella? She's in the wind. But you can bet we'll be talking to Derrick."

"Good luck finding him. I've tried."

"We have him. They're bringing him in now."

Rosalyn blanched. A cold pool of sweat welled in the shelf of her bosom.

True to Bergin's word, within the hour, Derrick was escorted into FBI headquarters. By then, Rosalyn was seated in the hallway, purposefully planted there, she supposed, to witness his arrival. On his way to the inter- rogation room, he sent her a snarl that said he didn't like being hauled in to answer for her con games. But *his* worries were small, she knew. He hadn't taken the cash or written the check. Not long afterward they released him, and she never learned what he'd told the investigators.

Although her testimony wasn't very useful, Bergin made good on his promise and got the charge dropped to a misdemeanor. Rosalyn was disbarred and served four months in a minimum-security facility. For 120 long nights, alone in her room, she shared laughs and cocktails with Paul Bergin, grazed the steel wool on his head with her fingers, listened to his big, booming voice diminish to a whisper in her ear, over and over again, promising, *I could see you out again in no time. I could see you...see you...*

The day came, bright and clear, when they unlocked the gate and she emerged onto the empty street, swiveled right and left, stood silent to slow her pulse against the shattered dream, and stepped out along the concrete path toward her next, unknown destination. Disappointed, alone, and afraid.

It didn't take long, twelve hours maybe. The morning after Sergei's proposal, a subtle itch suggested itself with her involuntary reaction, left thumb pushing at the ring, rotating it, jiggling the rock on top. Within another few hours the irritation flared and the skin under the band grew pink and puffy.

Still, she wasn't aware of the itch so much as a dark, anticipatory excitement growing in tandem with it. She sat behind her desk, rotating, jiggling, eyes roaming the wall, finding the diploma still slightly askew, the shelf bulging with collectibles, and the dozens of ancient file folders, now pushed into a neat column in a corner.

A memory was triggered. Early in their law practice, the young lawyers still fresh and in love, Derrick and Rosalyn naïvely accepted a client with ties to organized crime. Gradually they learned just how connected he was, a man who authorized executions and arranged torture for his debtors. In the end, the eavesdropping evidence was too garbled to prove the charges, and Spitts & Bleinstorter won their client an acquittal. He was grateful, paid big money and had plenty of friends in need of their services.

The possibility held the lure of power and illicit wealth. But she and Derrick understood the danger and made a pact never to accept another case like that.

And now, here was Sergei, inspiring the same feeling.

She sobbed bitterly, and an hour later, when the shaking and choking subsided and her mind was a white blank, the itch announced itself with unbearable urgency. Her thumb probed the ring, unable to budge it from its nest, embedded in swollen, red flesh. The ridiculous discovery squeezed a laugh from her lungs. As careful as Sergei had been, he couldn't have foreseen her skin allergy—the metal alloys in costume jewelry did it every time. Would she confront him on his next visit? Poke the turgid red digit in his face? But as soon as this thought surfaced, another took its place—there wouldn't be a next time.

Still, why hadn't he given her the real thing, something nice as a farewell gift? To him, the cost was negligible. The answer had to lie in his estimation of Rosalyn, the way he truly regarded her, worthy of only cheap trinkets. Like the mallard, a two-dollar novelty that fetched him twenty-five.

1994, three years after her release, Rosalyn's second petition to reinstate her license had been denied and she was earning pennies in a graveyard typing pool churning out legal briefs. One morning at the end of her shift, she was making her way down a crowded sidewalk when Derrick nearly ran her down, weaving in and out with his nose to the ground.

She hadn't seen him since the day of her arrest.

Making a split-second decision, she stepped directly into his path. He looked up and took a step backward.

She was the first to speak. "Well, hello."

"Hey, Roz." His clothes were new and expensive and his face older, the skin still pasty, the eyes bloodshot and wild.

"Where you going so fast? Running to court?"

Derrick hesitated, eyes shifting sideways around her shoulder and back to her face. He laughed. "Hell no. I took down the shingle."

"So, what's the new line?"

"Insurance. I sell life insurance. Making a living, no thanks to you."

His smirk stoked her dormant rage. "You ruined your *own* career, screwing up your cases. I could have gotten you disbarred the way you dumped everything."

He shifted from side to side and finally kept his ground, averting his eyes. "I had it up to here, you know. I had it up to here with you, Roz."

"Who still has a license to practice? Not me. You did *nothing* to help me. Saved your own neck and let me stew—"

"You don't get it, Roz." He shook his head. "You have no idea what you were dealing with, do you? Damn lucky I got it straightened out. Now, excuse me. Maybe you jailbirds don't run by the clock, but I'm late..."

She jabbed a broken fingernail into his sternum. "I'll be back, boy. I'm going solo, without your name to drag me down!"

"Okay. I'll look you up in the *Law Journal*." He pushed around her. "Under 'Reinstated Convicts,'" he called back over his shoulder.

For the past two years she'd been thinking about Derrick's words, wondering what she wasn't "getting." She wondered about it every night on graveyard, wrists sore, fingernails broken from endless pecking at the keyboard, and she wondered about it during the interminable proceedings on her third petition for reinstatement, the successful one, and as she moved the old desk, leather chair, and file cabinets out of storage and into her new office. Sergei had made her forget for a while, but her questions were still unanswered.

Damn lucky I got it straightened out. Derrick had done something to save her, but from what?

The shadowy part of the story was well within her power of imagination, yet lingered beyond her desire to know, even as it plagued her with an ominous certainty that the truth would, one day, descend full force upon her.

This was the day. Before entering, the men must have heard the laugh that accompanied her bitter discovery of Sergei's counterfeit offer. Gazing at her puffy finger, she was too absorbed in misery to hear the shudder of the outer door and the click of footsteps in the reception area.

The first one came to stand squarely in her inner doorway, suddenly filling the frame with an immaculate presence. The years had been kinder to Special Agent Paul Bergin than to Rosalyn. Still that thick scrub of hair and the big-man, padded and friendly physique. She'd always liked that about him, the fact that he was so much broader and bigger than she. Paul. He stepped in and looked at her like an old lover, she thought, but then the slight man behind him ruined it all, squeezing around to take his little jab. She couldn't be sure if he was the same one, Paul's partner of five years back, but then he spoke, eliminating all doubt. "Good to see you again, Rosalyn. I understand you're still doing the dirty laundry?"

This nameless one took out his handcuffs and started toward her, but Paul waved him away. "We don't need to do that. You're not gonna run, are you Rosalyn?" His eyes roamed her face, the puffy pink eyelids, smeared makeup, and naked mouth with all traces of maroon wiped away. She shook her head "no."

"You know why we're here, don't you?" Paul asked gently. She did and she didn't. He pulled the cracked leather chair around the desk, sat down and leaned forward, elbows on knees, his giant lion's-cub face inches away. "I know everything, Rosalyn. Everything about before. I wish you'd told me. It was revenge, wasn't it? Estrella and Derrick? That sonuvabitch was screwing around on you, wasn't he?"

In a trance, she nodded in agreement.

"If I'd known, the prosecutor wouldn't have touched it. You wouldn't have gone to summer camp. Can we do it different this time?"

She nodded again.

"Can we get Derrick this time? And Sergei."

Her eyes widened at the mention of his name.

"He's the real sonuvabitch here, isn't he Rosalyn?"

Tears came to her eyes, but she summoned the will to speak. "I want to cooperate."

"I'm glad you do. There's others I could ask…"

"Other women?"

"Yeah. Sergei's collection. The living collection. The ones who smartened up in time."

Roz hadn't smartened up, but she'd been saved. Back at FBI headquarters, a giant weight was lifted, evaporating into the residue left by all those confessing felons who'd gone before her, coming clean in that little room. She laid herself bare to Paul's drilling penetration, relishing his excited responses to every one of her revelations, the evidence he could use to fill the gaps in his investigation, his surveillance notes and photographs. She learned of the seizure that had gone down that very morning—a thousand kilos of cocaine from Sergei's warehouse, and worse, the cadaver hounds sniffing out the remains he'd buried there, his departed collection, the ones who hadn't smartened up in time. She learned that agents had located Sergei and Derrick and were arresting them at that very moment.

She asked Paul what she'd been wanting to know, and he told her, because the truth about the past wouldn't harm his investigation. Estrella had enticed Derrick into laundering for the cartel, and the ten thousand was a test of his reliability. Bad luck that he was unavoidably detained in court on the day of their crucial second appointment. But Estrella, foolish girl, read the cues wrong, understanding the word "refund" as code for laundering, believing that Rosalyn was in on the plan. *Damn lucky I got it straightened out.* Derrick ultimately saved them both from cartel retribution, sure death. He scrambled for the unpaid balance from personal assets. In the process, he passed the test and signed on for the life of the underworld. Estrella wasn't so lucky on her next assignment, her incompetence putting her under.

"But why am I going through this again? Why did he do this to me?" she asked Paul.

"Sergei?"

"No. Derrick. He already did me once."

"Sure, well, he recommended a lot of people to Sergei. He was in the business. And *you*..."

She smiled with trembling lips, relieved to unload her shame. "I was the obvious choice, wasn't I?"

Paul didn't answer, just touched her shoulder and offered his hand, coaxing her up from the chair in their intimate little room. The interrogation was over, for now. She would be preened as their star witness. She placed her left hand in his, wincing on the way up.

"That looks nasty," he said.

She extended her hand at arm's length in mock exhibition of her "diamond." "I actually believed this was real."

Later that afternoon, Paul summoned a jeweler, who arrived with a little bag of tools. Carefully, he cut the band from Rosalyn's finger at taxpayer expense.

Within a day, the swelling subsided.

Within a week, the rash scabbed over.

Within two weeks, Derrick and Sergei were under indictment and Rosalyn was home free, marked with a wide band of new, pink skin. It left a permanent, faint impression, a subtle reminder in the years to come, back in the typing pool—hands on display, rattling the keyboard—that her ring finger was, and would always remain, naked.

love and crime reprise
stories from
Dust of the Universe, tales of family
Everyone But Us, tales of women
Malocclusion, tales of misdemeanor

ℕ *The Zephyr*

THE OTHER CHILDREN had nearly finished their Jesus TV sets when I joined the Bible class that summer. They'd run out of black paint by the time I was ready to decorate mine, and the best Miss Nancy could offer was yellow crepe paper leftover from Easter.

I slapped it on the outside of the box as best I could, applying little globs of paste with the dried-out brush in the middle of the jar cap. Just like the others, my set had white rounds of construction paper for the knobs, and I drew numbers on them for the channels and the volume, but still, my yellow TV ended up looking so different.

It was June 1962, and we were staying six or eight weeks in Reno, however long it took, "pretending to be residents." Bible school was one of my mother's attempts to break up the long, hot, blank spaces of time. The church in Reno wasn't anything like ours in California, just another strange thing to get used to. I didn't know it then, but we wouldn't be returning to our regular church anyway, once all the business of divorce and marriage had been accomplished.

The Zephyr Motel, on the far outskirts of Reno, was

our temporary home. I hadn't a notion what a zephyr was, and a chill went up my spine from the ominous sound of it. *Zephyr*. I told Mom I wanted to stay the whole summer without mentioning that, really, I refused to go back to a place that wasn't home anymore but a different house with strange, extra children and a new father.

The others, my siblings and soon-to-be stepsiblings, took turns one by one visiting Mom and me in our two-room bungalow with kitchenette. The two kids (me and the child of the week) slept on the twin beds in the bedroom and Mom slept on the foldout couch in the living room/dining room/kitchenette.

A couple of times the outgoing father, the one I was more used to, came and took me to a restaurant and asked a lot of questions about things like my favorite subject in school and how the weather had been in Reno. I would turn my head to the side when he kissed my cheek goodbye, and the next morning, I'd find a present on the end of my bed, a paint-by-numbers or a Nancy Drew. If the other bed held a stepsibling, there'd be no present on that one.

There wasn't much for an eight-year-old girl to do at The Zephyr. None of my brothers or sisters could under-stand why I stayed, but I didn't want to go back, sus-pecting it would be worse to be scared in a new place than bored in a less-than-new place. My mother and the new father, Bill, would put heads together and whisper, stealing looks in my direction, whenever he came to pick up the departing child and deliver the latest arrival.

"You can just call him Bill," she'd said. He was

"Daddy" to the new kids, who called her Betty because she wasn't exactly taking the place of their dead mom.

"Call me Bill," he'd agreed, saying all those same kinds of things about not trying to replace my father and not coming between us. Maybe he didn't understand that my daddy was on the way to becoming just a present on the end of the bed.

I would spy, watching their moving lips and their shining, smitten eyes that would somehow lurch free of each other to cast a knowing gaze upon me. They'd contrived a justification for my recalcitrance: time for quiet little Debbie to bond, one-on-one, with the old sibs, Allison and Teddy, and to become better acquainted, one-on-one, with the new ones, Trudy and William.

Not in the mood to cooperate, I preferred to sit alone in the poorly lit bedroom with curtains drawn, reading my Nancy Drews or methodically filling in the squares of my outgoing father's graph paper with colored pencils while the current sibling-of-the-week sought company outside, latching on to any available kid looking for action in the parking lot or by the pool. Sooner or later, I would be shooed outside to "go and play."

My brothers and sisters didn't go with me to the Bible school. They always seemed to find something normal to do, and besides, I was the only one who could attend twice a week consistently for six or eight weeks or however long it took to get the divorce papers signed. From my first day, I saw what had to be done. The other students were already on week three, and I had to catch up.

Busy with all that cutting, coloring, and pasting, I had

no time to talk to anyone except the pretty and young Miss Nancy. At most other schools you had to say Mrs. Morris or Mrs. So-and-So, but she let us call her Miss Nancy. She prepared the cardboard box for me by cutting out the large hole in front for the "screen" and four small holes, top and bottom on either side, to insert two bamboo sticks. The ends of a long scroll of Jesus pictures were wrapped around the sticks, which could be turned to view the pictures one at a time like still frames of a motion picture on the screen.

There was Jesus blessing a pile of bread loaves and fish, Jesus touching the forehead of a kneeling blind man, Jesus with blood dripping down his cheek from the thorns. About a dozen of them, with a little caption at the bottom of each.

After four intense sessions, Miss Nancy told me, sadly, it was time to move on, although I'd finished only three pictures, all colored neatly and uniformly inside the boundaries and outlined with an extra-dark layer of the same color, traced on top of the purplish mimeographed lines. Miss Nancy helped me roll it onto the two sticks, saying she was "so sorry" we had to "finish up our projects now," but once I got "home," she was sure my mother would help me to unwind the scroll so I could color the rest.

On the way back to The Zephyr that day, I held the precious set, lumpy and puckered, on my seatbeltless lap in the front seat of the Rambler. My older sister Allison sat in the back seat, singing Pat Boone's "Love Letters in the Sand." My mother looked sideways at my TV, one eye on the road.

"That's very pretty."

I doubted she actually noticed how well I'd colored between the lines because her glance was so fleeting before she looked back at the road, dreamily, with a little smile on her lips and wild, shining eyes full of her new man. That look reminded me of Miss Nancy's eyes when she spoke of Jesus, even though Miss Nancy seemed so much younger and prettier, the shine a bit softer. I dropped my gaze to the box with a throat feeling suddenly just as lumpy, lips just as puckered. The only sound was Allison's raspy, pretend love-sick voice crooning above the engine noise about how her broken heart aches.

"I like that yellow paper on it," Mom tried again. I hunched over the set, peeking up at her. The ardent gleam had vanished, replaced with restless boredom. "You glued it on real nice and even." I'd said nothing to her about the black paint or the crepe paper or the paste jar. Or about Miss Nancy standing next to me with her perfume smell, helpful and patient, saying things like, "We should be able to get enough paste out of this jar, don't you think?"

My eyes stung like I'd opened them in the deep end, diving for caps. Now there were wet splotches to pucker the crepe even more.

I didn't think she'd seen me and thought this would be the end of it, and for a while there was nothing but Pat Boone, when all of a sudden she slapped the steering wheel with the palm of her hand and heaved a sigh: "Ah!" I jumped in my seat and began to shiver.

*　　*　　*

The next day, Sharmane was at the pool without her little brother, Buster. I was happy that Buster wasn't there to throw his army men at us but expected the worst from Sharmane's tongue, since Buster always provided such a convenient target for it.

I didn't know how she spelled her name, but it sounded like a "shark" with the mane of a horse instead of a "k." I'd been shooed outside after many minutes of rolling the pictures, one by one, past the screen, too afraid to dismantle the TV or to ask for my mother's help so that I could finish coloring it.

Allison was already at the pool with Sharmane. They were almost the same age but not at all alike, my sister just ten and going into fifth grade, Sharmane nearly eleven and going into sixth. The only thing they had in common was a copious amount of peeling skin, Sharmane's many layers deep and brown, Allison's newly acquired and raw underneath.

Allison was short and plump for her age with a thick waist and no hint of the figure to come in her one-piece-with-skirt bathing suit. My suit matched my sister's except for the different color: purple flowers instead of orange. We weren't allowed to get two-pieces like the one Sharmane wore in blue gingham. She strutted around the concrete so tall and proud with two little lumps pressing out the front of the top half.

There were no trees by the pool, no plants, no umbrellas, no cabanas, no tall drinks, no floats. Just cracked cement and glare, a metal picnic table with attached benches that wobbled and scorched your behind if you sat down without the protection of a wet towel.

The only source of refreshment was a Coke machine next to the front office, a few searing steps from the pool across the parking lot. The machine ate your nickels and clamped its rusty jaws about the necks of the frosty bottles, not letting go no matter how hard you tugged.

I'd given up early on, not wanting to step inside that office again to ask Mrs. Tillman (Sharmane and Buster's mom) for my nickel back. I'd come to believe that the machine didn't like me and me alone because the ground was littered with bottle caps under the opener. We would collect them, toss them into the pool, and dive for them when Mrs. Tillman wasn't looking. Some had cork inside and would float. Others would sink.

"If she doesn't see us doing it she can't kill us," declared Sharmane with the authority of one who knew her mother well. But secretly I hoped Mrs. Tillman would watch Sharmane from her window and come out from time to time like my mom did, because there was no lifeguard around. Most other kids didn't seem to worry about things like that.

If I'd never seen Mrs. Tillman's face, I would have thought she was the nicest mother imaginable, letting her daughter wear a two-piece and go around in curlers—in public—all summer. Tight to Sharmane's head were rows of little pink sponge rollers from the Clairol home permanent wave box, lined up just like the picture on the instruction page. She was going to keep them in all summer so she wouldn't have to curl her hair again for the rest of the school year. The experiment included many hours by the pool, swimming, saturating her hair with chlorine, and baking in the sun for a stiff, chemical set.

On account of Sharmane's experiment, and because our hair was short, we got away with not wearing swim caps.

When I got to the pool, she and Allison were diving for bottle caps. "You again," said Sharmane, spying me when she surfaced. "You never come out here, do you?"

Even *I* could hear the contradiction, but something about Sharmane's contradictions just drew you in. She swam to the edge.

"Not much," I admitted.

"What you been doing in there?" She stared up at me from the water, her body making a crucifix with her chest pressed against the side and arms stretched right and left along the edge. A handful of caps lay in front of her on the cement. Allison came up alongside, deposited her caps on the edge, and propped herself identically, in imitation. "I bet you eat a lot in there." Sharmane eyed my waist critically.

Allison gave a little complicit laugh, but then seemed to remember her own waistline hidden underwater. She glanced down and looked up at me, guiltily.

"Not any more than you," I said, surprised to be so bold.

"Not so much," agreed Allison quietly, in the midst of torn loyalties.

"How do you think I keep this figure?" Sharmane appraised the lumps one at a time while lifting an index finger to scratch, absently, along a line of scalp between rollers. There may have been blood on her cheek. "What do you think I eat?"

"Yeah, what?" added Allison, although she should have been asking Sharmane, not me.

"I don't know."

"Just three slices of Wonder Bread a day. Breakfast, lunch, dinner. I wouldn't touch all those TV dinners you eat. That's the fattest kind of food."

I stared at her, wondering if she'd been through our garbage. In California we ate other things, but here, or maybe it was just now, our mother was different. I could already see myself, tonight, sitting in front of Dick Van Dyke, or maybe the Jesus TV, eating from a tin. I looked at Allison, who was smirking and fidgeting at the same time. Of course, she had told her.

"What about your roughage?" I asked, but Allison interrupted with a loud voice, "Debbie made a Jesus TV set!"

"Jesus *what? Jesus H. Christ!*"

Allison's eyes widened at this, and she gaped in awe while Sharmane lifted her eyebrows and skated a blasé glance between us. "That's what my mom always says when she's about to kill us. *Jesus H. Christ!*" A strand of hair had escaped a curler and was plastered to her cheek, a rivulet of blood.

"What's the 'H' for?" asked Allison.

"Hell and High Water." Sharmane's eyes became glittery, the way they always did when she was impressed with herself.

Allison's mouth dropped open, the contradictions drawing her in and turning her own eyes to shine, while I grew angry just to hear these words alongside the Lord's name.

Caught up in her own smartness, Sharmane seemed to forget entirely about TV sets. "I bet you don't leave any food for that skinny brother who was here last week. He doesn't even look like your brother."

I almost said he wasn't, but Allison jumped in with, "He is *too!*" as if to convince herself.

My feet were burning, and I walked down to the shallow end. Sharmane yelled at my back, "He better not be coming back."

I didn't answer, but I hoped she was right because we had nothing to talk about, even though William was my age. Allison and Trudy were both in fifth and could end up being twins, but William and I would never be twins, I just knew it.

"Buster said he was so weird, just like a girl, he didn't even like to play army men. He didn't even like to be called Billy or Bill. We had to say *William* because he was a Junior or something and didn't want a name just like your dad's. Hey, why do you call your dad 'Bill' anyway? That is *soooo* weird!"

I could have asked her why she didn't have any dad at all because there didn't seem to be one, and we had two, even if each one might amount to only half a dad.

Sharmane didn't wait for an answer but launched into a low-voiced father imitation: "I'm your daddy, *William*. You have to eat something, *William*. Here, *William*, have a TV dinner. Oh no, sorry, you can't have it. Debbie needs two!"

She laughed crazily, pinched her nose and slid underwater. Bubbles surfaced while Allison and I waited and watched, long enough for me to remember the time I ate William's leftovers off his plate. And it was only the second time we'd had dinner with the new kids.

When she emerged, the blood was washed clean.

On Allison's last night, we did what we always did.

Now I lay me down to sleep…

Allison and I were kneeling next to my bed, Mom in between, our heads drooped over prayer hands. The electric fan in the corner whirred and made a steady, rhythmic clang with each round of the crooked blade.

I pray the Lord my soul to keep…

We wouldn't have done this if a step were here instead of Allison.

And if I die before I wake…

I peeked at Mom sideways, trying to find the shine. Miss Nancy's eyes would have shone.

I pray the Lord my soul to take.

Trudy would have lectured like a science teacher on evolution. That's why we only did this without the other two. But tomorrow, Trudy would be coming to replace Allison, and then we would see.

Amen.

Lights out, tucks and kisses in darkness edged with flashing red. *The Zephyr Motel. Vacancy.* Everything seemed to flash in Reno once you got into town, past all the desert. Step out the door and look away from the pool behind the bungalow and there was nothing but whiteness and glare, a fine kind of pebbly dirt-sand, shimmering and waving into the distance. A long road to town. Beyond that, at night, we could see the throbbing, orange-red glow of a nuclear holocaust on the horizon.

I lay in bed, awake, sweating under the single sheet in my summer PJs. My heart was beating to come out of my chest, as if tomorrow were the first day of school. There were two kinds of nights, the kind when I was sure I would die if I closed my eyes, and the other kind when I almost wished I would die just to get it over with. Miserable as I was, these thoughts would give me a terrifying kind of excitement.

This night, though, was a little different: I was sure that if my eyes would only gleam like Miss Nancy's when I said my prayers, I wouldn't have to worry about any of these things. She had the kind of shining eyes that made you feel comfortable, not scared.

"Z," I whispered, and put my finger up to trace it in the air, following the image behind the translucent curtain. "E-P-H..." I traced.

"Shut up!" complained Allison.

"Y-R..."

"The zephyr's gonna get you if you don't shut up!"

"What's a zephyr?"

"You don't wanna know."

"Some kind of animal?"

"You *really* don't wanna know!"

I shut up then and let Allison get away with being changed, just like everyone and everything else. The arm under my tracing finger dropped to the bed, and my chin pushed my lower lip into buck teeth, trying to control the quivering, but it just wouldn't stop and tears rolled down into my ears.

Even Allison was different. Last year, I could have said something to her and she would have listened and then talked to me, all night if I needed it, just to make me feel better. But now there was Sharmane, and also Trudy, to change her, and Trudy and Allison would end up just like twins, leaving me behind.

I cried myself into a terrible, choking excitement, almost unable to breathe, and was suddenly so tired I fell into sure death, praying for the Lord to take me. Toward morning, as the flashing Zephyr faded into dawn, it pursued me, colossal and fiery red. I struggled to open my eyes and gagged on the knot in my throat, closed tight against the sound of my screams.

The next day, I found myself at the pool, alone with Buster. We were never alone together, and I wondered how I'd gotten there, thought back, and couldn't remember the steps that had taken me outside. I'd been rolling the pictures past the screen, and then, before I knew it, I was at the pool without Allison, just me and Buster. Allison might have been somewhere with Sharmane, I didn't know, and I may have been angry about that, or about the fact that she hadn't been in her bed when I awoke from my dream, or the fact that she would be leaving later that day.

At first, Buster was lying on his stomach, a towel underneath and an army man in each hand, shooting at ants spilling out of a crack in the cement. His ballooned cheeks were pushing loud explosions from his mouth. I put my towel on the metal bench of the picnic table and sat and watched him. His face was one big run-together freckle with a few white spots. He didn't look at me while he relished his continuous eruptions of flying spit. When Teddy got here, I thought, the two of them would have a great time because Teddy was the same age and loved army men. So far it had been William for a week, then Allison, and now, later today, Trudy.

After Buster got tired of his game, he jumped into the shallow end. He was only six and a half, but he was allowed in the pool by himself, as long as it was the shallow end. This seemed terribly wrong, even though Mrs. Tillman had come out to the pool with her kids a week ago and declared that Buster was a "water rat" who learned to swim when he was two. "Just throw him in and he floats," she said. She was wearing curlers that day too, and when you looked at Sharmane standing next to her mom, you'd think she'd been born with those things on her head.

Later that same day, Bill had come to deliver Allison, and we were all standing by the door of our bungalow when we heard a commotion by the office. Mrs. Tillman, with the curlers still in her head, was clutching Buster under the armpit and dragging him away from the Coke machine, yelling, "I'll tan your hide!" and giving him a whack right there for the world to see before she got him inside. We heard a good amount of screaming then, and Bill shook his head and professed that he didn't believe in "tanning."

Feeling strange to be alone with Buster, I was about to go back inside, but when he jumped into the pool, I realized I couldn't. He wasn't just wading in the shallow end. He was swimming like the steamboat in Huck Finn with big circling arms and splashing kicks, sometimes coming too close to the "4 FT" mark, and I knew he wasn't four feet. I sat clutching the edges of the bench, my hands on top of the towel next to my thighs, and kept my eyes glued on him, even though I had to pee and the sun was burning my back. He kept swimming back and forth, 3 FT, 4 FT, 3 again, and anything could happen to him.

Something would happen to Buster if I left. So I stayed.

Trudy was silent in the back seat on my way to Bible school. She'd said only one thing before she got in the car, after Mom had answered her question about where we were going.

"*Bible* school," she'd said. Just like that, and that's all.

I would rather have heard Pat Boone than the silence Trudy was making.

But I ran into the classroom with relief, leaving them behind. For two hours I'd be with Miss Nancy.

Her eyes were shining a welcome, and we sang our favorite song. *Jesus loves me this I know, for the Bible tells me so.* Nights, when my roommate was asleep, I'd sing this song softly to myself, working on the gleam in my eyes, trying to feel what it ought to feel like, in the dark.

But toward the end of class, something unexpected happened. Mom and Trudy would be coming soon, and for no reason I could think of, a sick feeling pushed up into my throat and tears streamed from my eyes. Miss Nancy took me aside and put her arm around my shoulder and pulled me so close that her perfume was still on my skin when I got back to The Zephyr.

She asked me gently, over and over, what was wrong. I wouldn't say, because it seemed, really, that nothing should be wrong except that all I wanted right then was for her to hold me. Finally I said, just to say something, that I'd had a bad dream.

"Oh, Debbie!" She stroked my shoulder and arm. "Don't worry. Bad dreams are there only to remind us to come closer to the Lord." She put her face very close to mine so I couldn't avoid her big, eye-gleaming smile. "Have faith in the Lord."

More sobs erupted and my shoulders shook. I'd let Miss Nancy down because I wasn't close enough to the Lord.

"Have faith, Debbie. Jesus loves you."

I wanted to ask Miss Nancy if *she* loved me, and if she had any children or if she might want just one more, but I could manage only to look up at her through bleary eyes, hoping she could read the question there.

That afternoon, Trudy and I played jacks in the bungalow. The only part of the floor good for jacks was the little section of beige linoleum next to the oven in the living room/dining room/kitchenette. The part where my mother slept had a bumpy sort of carpet the texture and color of oatmeal cookie dough with dirt spots that could have been the raisins.

While we played, Mom slouched down on the sleeper, all put away into a couch, with her feet propped on the coffee table, pretending to read a magazine. Most of the time she would turn her little smile with Bill in it toward the window, where she would dreamily gaze with her shining eyes that turned dead again when she looked back at the magazine and gave its pages a restless rustle.

There on the linoleum, Trudy and I could fit our two

bodies, sitting crossed-legged or on one hip with legs bent under, a little space in between us for the jacks. We couldn't toss the jacks too hard, or one of them might go under the oven, and then you'd have to stick your fingers underneath in the grease and crumbs from other people. Luckily the ball was just a bit too big to be able to roll under.

Trudy was an expert at jacks, almost always making it up to ten-sies, even if one of her jacks got stuck in the tiny triangle missing from a corner of one of the linoleum squares. Allison usually only managed seven-sies, and I was lucky to make five-sies.

"I don't know how you can stand that girl," she said to me. We had just been at the pool with Sharmane, whose tongue had been worse than ever until Trudy got the better of her. Trudy was just as self-assured as Sharmane, but a whole lot quicker, smarter, and kinder.

"What kind of name is *that?*" Sharmane had asked Trudy.

"It's short for Gertrude."

"*Ger-troooood!*" Sharmane let loose her crazy laugh.

Trudy didn't flinch. "I'm named after my grandmother, a famous suffragette and union leader."

Well, Sharmane had nothing to say to that.

"I don't really like her too much," I answered Trudy over jacks.

"Then you have to come back to the new house. We built a tree fort."

I didn't answer but sat mesmerized by Trudy's skill, nailing eight-sies and talking at the same time.

"Grandma taught us how to make chocolate chip

cookies." It was their Grandma, the one who stayed with the kids left behind when Bill came up to Reno. "And my uncle came and took us out to the Big Slide and we had Neapolitan ice cream. I swapped my strawberry for William's chocolate."

For a while now, I'd suspected fun goings-on at the new house as I wallowed in the pleasurable pain of my self-imposed exile. I forgot about the jacks and stared past them into the lines and intersections of the squares of linoleum, following a line straight down the length of three squares, then back up for two and, at one down from the top, across for two. A crucifix. Three down, two across.

But someone was talking. "It's your turn," said Trudy in a loud voice. My finger was on the floor, tracing the line. I looked up and saw Mom staring over from the couch, no longer dreamy, and I understood that Trudy had been saying it, over and over, louder and louder.

That night, just as I expected, there was no kneeling by the bed. Once during the first week, when William was in the bathtub, Mom and I had knelt and said our prayers, but this night Trudy didn't need to take a bath and was ready for bed. Mom stayed a little longer than usual, sitting on my bed, stroking my hair, while I looked out the window and followed the outline of The Zephyr, wishing she'd go away.

Now there was no one to go to, not even Miss Nancy, because in Mom's lingering hand I felt that Miss Nancy had told her something about me when she'd called Mom back inside. "You forgot something, Mrs. Hilliard," she'd called out, using our old name. Mom said

I would be keeping it, but she would be taking Bill's, and we would end up with different names but the same family. After stroking my head for a very long time, Mom went over to Trudy's bed, leaned over stiffly, kissed her on the cheek and said, "Good night, dear," sounding like the saleslady at the five-and-dime.

When the lights went out, I wasn't going to sleep, or for sure they would find out whatever was inside my head, or I would die, one or the other. Maybe Trudy had felt the same way when she was my age, just after her mother died. I wanted to ask her this, and about the sickness and death that people only hinted at before looking off into the distance. Trudy would tell us little things about her mother, what she wore, what she said, but never about the sickness and death part, and so, how could I possibly ask her about it?

The cardboard box on the dresser had become an empty, black square in the red-tinged darkness. Still, it stared back. Trudy might have been asleep by then, but I no longer had the urge to sing "Jesus Loves Me," and I used every muscle in my face to hold my eyelids open in the dark.

My plan failed, because the Zephyr chased me again at dawn. I screamed and screamed, the sound trapped inside under the knot in my throat.

Trudy spent her week besting Sharmane, and Teddy spent his being twins with Buster, and then it was William's turn again but he didn't want to come, so Allison came instead. I sat near the window of my room, in safety with the lights out behind the gauzy fabric of the curtain, watching their indistinct figures in the sunlight around the front door of the bungalow: Mom, Bill, Allison, Allison's little suitcase, Teddy, Teddy's little suitcase.

The place was so small and the Reno air so dry and empty that I could hear them. Mom was saying she thought I should go back. "But then I'll be alone!" screeched Allison. "Maybe it's best to leave her be," said Bill, while Teddy kept picking up his suitcase by the handle and dropping it to see if it would fall over. Later, at the new house, Teddy would unpack that little suitcase, or Bill would do it for him, so the next kid could use it. William would have to come whether he liked it or not, because it would be unfair to make Trudy come again so soon. With Allison, it didn't matter. She was my sister.

"She's just afraid of the zephyr," said Allison.

Mom and Bill looked at each other and said, "The what?"

"Trudy told me. She says it in her sleep."

A shockwave turned their voices into blur and expanded their bodies grotesquely behind the gauze. Bill loomed bigger than the rest but seemed much smaller than I remembered, his legs skinny below the khaki shorts. He touched my mother's arm lightly and they leaned together in a whisper. I blinked and Bill was gone. I blinked again and turned around to see him standing in the doorway to my room.

My heart jumped and my breath went out of me until all I could see were the particles of dust in the air, dancing in the filtered light. Bill didn't exist, I didn't exist, and we might have been no more than two specks of dust, dancing with the others.

Without knowing it, I stood and followed him, walking through the dust, out the door of my room into the living room/dining room/kitchenette, out the front door, past Mom, Allison and Teddy, into the front seat of Bill's station wagon. We drove along the gray line surrounded by a vast, white shimmer while Bill spoke words I couldn't understand in the way you might hear an announcer on a transistor radio far down the beach, under the sound of the waves. The announcer had a comforting, familiar voice, unchanging and constant, there to be ignored until the noise of other voices died down.

That moment happened when we were standing in the middle of a big, bright room in front of a little table with an enormous book lying open upon it. All around were bookshelves and tables and chairs with a scattered handful of people, silently reading, and I knew we were in a library, although it looked different than the one back home. Bill put his hand under the bulk of pages on the right side of the book and lifted them up and over to the left, then leafed through a few more, stopped, and ran his index finger down the length of the page. I was standing at his elbow, just tall enough to see where he pointed.

"Here, read this," he said in a voice so quiet it could barely be heard, but at last I understood him because of that whisper, and the quiet all around, and the firmness of the tip of his index finger pressing down at its destination.

I did as he asked, immediately recognizing the dreaded word: "zephyr." He saw my difficulty with the rest and used the index finger of his left hand to cover a long section in italics, using his right index finger to underline the words he wanted me to read: "a gentle breeze from the west."

We may have stood there a minute or an hour, long enough for the words to cause tears in my eyes. "Come," he said, and I allowed him to take my hand and lead me out into the sun. The skin of his hand was warm, dry, and scratchy, a good feeling.

He took me to an ice cream shop, and when I still hadn't spoken after both he and the waitress asked what flavor I might like, he ordered Neapolitan for me. I said, "Thank you," when it came.

I was feeling better than I had in weeks, comfortable enough to allow an excited circulation of questions in my head with the buzzing possibility of their being asked and answered. There were the obvious ones, like why the motel had been named The Zephyr when there wasn't any wind in Reno, and whether Bill's family had ever tried chocolate chip ice cream instead of Neapolitan, but still I couldn't bring the words to my mouth and I let him talk to me about the new house and William and Trudy. I tried hard to eat the strawberry part too but took only one bite and left the rest in the bowl, thinking of Trudy.

Suddenly, he became very serious and said this: "You know, Debbie, after William and Trudy's mother died, I was very, very sad for a long time. And it made all the people around me sad too. So, one day, I realized it would be better for everyone if I was happy, and I decided to work on it. It takes some work. I knew that I would always love and remember William and Trudy's mom, but I could also love other people and be happy with a new family. And I'm so glad that you're going to be a part of that new family."

He smiled then, and his eyes were shining in that comfortable way, because he was seeing me and not just himself.

When we got back to The Zephyr, Teddy and his little suitcase got into the car with Bill, and Allison unpacked her little suitcase, and I stayed planted after all. I was feeling better, but not better enough to change things immediately, and I couldn't very well leave Allison alone, even if she had Sharmane. Just before Bill left, he looked at me over the top of the station wagon and winked. Allison and Mom and I stood waving a long time as they drove out of the parking lot and down the long gray ribbon, until all we could see was a speck of a car, even though there was no possibility they could still see us. Next week that would be me in the front seat.

Later, all three of us were at the pool when Sharmane came out, looking different somehow. Maybe it was because my mom was there, but Sharmane didn't immediately come up to us with her glittery look and a fast comment, and Allison didn't make the big puppy eyes as usual. We were splashing and smiling a lot more than we ever had that summer. Mom, sitting on the picnic bench, was dividing her time between laughing at our antics and reading her magazine. But on this day, she was really seeing, really reading.

Sharmane didn't jump in the water right away and was standing so quietly that I stopped splashing and took a good look at her, tall against the sun, gazing down into the pool at the deep end. She seemed to be waiting there, deciding what to do, and it was then that I saw blue through the holes. Funny that her head looked almost the same, but now there was only air inside each of the rolled shapes instead of a pink curler. And something else. Her face was round and soft, released from the tightened ends of the rollers.

After we'd stopped splashing and said nothing for a long time, Allison suddenly yelled, "Jump!" Sharmane didn't respond, didn't look at us, but kept gazing down into the water. She was working on something. *It takes some work*, Bill had said. "Jump!" yelled Allison again, and soon I joined in, and our screams escalated into a frenzied chorus of "Jump, jump, jump!"

There was a split second when anything could have happened. Sharmane had that power to leave you doubting but at the same time believing in the impossible.

And then she jumped.

Allison and I waited, watching the bubbles surface. Mom waited, I could feel her waiting at my back. The waiting lasted a very long time.

Sharmane surfaced a very different animal, shoulder-length hair plastered flat to her head, a genuine smile spreading from ear to ear. She looked all around, met us each in turn, and let out one of her crazy laughs, but there was fun and company in it this time.

Much later, after her hair had dried, it seemed to fly softly from her head, lifted by the gentle breeze.

◫ *Cactus Flower*

ROY SAT ON his haunches squinting up at the clouds, thick and white as whipped cream piled high on a glass plate. His nostrils sucked dust and the air pulled moisture from his eyes before it could surface.

He had been to other, damper places, but belonged here. Red-brown like the earth, he felt like another, larger morsel of it. He lived inside it, erecting no structures, no barriers, carrying his possessions on his back: a bedroll, canteen, knife, revolver, tin pan, a few other things. Everything he needed, and his wits besides.

His eyes followed the path of the sun, leveling on distant peaks at the horizon. Around him spread an extraterrestrial canvas: miles of pock-marked dust sprouting pockets of Indian paintbrush, century plants, and the vivid blooms of beavertail cactus. A few outcroppings of layered rock—shelter from the sun. Home to Roy, snakes and lizards.

A dot moved, grew larger, became a human figure shimmering in the heat. Roy stood and tried to swallow, finding nothing in his mouth but a thick coat of dusty phlegm. He spat and tugged at the spines on his chin

249

where he'd hacked at his whiskers with a knife to keep the heat away.

Minutes passed.

The figure slowed then stopped, dead still, not ten feet away.

Roy stared. The newcomer stared back then moved slightly, hand touching rifle slung over back, body shifting under denim shirt. It was then he could see she was a woman.

Her gesture toward the rifle was a matter of habit, not of threat. But his heart, instead of slowing, galloped a few paces as he looked into her milky blue eyes, light as opal. Tumbleweed for hair, front teeth poking out long and brown like a prairie dog's. Skin thick and tough as rawhide, covered with bristly fuzz like thistledown.

She removed her hand from the rifle and hitched up her silver buckle, shaking the inhabitants of her belt: a dozen or more rattler tails, some near dust, others fresh kill. Roy's head chased words, finding none; he didn't have much use for them.

She was the first to speak. "Goin' east?" Not an invitation, but a warning.

"Nah," he choked, then turned his head and spat to clear room for more. "Goin' west."

That night, bedrolls laid together under the stars, they tussled a mite, but nothing came of it. She was dry as the air and tight as a rusty pocketknife.

"Move y'r paws," she said, pushing him away.

He rolled over onto his back, hands behind head, gazing at the moon. He lay that way a long time, and when he turned to look, she was five arm lengths away, asleep with her hand on the butt of her rifle.

At dawn, he opened his eyes without her knowing. She sat with her back to him, licking her knuckles like a bobcat and stroking her tangled head, smoothing and matting the fur as best she could. He closed his eyes again when she turned around.

Pure east or west didn't work, neither one of them willing to give in. For an hour or more he trudged southwest, two paces in front, until she began her determined, steady drift to the southeast. The distance between them grew while his heart loped along just fine to a point, then froze up the way it always did when he stepped near a rattler, coiled up for the strike. To find his breath again he closed the gap, staying back a ways as if she couldn't see, until he was no more than two steps behind, getting hot under his collar, feeling his blood boil worse than being stranded in a 110-degree sun without a rock for cover. To cool off, he broke away and found his own path again, increasing their distance, plodding along toward the southwest.

Who needs a woman anyhow? Roy's head told him.

A while later he heard her muttering, close behind.

Three days of zigzagging and they were twenty miles due south of where they'd first met. Good and sick of agave and jerky. Running low on water. And here he was, letting her take him south.

But Roy knew of a stream ten miles off, southwest. He wouldn't allow himself to stray. He wouldn't be led to die of thirst.

Plodding along, he drifted off when it wasn't his turn, half wondering if she would follow. The distance between them grew the longest yet, but he kept his eyes forward, refusing to see her.

A rifle shot turned his head. He froze, watching her in the distance. She stooped, pulled her knife and hacked off the tail, found a place for it on her belt, then hacked off the head, leaving it in the dust. She stood, winding the thick body around her hand like a coil of rope.

She looked at Roy but didn't budge. He looked at her, motionless.

Then she took a step toward him and called out. "I ain't goin' west, but I need the water." Roy's eyes popped wide in awe. She walked to him and he waited until he could see the raw end of the snake, dense and meaty, before he started walking again. She followed.

A strange excitement crept over him like the way he felt sometimes looking at the deepening orange-purple of a sunset. He wanted to talk. He thought of some words, then spoke while they walked. "Ya got a name?" he asked.

"S'pose so," she said.

They walked another ten yards, dust billowing.

"Well, what is it anyhow?"

She cocked her head to the side. "Don't rightly 'member."

Roy searched for more words, tugging at the straps of his pack. In another dozen steps his excitement slowly vanished, replaced with lonesomeness, his sunset darkening into night.

"You c'n come, I guess," he said, finally. "But you

hafta give me some of that." He nodded in the direction of the snake.

Later, they had a tasty meal.

On the fifth night, their canteens full, he decided to try her again. She didn't push him away right off, but she didn't like it either. Nothing seemed to fit or work right, so he gave up.

"Don't have no use f'r it," she muttered.

"Well—ya ain't hardly tried."

She moved away to where he couldn't touch her. "Once, a baby come outta me backward," she said. "Ain't worked right since then. That's all." She moved another couple yards away and settled down, turning her back to him. When she spoke again, her voice was fuzzy and muffled. "Had a coyote face, so I left it f 'r the coyotes."

He rolled onto his back, hands under head, thinking of the coyote-baby. She won't want to stay after this, he thought.

At first he couldn't sleep, and then, as soon as sleep tugged at his eyelids, he became determined to stay awake. He looked over at her, sleeping on her side, hand on the butt of her rifle.

He gazed at the stars again until they were a blurry mass.

A second or an hour passed. He awoke and turned his head. She was still there, in the same position.

He rubbed his eyes, set his eyelids hard in their sockets, but they lowered in spite of himself, sending him into a deep sleep.

His eyes opened again in the first gray light of dawn.

He sat up and looked to the left, to the right, and all around. She was gone.

No more south or southwest. Pure west, following the path of the sun. The pink ball drew him on, and he watched it turn white as he headed toward it. The coyote-baby shimmered before his eyes. He spat and it was gone.

His feet moved one in front of the other, but his body stood still and unsure at the edge of a canyon, too deep to go down, too wide to go around.

The sun rose directly in front of him from his chest to his crown, reaching straight overhead as he came up beside a prickly pear with a lone flower, fire orange.

He stopped, looked again. Not one, but two blossoms merged.

His heart beat hard up in his throat. He turned around on his heels and shook his head. The sun should've come up from behind. He'd been going the wrong way all along and just now saw it.

He turned back, facing east again.

She was there, a good ways off, quivering within a transparent wave of heat. He squinted hard. She had stopped, her head tilted slightly sideways and back as if sensing his approach.

The sides of the canyon clapped together. His footing was sure. He walked on, and she waited for him.

✝ *Cat*

KAREN PONDERED THE aftermath. Angelic in death, Cloud lay silent, pristine white, legs extended straight down in two, perfect inverted Vs. Perhaps not dead, but on further look, yes, certainly so. Motionless, at rest, a tiny trickle of blood from the side of the mouth, the fatal injuries—broken bones, punctured organs—all internal and mercifully hidden from view by that silky cumulous thickness.

Gazing upon the animal in the falling light, Karen felt empty of emotion, suspicious only of incipient dread. Something was going to happen to her because of this, an irreversible something hidden under that voice in her head, a rational, pallid monotone: *The cat is dead. You have killed the cat. But it was an accident that couldn't be helped.*

She looked up to her right at the mouth of Jaclyn Temple's long driveway. Further in, shielded from view by a jungle of overgrowth, stood the contemporary redwood home. Private, secluded. Jaclyn couldn't have witnessed her cat's death. Karen glanced to her left at the Overmeyers' house across the street, then at the Brewsters' next door. Quiet. Dusk. Families at their dinner tables, unaware. At the end of the cul-de-sac, Ben and the twins would be awaiting Karen's return from a quick trip to the market, bringing milk for dinner.

She stood and leaned against the hood of her car, allowing her eyes to fall on the cat once again. No, she wouldn't lift it; she could imagine the feel of those soft-jelly insides beneath the thick coat, and perhaps there was blood matting up underneath, absorbed by the fur. A rhythmic clicking was the only sound, marking the pulse of orange light from the Peugeot, her steady and safe chariot. Apparently, quite automatically, Karen had applied the brake, turned off the engine and hit the hazard light button, although she had no memory of these actions.

Parallel lines of sparkling dots blinked on, outlining the perimeter of the Temples' driveway like a smuggler's runway snaked into the trees. Beckoned, Karen sidestepped Cloud and traversed the runway until she stood at Jaclyn's threshold, facing that large etched-in-oak WELCOME sign hanging by a chain on the front door under a bright, halogen lamp.

Despite the lights and the WELCOME, Jaclyn's door oddly lacked a bell. Beneath the sign jutted an old-fashioned brass knocker that, Karen had always suspected, required the use of considerable force to elicit a response from within. To be heard and seen by Jaclyn took effort, an effort that Karen had expended on many occasions with objectively satisfactory results, Jaclyn's response always appropriate, defying any real need for complaint.

She hesitated, lifted the knocker high and aided its

fall. In the twenty seconds before Jaclyn came to the door, Karen's mind opened to a picture of that first day, now over a year ago. She'd waited a decent amount of time, a week after the moving trucks had come and gone, before baking a zucchini-nut loaf and arriving at the Temples' doorstep, bread still warm inside the foil wrapper. The WELCOME sign, recently hung, was coincidentally positioned within a spot of sunshine, burning down into the clearing shaved from the woods for the house.

As the door opened, the sign swung out from its chain and gave a wooden clunk at the moment her new neighbor appeared, wearing an earth-toned caftan, tall and striking, her black hair pulled into a French bun with a single line of natural white growing from the temple, dipping down at the side, ending inside the knot in back. The white streak suggested a wisp of Cloud, cradled snuggly, slit-eyed and purring, in the crook of her owner's left arm. Jaclyn smiled softly with raised eyebrows at Karen's welcome-committee "hello," her right hand floating up without thought to the arched mound of white fur, as if she were stroking her own arm or neck.

This time, of course, Jaclyn appeared at the door catless and alone. She had a husband, but Mr. Temple was rarely seen, no more than a shadowy figure at the wheel of a new Lexus, emerging from that driveway early in the morning. Always, for every neighborly sort of contact, Jaclyn and Cloud had been the Temple family representatives.

Karen said nothing immediately, suddenly panicky, wondering at her involuntary need for exposure. After all, she could have driven away and no one would have been the wiser.

"Hello," said Jaclyn with a sort of smile-frown, something appropriate for an unannounced visit at the dinner hour.

Karen screwed up her courage. Nothing to do but say it straight out. "There's been an accident."

Jaclyn's brow wrinkled, her eyes searching for obvious injuries. "Are you all right?"

"Well, yes." Too late. Perhaps a "no" would have been better. "I'm not hurt, that is. But, I'm so sorry, your cat..."

The wrinkle deepened. Her face remained unchanged except for the furrowed brow that said everything. "Where is she now?" Jaclyn looked beyond Karen's shoulder into the driveway, as if Cloud might be limping home.

"Out..." Karen motioned toward the road. "I didn't know whether to lift her. I'm so sorry, but she just *darted* into the street."

Jaclyn's dark eyes shifted slowly onto Karen and stopped there. She suspected the worst, Karen could tell. There was nothing more to say. In silence, the women turned from the door and marched out the driveway, Karen two steps ahead with her arms crossed tightly, holding her insides rigid and protected from Jaclyn's cool exterior, pressing in at her back.

Night had now fallen, allowing the hazard lights to define fleeting orange outlines of trees in blackness, each flash ticking off another second between here and there, the moments remaining before the full impact of Jaclyn's grief and Karen's plummet.

As they emerged from the driveway, Jaclyn at once spotted Cloud's white glowing mass, eerily more visible than it had been at dusk. Stepping around Karen with long, intent strides, she came up to the animal's side, crouched, felt here and there, gingerly. She touched the cat's neck, ran a finger along the pads of one paw, stroked the body, lifted the tip of the tail and laid it to rest, placed a finger under the nose, cupped and cradled the head. After she'd done all these things, she fell heavily from her squat onto the side of her right thigh and placed a hand on Cloud's abdomen. "Already cold," she said.

"I'm so sorry," said Karen, more for herself than for Jaclyn.

After the delivery of the nut loaf, there'd been a few coincidental meetings and pleasant chats at the entrance to Jaclyn's driveway, once when Karen stopped to lean out her car window, the second time as she walked her eight-year-olds back from the school bus stop. Each time, Cloud sat snuggly in the crook of her owner's arm while Jaclyn completed her task with the free hand: setting out the newspapers for recycling or retrieving mail from the mailbox.

Karen's twins, Devon and Kimberly, fell immediately in love with Cloud. In the way of young children, spontaneous and uninhibited, they ran up to Jaclyn without hesitation or introduction, yet mindful of their mother's lessons on manners, asking "Please, please," could they pet the beautiful cat? Jaclyn smiled warmly while delivering a caveat along with her assent: "Yes, but

I'm afraid that Cloud is somewhat wary of strangers."

An odd way to put it, thought Karen as she watched Devon slowly reaching up with amazing self-restraint against her eagerness, *little children and neighbors at that*, inching closer to the silky mound of fur while Kimmy patiently waited her turn, *"somewhat wary of strangers,"* extending her fingertips and touching gently, when suddenly a "hsss!" and a darting claw! Little Devon's face crumpled with disappointment. "She doesn't like me!" exclaimed the girl. Karen lifted her daughter's hand, found the raised pink streak and asked, "Are you hurt?" Between the two of them—and only the mother of such *identical* twins would know this—Devon was the more sensitive and least likely to rebound from an assault. And although Jaclyn's face was filled with compassion, she did not apologize. After all, her eyes seemed to say, children should learn the value of a proper warning.

When Karen returned home with the milk, she said nothing to Ben and the twins, who didn't seem to notice the extra fifteen minutes she'd been gone. The girls were petty and quarrelsome, something that Karen usually wouldn't tolerate, but she remained silent. Not un-pleasantly so. She was partially present at the dinner table, her eyes opened to her husband and children but seeing other things while her face maintained the placid expression of inner peace. *Even the best of us have accidents—it couldn't be helped.*

She ran a replay of Jaclyn slowly rising to her knees, bending forward to scoop up the animal, one hand under the head, another hand under the hind quarters, lifting and pressing the cat firmly against her breast, unmindful of the blood, dirt, gravel, and oil that would stain her caftan, standing awkwardly with a tiny stumble, coming to right, not seeming to notice Karen's second, or perhaps third, apology with an ineffectual, "If there's anything I can do…" Jaclyn turned away and whispered, "I'll just lay her to rest," as she drifted toward her driveway, an apparition swallowed by the trees.

Ben noticed the pictures in Karen's eyes. Later that night, when the children had gone to bed, he asked what was wrong, and she conveyed the story in a vague sort of way, which was exactly the way she remembered it.

"So, the cat just…?" he asked.

"All I know is the cat was suddenly there."

"…darted out?"

"I remember the sound. The thud. Oh, my God!"

"I'm sorry," he said. "In a way, though, it's better that you never got to know her well. Jaclyn, I mean. You never quite hit it off." Stunned, Karen looked at her husband, wondering how he could know that it mattered to her.

"But you should tell the girls. They were fond of the cat."

"I will," she said. "Tomorrow."

Despite the bad start, the girls eventually eased into a relationship with Cloud. There were days when they were playing in the neighborhood and saw Cloud at the end of the driveway, near the street. Free of her owner's protective arm, Cloud would act differently, aloof without the hostility. Standing or sitting still, she would pretend she didn't notice the children as they approached her, cautiously, hands at their sides. Once close enough, Kimmy and Devon would crouch down and coo things like, "Nice kitty," and soon, they graduated to brief and tentative touches. Depending on her mood, Cloud would bat a paw—playfully this time—or lay back and enjoy being stroked and tickled on the neck.

Karen saw some of this and knew the rest because her twins told her. Anything having to do with animals was big news and eagerly conveyed, unlike other information that required subtle forms of coercion to elicit. The children frequently asked for pets, anything from dragonflies to dogs, but ever since Jaclyn and Cloud moved in, they very clearly wanted a cat. Not just any cat. A cat with thick, long white fur. Karen delivered the standard answer: "No. I have enough animals in the house already."

To Karen's mind, children were the only kind of animal worth serious consideration. She'd wanted more of them, and there'd been the two miscarriages after the twins, and maybe she and Ben would try again, but pets instead? She'd rather devote her time to the twins, not to an animal they would abandon as soon as the novelty wore off. Her thinking on this might be different if she were older and had no children at all—if she were a person like Jaclyn. Childless by choice or cruel fate? Perhaps Karen had it wrong and there were adult Temple children somewhere, living away from home. But she suspected not. Childless women were so prominently childless, their barrenness evident in the way they smiled and talked to the children of others.

And in Jaclyn's case, one indication seemed to be her glaring lack of interest in Devon and Kimberly's identicalness. As if she simply hadn't noticed. Didn't *everyone* have something to say the first time? Karen had gotten so used to the comments and compliments that she kept a repertoire of pat responses on the tip of her tongue, always ready for quick, good-natured repartee. But Jaclyn, upon first sight of the twins, had said nothing, hadn't even done the usual double take.

Surely Jaclyn wouldn't be shy to comment the next time. Without hesitation, Karen invited her over for coffee, choosing a morning when the children would be in school, Ben at work. Jaclyn graciously accepted, and as the appointed day approached, Karen half wondered if she would arrive alone or with Cloud on her arm. So easily and naturally they would come in and sit down, those Siamese sisters—forearm glued to furry ribcage—Jaclyn lifting her coffee cup with the free hand, pinky extended, bringing the cup gently up to Cloud's lips, the sly smile and cobalt eyes, the dainty, human-like sip and a *meow, more cream please.*

But Jaclyn arrived without the cat, wearing a caftan of sky and water tones, blues and gray-greens. She stepped through the door looking doubly childless and alone, yet taller and straighter because of it, broad shouldered and confident without a hint of ill ease. Her sudden presence in the foyer, filling it up with dramatic closeness, rendered Karen momentarily speechless, something unusual. At once exotic and down-to-earth, Jaclyn possessed distinction without eccentricity and a pull that seemed to invite proximity. Especially now, standing alone, without the cat.

Karen led her guest into the kitchen where she'd laid the table with flowers and her prettiest stoneware in neat place settings amidst good coffee and cake smells, with a hope that now seemed transparent for its desire to impress with simplicity and goodness: a childlike tea party dream.

"Lovely kitchen," said Jaclyn.

"Thank you. Would you like to see the rest of the house?" Karen made the offer, knowing she would like to see every room of Jaclyn's house someday.

Jaclyn smiled. There was an evident pause before she answered, "All right, then."

Slightly rattled, Karen commenced the tour, explaining the obvious and pointing out photographs and mementos while a pleasant-faced Jaclyn followed, uttering polite assurances: "The children's room, yes," and "Ah! the dining room," and "I can see why it's your favorite; they're smiling so nicely." Ten minutes later, her life in four walls thus explained, Karen was ready for the certainty of her stoneware place settings and the secure hardness of cane-backed chairs.

Jaclyn took her coffee black and sipped slowly, ending only halfway down, remaining cool and unbent by Karen's urge to move faster. Inexplicable: her guest's perfect composure and seeming indifference to their lack of progress. Karen's usual ease with language and skill at maneuvering the S-curves of personality had all vanished beneath the banner of her desire to delve deeply and her inability to understand. At the end of an hour, she'd volunteered most of her life history and had learned little of her new neighbor's.

Jaclyn pushed back from the table. "It's been lovely, but I should get back to work."

Work? Karen was taken aback. "Oh? Where do you work?"

"At home. I travel occasionally, but most of it can be done from my desk. The wonders of telephone, email, and computer!" Jaclyn was out in the foyer by then, in transition between coffee hour and the better part of her day, unaware of her hostess's need to know and struggle with language. A question was blurted and an answer given, a complete statement of the nature of Jaclyn's employment, said in a way that betokened its everyday-ness. But Karen, who'd found nothing obvious about Jaclyn, remained stuck in her own formulation of the question, unable to render meaning to the answer that followed. There was a company name and a short job description with technical sounding words.

After this, the next part was easy to interpret. "Thank you so much for the coffee," said Jaclyn, stepping onto the front walkway.

"You're welcome! Thanks for coming! We should do it again sometime."

To which Jaclyn simply smiled and waved before turning away.

The return invitation, the one that Karen expected, never came. There were more chance meetings at the end of the driveway, polite and pleasant conversation. Nothing even as intimate as Jaclyn's work was discussed, since Karen feared that her questions would be embarrassingly indicative of her ignorance or inattentiveness.

Soon after, the uninvited visits began. There were many of them, every one perfectly justifiable. A diversion up the long driveway to Jaclyn's door required a legitimate explanation, and Karen always had one, even if she sometimes stretched the limits of legitimacy, like the time she was out on a brisk walk and strode into the thicket, traversed the runway, banged the knocker hard, and asked Jaclyn with a big healthy smile if she might like to join her for the exercise. Jaclyn, wearing a caftan in muted lavender, mauve and burgundy tones, gave Karen a tepid look and said, "Thank you, but I'm afraid I have a deadline to meet." Cloud's gaze, from the comfort of Jaclyn's arm, was equally lukewarm. Noticing the cordless phone receiver in a dangling hand, Karen apologized for the intrusion, explaining that she had tried to call but the line had been busy.

Landing, decelerating on the way out the runway, she attempted an image of Jaclyn in exercise clothes, feeling uneasy but not cognizant of mistake. The tepidness could have been only shyness.

And so there were several other attempts, Karen couldn't be sure of the number. She wasn't counting. If Jaclyn wasn't impressed with homemade cakes or well-behaved identical offspring or exercise programs, Karen would find the hook that sold. She sensed repetitiveness and rising desperation in her behavior but ignored it, wondering only vaguely at the growing uneasiness in these manufactured contacts. After all, there was nothing wrong with showing neighborly concern, like the time she warned Jaclyn about the rabid raccoon wandering the street. And it was only friendly (wasn't it?) to invite her new neighbor to join a book discussion group with friends, or out to lunch, or over (again and again) for coffee. Yet, each invitation was met with a polite refusal.

Then there were visits that could only be deemed absolutely necessary. Like the time Karen was canvassing for signatures on a petition to shut down a local nuclear facility. Jaclyn, cat on arm, signed without question. And the time she went with the twins selling Girl Scout cookies. Jaclyn and Cloud purchased three boxes in a hurry. And the last time, after Devon had recovered one of Cloud's toys, a chewable mouse, from the pachysandra near the end of the Temples' driveway. Karen assured her daughter she would return the toy, and the next day she paid a visit, unaware that it would be the last time she saw the cat alive. "So sorry to bother you," she said, now habitually prefacing her demands with excuses, "but my daughter, bless her heart, found one of Cloud's little toys, and I promised her I would return it personally, she was so sure that the cat would miss it!" Karen dangled the toy before Cloud, who regarded it noncommittally.

With her stoniest look yet, Jaclyn accepted the well-used article and said, "We have several of these, but I *do* know how important it is to honor a promise. Thank you."

Now, what did *that* mean? Further conversation was not forthcoming, and so, once again, Karen turned and walked away, without an invitation inside.

The morning after, confessions out of mind, forgetfulness was conveniently excused by the rush of daily routine.

Breakfast to eat, hair to comb, lunches to make, school backpacks to check. The girls raced out the door to the bus stop, Karen two steps behind. Kimberly challenged Devon to a skipping contest while their mother lagged, wondering at the cause of her fatigue.

But then, as they approached Jaclyn's driveway, she was struck with the horror of it: her little girls skipping so close to that spot in the road. Could there be a telltale sign, a bloodstain? It had been dark and she hadn't seen, hadn't stopped to look. "Better run!" Karen yelled at her daughters. "You're going to miss the bus!" And run they did, right past the driveway, not stopping to gather the evidence of Karen's crime. *Not a crime, but an accident that couldn't be helped.*

And, funny, Karen's quick glance on her way past yielded no obvious clues, as if nothing had happened. So convincingly normal did everything look that she put it out of mind and focused on the children again, easily catching up to them at the bus stop because, after all, they weren't so terribly late. The twins jumped into play with their friends, while Karen merely nodded a hello at their moms, feeling slightly apart despite the utter normalcy of the morning, feeling, for the first time, that she belonged to a secret, shameful society ruled by aberrant desire and behavior.

But then, just as always, that familiar yellow hulk clamored toward them and screeched to a halt with flashing red lights. "Goodbye girls! I love you!" *I do love them so much.* But the girls, caught up in their own world, barely looked her way, something that children always seemed to do when their mothers needed just the opposite.

Once the bus was off, Karen waved goodbye to the neighbor moms, these women with whom she'd shared so much. Coffee, advice, carpools, favors, children's playdates. She'd seen the insides of their homes many times. Why wasn't it enough? "Going on my walk!" she chirped and strode off in the opposite direction. Nothing unusual, one of her brisk morning walks, a convenient façade to cover her intention of returning once they'd gone and heading straight for that spot, the source of her secret deviance, knowing she'd find it there.

On the way back, nearing Jaclyn's driveway, she moved into the center of the road where she might have stopped the Peugeot, her eyes searching the ground. Nothing, just as she'd thought, but no, out the corner of her eye she saw it, some distance away on the side of the road. No more than several inches out from the curb. A large reddish-brown splotch, the distinct color of blood. Not in the middle of the road, but close to the curb. So close. She walked up to the stain, inspected it, knew what it must be, still doubting, refusing to accept this new evidence that threatened to violate her neatly sealed protective box. She tore her eyes away and headed for home, for the comfort of ritual.

But when she returned, she could only stand silently, helplessly, in the middle of her disheveled kitchen, the single room out of order in her neat home. The breakfast dishes, the bills, the errands awaited. Yet she couldn't move and simply stood for a very long time, wishing only for relief from her anticipation, the nagging certainty she'd glimpsed the night before: something, an irreversible something, was about to happen.

The doorbell rang. Longingly, she glanced about the kitchen, at the breakfast dishes, the rose-covered tablecloth, the ruffled curtains.

The doorbell rang again.

With another aimless glance, Karen shuffled to the front door and opened it. Finally, Jaclyn had come to visit.

The stunned silence and quiet grief of the previous evening had vanished. In its place, a monstrous anger simmered under the perfect exterior, the French bun, the elegant caftan in black and gray tones. Karen remained silent, awaiting her punishment.

"I've tried to tell you in every way I know how," said Jaclyn, bold and defiant. "I didn't want a confrontation. But you refused to see things, and now you've done *this*."

This, the shameful thing, exploded with the flashes of memory of all those polite refusals, all the proper warnings. "But...I did see. I just didn't... Maybe I couldn't—"

"Accept it." Jaclyn leveled her gaze at Karen and shook her head slowly, eyes cold and accusing. She spoke distinctly, enunciating each word. "Then accept *this*. Cloud does not *dart* into the street." Jaclyn turned around, took three steps from the door, and swiveled to face Karen again for the last time. "*She never darts*."

Karen froze, grabbing at the sickness in her gut as she watched Jaclyn float away under the billowing fabric. Tears would come later, along with the futility of remorse and enlightenment—too late.

For now, the buried images beckoned and resurfaced

with the clarity of fact: Cloud stepped sedately off the curb, taking a single step, then another, head turned up, eyes shining in the headlights. Cautiously, she waited for the car to pass, remaining fixed near the curb like a white marble statue.

But then there was a pull to the right, the wheel was pulling toward the curb, and Karen's hand was guiding it…

epiblog

HERE, I OFFER three blog pieces which were originally
posted online. "The Story of August 3, 1964," was first
posted on *VBlog* at www.vskemanis.com. "Truth or Point
of View," and "Ballet, Law, and Mystery," were written
for *Something is Going to Happen*, the blog of Janet
Hutchings, editor of *Ellery Queen's Mystery Magazine*.

In these pieces, you will find some love and crime,
with a little bit of my life mixed in.

— V.

The Story of August 3, 1964

Based on actual memories

THE NEARLY NEWLYWEDS were to celebrate their second anniversary. A big surprise was in store for them, although the secret was not well-kept. Too much was going on in the house. Their six children plotted and planned. The seventh was yet to be born.

In those days there were no summer camps, no structure, no money, only imagination. The family had recently moved into a tumbledown redwood shack on a treacherous California hill. For weeks in advance of the anniversary, the eldest boy—the mastermind—arranged rotating shifts of work crews among his siblings to clear the path up the hill. He was fourteen, strong, and loved the out-of-doors. He ended up doing most of the labor himself.

What were their tools? Hands, sticks, and maybe a few garden implements, spirited away from the shed. They sculpted their work of art, snaking it through the oak trees along the contours of the hill, pricked by the sharp points of fallen oak leaves, surrounded by the dry

275

smells of summer, the California bay laurels and eucalyptus. They ripped at the coyote brush and greasewood and copious amounts of a beautiful three-leafed plant: the poison oak.

Construction delays. Workers took sick leave, battling the painful, itching, weeping pustules. Cotton balls were soaked in Calamine lotion and dabbed on, allowed to harden, no defense against the yellow ooze that broke through and crusted atop the pink cupcake glaze.

The eldest toiled on. The job was finished under the wire.

On the big day, the children awoke early and began their preparations in hoarse whispers that broke into urgent instructions and unyielding opinions. The honorees began to stir in their bedroom, patiently waiting to be called. They knew better than to emerge in the midst of the "secret." A lot was going on in the kitchen.

The gourmet menu was conjured from magazine articles: prune whip and eggs benedict. When breakfast was almost ready, the younger boys were dispatched up the path to place a blanket in a clearing on the hill, affording a view of Mount Diablo. The parents, by then famished, were summoned. They put on their most surprised and delighted smiles and followed their eldest son up the winding path, the other children following single file, each holding a crucial element of the special repast. When everything was set up, the children descended to the house.

Alone on the hill, with a view of the valley and the mountain beyond, the mother and father ate, or pretended to eat, the runny prune whip and the congealed, cold eggs. Perhaps they talked about how blessed they were to have each other and these children. Perhaps they laughed and wondered what they had gotten into, creating this family. Perhaps they said nothing at all and looked at the view.

We will never know.

Did any of this happen? Is it fact or fantasy?

At the movies, we've seen phrases like the ones I've listed here, presumably, in descending order of reality: "based on a true story," "inspired by a true story," "based on actual events," and "inspired by actual events. Which applies here?

To start by point of comparison, when I write fiction, the characters and events in my short stories and novels are fabrications compiled from bits and pieces of experience. Years after I've written a story, my characters live in my memory. I think about them and what they look like and wonder how they think and remember the words they spoke.

This story, *The Story of August 3, 1964*, originated in memories from childhood, images accompanied by tastes, sounds, and smells. I think about these people and what they look like and wonder how they think and remember some of the words they spoke. I believe I remember these things. Today, I assembled some words and placed them on my computer screen. This story, taken from memory, is conveyed to you imperfectly, as most things are. For this story, I devise a fifth category: "based on actual memories."

This would have been their 53rd anniversary. John Meredith Swackhamer and Kathryn Trask Swackhamer. [Posted August 3, 2015.]

Truth or Point of View?

Q: How many lawyer jokes are there?
A: Only three. The rest are true stories.

I'VE HEARD THEM all. We've been called sharks, ambulance chasers, hired guns, shysters, and at the other extreme, bookish nerds. But for every "true" story you hear about a lawyer, a litigator will have a great tale to tell. The courtroom is a place of high drama, and our legal system supplies the contradictions that so intrigue me as an attorney and fiction writer. My two favorites: instinct versus rule of law, and truth versus point of view.

Early on, I knew I was destined for the criminal arena. Corporations, contracts, tax law—*bo-ring*. The dream went something like this: I would be a champion of the innocent, the next Perry Mason. The framed and unfairly maligned would flock to the law practice of Ms. Periwinkle Mason, Esq., mistress of the art of cross-examination. Lashed by her cutting inquisition, every lying accuser would crumble on the witness stand, inspiring that emotional outburst from the real murderer at the back of the courtroom.

279

Improbable endings aside, here's what really happened.

First year law, I enthusiastically applied for a summer internship with the Public Defender. The young man who interviewed me couldn't have been more than five years my senior. He started out with a hypothetical. We lawyers love hypotheticals.

"Your client, Mr. X, is charged with rape and murder. The prosecutor has an airtight case against him. Here's the evidence. [INSERT: gory details, enough to make a naïve 23-year-old blanch and tug at the hem of her recently purchased interview suit.] Tell me, Ms. Kemanis, what is your objective in that case?"

Of course, I had the perfect answer. I had just gotten an "A" in Criminal Procedure. "Our Constitution guarantees everyone a fair trial, and it would be my job to uphold his rights." Even the lowest worm has rights, don't you know.

"Sorry," he said. My face fell. "Your objective is to *walk* him. Get him out on the street!"

Really?

Perhaps he saw the disillusionment in my eyes. "If you want truth and justice, go to the DA's office."

Well, I like truth and justice. I went to the DA's office.

Fast forward five years. Alone with a handgun in a private ladies' room of the Manhattan DA's office, I blinked away tears, peering through a grimy window. A pair of pigeons on the stained ledge outside stared back. I had just suffered a felony acquittal of a really bad guy.

Don't get nervous. The gun wasn't loaded but

encased in a clear plastic evidence bag, the bullets jingling loosely inside. And I hadn't "walked him." (Wasn't that the other lawyer's job?) The bad guy was on his way to New Jersey where he faced multiple felony charges. None of this made me feel any better. My gun possession case was supposed to be a slam-dunk. But my defeat proved to be a lesson in instinct versus rule of law, truth versus point of view.

Just before his arrest, this defendant was driving a dented vehicle with New Jersey plates, attracting the attention of city police officers on radio motor patrol. Loping along behind, they called in the plate number and came up with a hit—the car was registered to a paroled felon wanted for recent crimes, including attempted murder. The officers figured that, even if the information didn't pan out, they had him on a busted taillight.

Siren and flashing lights didn't encourage the wanted felon to stop, but a traffic jam conveniently put up a roadblock—nowhere to run. The two officers alighted, coming up behind on either side with their service revolvers unholstered, pressed against thighs.

The situation required caution and guts. Inside the car—not good. Our felon in the driver's seat was fumbling with something at waist level, ignoring commands to exit the vehicle until...he cracked the door. The partners reacted, tugging the doors open on either side, pushing, pulling, and shoving the man to the ground, cheek to grit. A loaded semiautomatic clunked onto the asphalt beside him.

Having gone to such trouble, we decided to give the defendant a New York record before sending him home to New Jersey. Felony weapons possession. Easy shmeezy.

The truth and just a bit of instinct assured a guilty verdict. The gun was on the ground but, of course, the defendant "possessed" it under the penal code—he was trying to hide the weapon and possibly thinking of using it when the officers came upon him. Here, however, is where the rule of law stepped in. I was precluded from introducing any evidence about the radio run. The jury would not learn what the officers knew about the defendant before they approached the vehicle. Why? We just can't trust the jurors to ignore their nasty instinct that past behavior defines a person, or at least, makes it more likely that he committed another crime.

Oh, I put up a good fight, and a different judge might have allowed the jury to know that the officers received *some* sort of communication. But this judge gaveled away truth and instinct with the rule of law, leaving in their stead merely point of view, the tunnel through which this jury was allowed to see the arrest. And it looked pretty bad: gratuitous police brutality—for a mere traffic infraction! Add in a little personality problem and I was cooked. My testifying police officer was no Sergeant Joe Friday. There was just something about him—that little bit of surliness and slouch, a mildly suggestive evasiveness in his eyes. "You say that loaded gun just fell out of the car?" Defense counsel winked at the jury. *A likely story.*

Fast forward an undisclosed number of years, and I'd rather be writing stories. There's always something interesting to dig up in the nuances of the law, the personalities in the courtroom, the psychology of the battle. Exclusionary rules, inadmissible evidence, and the code of professional ethics are just so downright counterintuitive and fun! Okay, maybe that's the bookish nerd talking.

Lawyers don't have a monopoly on this stuff. You don't have to be Grisham or Turow to use a courtroom scene or gritty legal dilemma in your story. For the ring of authenticity, just ask one of your friends at the bar for some legal advice. There certainly are enough of us around—some would say a few too many.

Drunks, to be sure, but I'm talking about lawyers.

Ballet, Law, and Mystery

BEFORE WRITING FICTION, I was a dancer and a lawyer. Still am, both. Oxymoron? You'd be surprised how many attorneys I meet in ballet class. Maybe it's because law books and toe shoes are both hard—dancing attorneys are gluttons for punishment. On a positive note, ballet and the law share many nicer attributes. An idealized world, perfectionism, intellectual puzzles, exacting discipline, technical precision, and personal expression. The expressive medium of ballet is the more artistic, you might say, but I could debate the point (sounding like a lawyer here, even if we swap "point" for "*pointe*").

My experience in the courtroom informs my fiction more often than my experience in the dance studio (although the protagonist in my novels, prosecutor Dana Hargrove, does take a weekly dance class with her sister Cheryl, a Broadway performer). With pleasure, I dove into the world of professional ballet in writing *Journal Entry, Franklin DeWitt*, for EQMM. Memories from the time I owned a dancewear shop came in handy for this story. It could take hours fitting those potential instruments of torture, *pointe* shoes, on the feet of persnickety ballerinas—always a Cinderella-esque exercise in frustration.

As for this blog piece, I thank Janet Hutchings for humoring my obsession and allowing this small offering, a short-short mystery. The style is not my usual, but like every word buff, I look for any excuse to have fun with language—here, the beautiful language of ballet. Consider, for example, this direction for a lovely *petit allegro enchaînement*: "*Glissade précipitée en avant, temps levé, tombé, saut de chat.*" If the ballet instructor were to say it like this—"Quick steps forward, hop, fall, and leap like a cat"—I might just walk out of class.

You will find, at the end of the story, a glossary of the less obvious ballet terms.

Doctor Coppélius Meets an Untimely Death at the Opera House

As the only child of two physicians, Serena Musette was destined for a future in the healing arts. So it seemed, until destiny took a detour on the occasion of her eighth birthday, when she was treated to a matinee at the National Ballet. From that moment, every step she took was a *chassé* toward her dream.

At seventeen, she signs with the company. Passion is no guarantee of talent, and Serena's passion falls short of artistic distinction, her *grand jeté* an inch below soaring, her *port de bras* heartfelt but uninspiring. Ever hopeful, she languishes in the *corps*, one of many *cygnettes*, sylphs, and Wilis.

In her fifth spring season, at the casting call, the light of good fortune shines upon her. Ballet master Stanislav

Gliadilev, towering over the diminutive Serena, twirls a waxed end of his mustache and declares: "Friend!" She fights to remain *à terre*. It's her first supporting role! One of Swanilda's six Friends in the comic ballet Coppélia. Her heart nearly *sautés* from her leotard before the impresario qualifies the offer: "Understudy!" Serena wilts.

An exhausting rehearsal schedule fails to wilt *Les Amies*, who remain remarkably healthy and uninjured while Serena shadows them, unnoticed, a fly on the studio mirror. With too much time on her hands and no hope of stardom, she is, quite unintentionally, on a gradual *pas de bourrée couru* toward her true calling in life. Observation is the key. Nothing escapes her eye.

She studies the principals: *prima ballerina* Peony Torne in the role of Swanilda, Enrique Dagloose as her fiancé Franz, and Morton Avunculario as Doctor Coppélius. Peony is known for the delicacy of her *petite batterie*, Enrique for his *ballon*, and Morton for his *danse de caractère*. What is the secret of their success? They're strong and beautiful, Morton the most powerful, a favorite of Gliadilev. Fifteen years older than the others, Morton is made to look eighty-five on stage with a painted face, a wig of scraggly gray hair, and stooped posture, as he teeters about with the aid of a cane.

Hmm, Serena thinks, is Morton the reason that Peony made it to the top? Perhaps if I cozy up to Morton the way *she* does, gazing droopingly at him while Enrique scowls with glints of daggers in his slitty eyes…? The backstage intrigue is the complete opposite of the story in the ballet. Peony's character Swanilda isn't attracted to Morton's character, that crotchety, diabolical inventor

Doctor Coppélius. The Doctor is a disturbing figure with a toyshop full of spooky, life-size mechanical dolls. And Enrique's character Franz is not the jealous one. In the ballet, Swanilda is jealous of the faithless Franz, who's duped and smitten by the lifelike doll Coppélia, sitting on the balcony of the toyshop, reading a book.

On the eve of opening night, an hour before full dress, company class is held on stage with portable *barres*. Peony, Morton, and Enrique *plié* center stage, and the lesser dancers fan out from them—the Friends, the Dolls, the townspeople, and finally the understudies, lining the dark edges. Serena is feeling like a useless appendage. At least she would like to be close enough to observe the greats, but they're barely visible behind all the bodies executing *les exercices à la barre: tendus, dégagés, ronds de jambe* and finally, *battements en cloche*.

A small commotion erupts. Rats! What did Serena miss? Enrique mutters something to Morton, who gives an audible "harrumph" and stumbles away in the hunched posture of Doctor Coppélius, hand at the back of his neck. The dancers disperse to dressing rooms, wishing each other "*merde*." The *maître de ballet* spies the understudies and shrieks: "Get off the stage!" In the midst of chaos, Serena slithers behind a wing, unnoticed.

Second act, it's the dead of night, and something is astir, a menace of unknown origin. Swanilda and Friends break into the toyshop, setting the mechanical dolls to life. The Troubadour executes a stiff *tour en l'air*, the Spanish Doll a sharp *coupé fouetté raccourci*, the Scottish Doll a nervous *pas emboîté en tournant*. The Doctor bursts in! Friends scatter, Swanilda hides, Franz sneaks in through a window and is caught! Doctor Coppélius produces two tankards of an intoxicating brew, slyly mocking his captive as they drink to Franz's love for Coppélia.

Franz is passed out when Swanilda reappears, impersonating the mechanical doll Coppélia. Strangely, the Doctor does not seem quite himself. Deathly pale, he staggers off stage, totters and collapses behind the façade of the toyshop. With a brisk *brisé volé*, Swanilda runs to him. The music stops abruptly, the rehearsal comes to a halt. "Morton, darling!" Peony cradles the gray-wigged head in her lap and looks up, searching blindly. "Please, somebody, help!" The Doctor needs a doctor. The *maître* drops to her knees, frantically feeling for a pulse. It appears that Morton *est mort*.

From center stage, ballet master Gliadilev quiets the crowd. "Remain calm! I've called for an ambulance." From behind the curtain, Serena discerns, in the tensing of muscle, the pain that the impresario feels for the loss of his friend. Or maybe he's remembering the inferior technique of Morton's understudy? Opening night will be a disaster!

"How can this be?" The tear-stained Peony stands, *bras croisé*, mindlessly stabbing *piqués en croix* with her right foot. "There!" She points to the tankards. "He's been poisoned!" She whirls in *renversé*. "*He* did it!" Enrique is fingered. But Peony *pirouettes* anew, unable to make up her mind. "No…it has to be *him!*" She points at the mousy little props man, who scratches his head in confusion.

"Wait! You're wrong." Serena *chaînés* swiftly out

from the wing. Quickly, before Gliadilev can banish her, she grabs the tankards, one at a time, and drinks from each. "It's water." She licks her lips and puckers them. "Maybe a bit of iron oxide."

Dumbfounded, the company awaits Serena's next move. Like magic, a path to the body is cleared. Serena kneels, removes the wig, and palpates gently. "Basilar skull fracture, occipital bone, subdural hematoma likely. Suffered a blow with a blunt instrument. He's been dying slowly before our eyes."

There's a communal gasp amid darting, wary glances. What could the weapon be? Was it the Troubadour's lute, the Scottish Doll's bagpipes, the Spanish Doll's fan, or that little hardcover book Coppélia was reading? Maybe the assailant used the Doctor's own cane, or a dismantled section of the *barre*?

Serena examines the shape of the injury, mentally calculating height and velocity. She stands to face Enrique, his head drooping *en bas*. For weeks now she's been studying him, getting to know every habit and quirk of technique, the way he likes to flex his foot at the end of the leg that swings like a pendulum in his favorite warmup exercise. "You were standing behind Morton at the *barre*. It was your *battement en cloche*, wasn't it? Directed *straight* to that nice little groove between neck and skull."

"But," Enrique protests, "I didn't mean for him to *die!*" The suspect attempts an *échappé sauté*, but Gliadilev seizes him before he can run.

Intentional, reckless or negligent? A question for another day, a question for a jury. With a joyful *sissone fermé*, the case, for now, is closed. Serena, having discovered her true talent, is arisen from the *corps* into the hallowed halls of forensic science.

A Literally Figurative Glossary of Ballet Terms

ballon: lightness, the ability to remain suspended in the air.

battements en cloche: beats like a bell. Basically, you swing your leg front and back, very high, like the clapper of a bell; it's fun and relaxing.

bras croisé: arms crossed.

brisé volé: broken, flying. A beautiful light step with a small beat of the legs.

chaînés: chains, links. These are fast turns in a line, spotting your destination. Really fun to do and a good way to get dizzy if not done properly.

chassé: chase. Slide forward, one foot chasing the other.

coupé fouetté raccourci: literally cut, whip, and shorten. Does this give you any sense of what it looks like? Too difficult to explain.

échappé sauté: escape leap. As you jump, the feet "escape" from fifth position into second.

merde: I don't need to tell you what this really means. It's a dancer's "good luck" wish.

pas de bourrée couru: a series of tiny rapid steps on *pointe*. When ballerinas look like they're floating across the stage, this is what they're doing.

pas emboîté en tournant: a springy, boxed-in step in a circle.

petite batterie: small battery in the sense of beating.

There's a lot of beating in ballet terminology, although it's far from a violent art form.

piqués en croix: sharp piercing taps with the toe, front, side, back, in the shape of a cross.

renversé: reversed. You wouldn't think this word is enough to describe the actual movement. It's a turn with a pitched body and a high, circling leg.

sissone fermé: a leap from two feet into a split, landing on two feet in a closed position.

tour en l'air: turn in the air. Jump straight up, do a full revolution like a pencil, and land. Harder than it looks.

————

Dear Reader

As I write the afterword to this updated edition, I'm celebrating a few book birthdays.

Ten years ago, I gathered all the stories I had written in the '90s and the '00s and published them in three volumes: *Everyone But Us, tales of women*, *Dust of the Universe, tales of family*, and *Malocclusion, tales of misdemeanor*. Three of those stories are reprised in this collection along with eight "love and crime" stories I wrote after 2012.

During the same decade, I've published six novels of legal suspense in the Dana Hargrove series. Each one is a stand-alone, finding Dana at a discrete stage of her family life and career. If you enjoy courtroom drama, legal thrillers, mystery, and police procedurals, these novels may be for you, starting with the first one, *Thursday's List*. The sixth, *Power Blind*, releases in January 2022.

Let me know your impressions of my stories by posting a reader review of any length with your online book retailer. You can also drop me a line through the contact page on my website, vskemanis.com, and I'll respond directly. The contact page also has a link to a free e-book offer.

To keep up with the latest on my books and life, find me on Goodreads, YouTube, BookBub, Facebook, Twitter, and Instagram, and subscribe to the blog on my website.

Thanks for reading!

V.S.K.

January 2022

* 9 7 8 0 9 9 6 5 9 0 9 8 3 *